Reviving a Rose

Chantelle's Journey

by

Sally Ann Loveday

Bloomington, IN 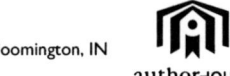 Milton Keynes, UK

AuthorHouse™
1663 Liberty Drive, Suite 200
Bloomington, IN 47403
www.authorhouse.com
Phone: 1-800-839-8640

AuthorHouse™ UK Ltd.
500 Avebury Boulevard
Central Milton Keynes, MK9 2BE
www.authorhouse.co.uk
Phone: 08001974150

This book is a work of fiction. People, places, events, and situations are the product of the author's imagination. Any resemblance to actual persons, living or dead, or historical events, is purely coincidental.

© 2007 Sally Ann Loveday. All rights reserved.

No part of this book may be reproduced, stored in a retrieval system, or transmitted by any means without the written permission of the author.

First published by AuthorHouse 5/1/2007

ISBN: 978-1-4259-9860-8 (sc)

Printed in the United States of America
Bloomington, Indiana

This book is printed on acid-free paper.

Preface

You might, find yourselves curious, about the village and town names in this story. Then I will save you the trouble of looking. They are there on the map, but I must confess to never having been to either or even Poole. Shame on thee, it will be rectified. As such, everything in the village is conjured up in this authors muddled come fuddled brain.

I must confess to have enjoyed myself very much whilst writing this story. I even have one or two more tales, relating to some of the other characters in the book. You'll have to wait and see which ones.

Many thanks must go to Philip, my dear husband. For putting up with a wall of silence, I get so engrossed when I'm working; I tend to forget he is there. Also, praise indeed for his sterling deciphering skills when putting my handwritten work onto the computer.

Lots of the encouragement and support came from my children Angharad, Grace and Aled and their partners. Also to my great circle of friends, who have been proof-reading as I have gone along? Including Anita, Sarah, Sam, Harry, David, Wendy and Sue, many thanks to you all for your support. Also the fab coffee we both have drunk at Maxwell's from Carla

They all seem to have enjoyed the journey, as much as I have.
I hope you do as well.

1

Slowly Chantelle looked up towards the ceiling, trying to picture what colour scheme she would need, to bring the old cottage to life. She would be 26 in a few weeks and this was her first job – commission after finishing college four years ago.

It was a small thatched cottage, the kind you see on chocolate boxes, only this little one, needed drastic care and attention. She had fallen in love with the cottage as soon as she had seen it. Now then... down to business.

The beams holding up the ceiling seemed to be sound, but she would have to get them checked properly by a builder. The main room had three small leaded windows which didn't let an awful amount of light in. Still, if she chose carefully, the room would have a warm cosy feel about it. Safe, yes that's the word she wanted, safe, but from what!

She had met Ben in the second term of college and he seemed to be the perfect man (if there was one). He was considerate, tender and very gentle with her. Little did Chantelle know that she would just be another notch on his bed-post; it had taken Ben nearly seven months before he had passed just petting, and a carefully disguised grope. She was the most unsure shy virginal creature he had ever seen and he definitely wanted to be the one to 'de-flower' her. What a coup! Still, he had to put his impatience to one side and win her trust. Tall and slender with ash blonde hair that curled slightly at the nape, he was the stuff that most girls' dreams were made of.

Chantelle couldn't understand why he'd picked her. She thought that no-one would want a skinny reed-like waif with (straight long) brown hair, green eye and legs which seemed to stretch for ever. What she didn't see, was what others did. A very elegant gazelle-like girl-child, whose eyes you could drown in. She had hair that hung long and straight, like a silk curtain and legs that a ballet dancer would have been proud of.

Still the romance (she had called it at first) went well. Roses, dinner, even the theatre, which she knew Ben hated, and all he ever took was a gentle kiss. That all changed after she finally let her guard down. The promise of marriage and a bright future, wore her into submission. Ben had planned well, just enough wine with the dinner to loosen her morals and then when she wasn't looking he slipped his 'special stuff' into her coffee. Because Chantelle had eaten the after-dinner mints, before draining her cup, she didn't taste the slightly bitter flavour. She felt warm and a bit muzzy, but because she was with Ben, there was nothing to worry about, was there!

He stopped the car and helped her out. Carefully up the stairs to the front door. As he opened it with her keys, he picked her up. At first, Chantelle thought he was putting her to bed 'What a kind man', but that soon changed as she felt her dress being slid up her body.

She tried to stop him but her arms and legs seemed to be made of cement. She closed her eyes, he didn't seem to be 'her Ben' anymore, and he looked evil as he ripped her panties down she began to blot out the unfolding trauma.

It took only half hour, but to Chantelle it seemed to last forever. Ben left straight away and said as he reached the door, "Don't think of telling anyone, they all think you're a 'frigid little bitch anyway', so no one will believe you." With a final sneer he slammed the door and went. Chantelle knew she should have gone to the police, but Ben would charm them just as he had done to her. (She shuddered).

Shaking her head to clear the bad memories, she pulled her mind back to the job in hand. A 'rag-rolled' Apricot colour on the walls should warm up the room. The old fireplace once cleaned and swept would also bring something special to the room.

She walked into the small kitchen writing as she went. It looked as if no-one had changed it in decades. The old 'Belfast sink' was still there under the tiny window. There were two cupboards on the wall and a very dodgy looking table that had seen better days. The place definitely screamed for modernisation. She would have to be really on the ball to make it practical but also keep the feel of the cottage together.

Strolling through the back door, she suddenly stopped and clapped her hands together in sheer delight, nearly dropping her note-book as she did. The garden, although overgrown, seemed to stretch on forever, down to a little stream. Two fully-grown willows seemed to frame the bottom of the garden. Following the winding path, she breathed in the scent of the honeysuckle and roses. There were herbs in there somewhere. What a challenge, she decided to tackle the garden herself instead of employing a gardener. Yes, it definitely had bags of potential.

Reviving a Rose

Back in the cottage, Chantelle went up the quaint winding stairs. They seemed to hug the chimney breast. There were two rooms, the roof was slung at a weird angle but that only lent to the charm of the place. The first room what would be the bedroom; it had two tiny windows just like downstairs. The second much smaller room would be turned into an en-suite bath/shower room.

Letting herself out and locking the door, she looked up at the cottage for final inspiration before getting into her little Silver Metro and heading off towards the village. The roads were very narrow and overgrown, obviously not used everyday. As she drove carefully round the blind bend, she just caught a glimpse of the red bodywork of a large powerful car. Wrenching the steering wheel over sharply to the right, she felt the car drop dramatically and judder to a stop.

It seemed to have taken quite a lot of hedgerow with it. Boy was she glad that her seatbelt had worked along with the airbag. The next thing she knew, a powerful hand wrenched the door open on the passengers' side and an extremely loud and angry face appeared and bellowed at her at her.

"What do you think you were doing, trying paint new lines in the middle of the road? It's a good job for you that my Mercedes can stop on a pin; I ought to have you charged with dangerous driving".

Chantelle was too stunned to say anything, so she just sat there and stared. Apart from being angry, he wasn't that bad to look at. A 'lived-in' face, that's what her mother would have called it. She un-clipped her belt and scrambled out the door, walking round to the front of the car, she tripped over and landed in bits of hedgerow, she grimaced and muttered under her breath.

"Oh brilliant, just what I needed." She turned to the loud man and said "What do mean blaming me.... I was going slowly..... You were obviously driving too fast..... Do you like being a racing driver? Well try doing it at the race track!" With that she stomped up the road. How far the village was, she wasn't sure, but it was better than staying there with the loudmouth bully.

2

Glyn Mathews just stood there and watched the 'nutcase' as he thought; stride off up the road. Was he going to fast, he wasn't so sure now. That'll teach him, trying to catch up on phone messages, instead of keeping his mind on the road. Well, if she wanted to walk to town, he wasn't going to stop her. What a lot of passion, he thought, stored up in such a quiet looking package. This was definitely something to investigate, but not now, he had a cottage to check out!

Roughly five mile down the road he found the cottage. 'Not bad.... There was a lot of work to be done though!' He would have to find out who the interior designer was.

He had been contacted via the internet by a 'C. Adams'. Obviously 'he' had priced the job for the buyer and needed extra help. Well he would have to 'log-on' and try to get a phone number so that work could start.

Chantelle's Journey

Chantelle finally reached the garage and a rather crusty old man in an oily overall slowly walked out of the ram-shackle office.

"Alright... What can I do for you lovely?" Chantelle's face broke into a smile which lit up her eyes and a mischievous glint appeared in them.

"My car had an argument, with a narrow lane back there and a very large Mercedes, driven I might add by an utter nutcase. He forced me off the road because he took the bend too fast."

Gedd chewed his bottom lip and studied the girl, 'Nice' he thought, but to lively for me though... I'm getting too old.

"Well now my lovely," he said with a very broad accent, "I'll just puddle on down there in my pick-up and...... erm pick it up then! Do you have a place to stay in the village...? I'm afraid it's probably going to be awhile before you'll be driving your motor again." With that; Gedd set off. The pick-up spluttered into life and trundled off down the lane to find Chantelle's car, or what was left of it.

She decided to try the local hotel and see if they had any rooms. It wasn't peak holiday time and she was cold and hungry. She also wanted a bath or shower at least, to wash the hedgerow and grass out of her hair. She would need her clothes too; *they* were still in the boot.

The 'Briory Bush Inn' was a picture to look at and Chantelle stood for a minute looking at the beautiful thatched roof and tiny windows. Maybe it was as old as the cottage she was to work on. She went inside and walked up behind the wide and beautiful booking-in desk. 'Ping'. The little bell on the desk echoed in the hall and a well rounded woman bustled in behind the desk from the room just behind it.

"Hello mi-dear... I 'aven't seen you 'ere before... Are you stayin' long then? You couldn't 'ave picked a nicer place... The blossom smells lovely this time of year." She stopped for a breath, Chantelle smiled, although the woman could win a talking contest she seemed to be very pleasant.

"I don't know how long I'm staying... My car is in a ditch down the road away, it's near the 'old cottage'. I'm doing it up for a 'Mr. Rodgers', he's a nice chap."

"Ooh, yes he is ... 'e's been comin' down 'ere for years looking for a retirement place.... lovely man.... Yes indeed he is." The woman behind the counter said Chantelle got the impression that the woman liked 'her employer'.

"Excuse me but what is your name in case the garage calls?" The woman looked up from the register and smiled. "Well" she said "It's quite unusual one, an' that's for sure... It's Honeysuckle... Honeysuckle Graham. Apparently my ol' dad named me after all the honeysuckle up at the cottage; 'e' said it smelt so sweet the day I come into the world."

"Oh how lovely.... Do you happen to know if the old cottage had a name?" Chantelle held her breath, if she had it right, it would be the same age as the hotel. "Why yes Miss Adam." Honeysuckle said as she glanced at the register. "It was known as 'Briory Cottage, because there was loads and loads brier on the plot when the old owner of the place bought it. Me ol' grand-dad said e's father was told it took 'im weeks to clear before 'e' could build."

Chantelle was overjoyed. If she could just poke around the rooms of the hotel, she'd get an idea of how the cottage looked originally.

"Excuse me, Mrs. Graham, would it be possible to look at how the rooms are decorated, so I can get some feeling for the decor of the cottage?"

"Call me Honey, Miss Adams, please.... I'm sorry to disappoint you love, but the rooms are all newly decorated. Have been every two years since I been 'ere.... And that's been near on 20 years this summer."

Chantelle's face fell, but her spirits picked up when Honey said "that as far as she knew, the attic rooms hadn't been touched, too small to bother with." Smiling openly now Chantelle said to Honey.

"Please call me Chantelle, and thank you for your help. Now if I could just have my key. I desperately need a bath or shower, and if it's not too much trouble, could you ring Gedd at the garage and ask him to fetch over my suitcase, I'll have something to change into then... it's still in the boot!"

The mention of Gedd's name brought quite a change to Honey's face. She blushed, a beautiful crimson colour and smiled shyly to herself.

"Corse I will Chantelle love... be a pleasure. What do you think of 'Old Gedd' then? I... um... like 'im a bit. Since my old 'Mr. Graham' passed... Oh must be at least 5 years since... I've been quite lonely in the quiet season. I think 'Old Gedd' has quite a lot to offer... but he needs persuading by me, if that is what he wants."

Grinning to herself, Chantelle said "I think that 'Old Gedd' as you call him is lovely too... best of luck Honey... I'll await further updates as they happen... well, while I'm here at least!" With that she made her way up the fantastic solid oak staircase, along the narrow oak bound corridors, to her room.

Number seven... Her lucky number and she hoped so, for the 'project' as well. Opening the door she was pleasantly surprised with the way it had been decorated and laid out. A small four-poster bed was positioned against the back wall and the wooden floor was polished to perfection. The furniture was sparse, but that only added to the whole effect. She noticed a smaller door in the corner of the room and walked across to have a look. On the other side of it was a very compact bathroom/shower unit, which had been fitted and it was very

Reviving a Rose

tastefully done too! Who-ever Honey or her predecessor had found to do the job, was very good indeed.

The steam filled the tiny bathroom as Chantelle scrubbed the last remains of the hedge out of her hair. As she did so, the 'live-in face' came back into her thoughts. "Who does he think, he his... flippin' cheek blaming me, when he was going too fast in the first place?" A flash of temper definitely helped to get the shampoo and conditioner out of her hair. She scrubbed her body with the same vigour, and using the fluffy white towels that had been left in the bathroom; she dried off and went back into the bedroom.

A gentle knock on the door alerted her and she gingerly opened the massive oak door and peeped round. "It's alright love... it's only me" Honey said "I've just brought your little case up". She blushed again as she had downstairs. "Gedd brung it over like you asked... He said it's going to be a long job... apparently you are wanting a new wing and that's the least of it. Well I'll let you get dressed... you'll be getting a chill."

Chantelle thanked Honey and put her case on the bed. On opening it, she took out a very small compact laptop computer along with a clean pair of jeans and fawn coloured pullover, with fresh underwear. She didn't go in for fancy stuff, just the plain and sensible kind, which covered everything. Yes that's what she liked; she didn't want to encourage any advances did she!

Once she was dressed and feeling a lot fresher, she plugged the laptop in and 'logged-on' to her internet page. "Oh". She had a message waiting for her from her builder, Mr. Mathews.

I've seen the cottage. Beams 'r' fine but the plasterwork and kitchen need drastic work... can start in the morning... see you there...Glyn.

Glyn oh well at least now she knew who she'd be working with. I hope he's pleasant she thought. Tapping her own message in and pressing the send box, she'd typed:

See you there... looking forward to a good working relationship... C. Adams.

Well she was his 'boss' after-all and she'd be the one reporting to 'Mr. Rodgers' if anything cropped up.

He was a pleasant man, was Mr. Rodgers. Apparently he was a headmaster of a private school, down in Dorset somewhere. Nearly 30 years he'd been there and he wanted to broaden his horizons as it were and the 'cottage' was just what he needed to start off from. He had seen Chantelle's advert in the local paper and something about it just sparked his imagination. Whoever had written it was definitely the person he wanted to bring his new 'home' to life. Mr. Rodgers was staying in the school house at present, but he hoped by the time he retired the following year his 'house' would be finished.

So after phoning the number, he was quite surprised to hear a woman's voice, after all it did say "C. Adams" on the advert. Mind you, when he did meet Chantelle he was won over immediately, there was something about her that said 'I need this to help me through' but what ever the 'through' was she didn't elaborate and he being a gentleman didn't ask. So, he commissioned Chantelle to do the job, and keep him posted regularly. He also said that at half-term he would come and see how she was getting on.

3

The following morning, after a wonderful night's sleep, it took Chantelle a couple of minutes to remember where she was. The bed was extremely comfortable. The phone rang and made her jump.

"Morning love, I'm just ringing up to let you know that breakfast is on for another half hour and after that.... It's a case of wait till dinner," said Honey.

"Thank you," said Chantelle "That was very nice of you. I'll be down in two tics. Oh... would it be too much to ask if I could have a lunch box packed... I'm to start work on the 'job' this morning."

"No bother at all love" said Honey "I'll make sure you've got a tidy lunch, don't you worry on that score Chantelle." 'Chantelle is such a lovely name.' Honey said, more to herself than down the phone. Chantelle had already put the phone down and scrambled into the bathroom to wake her self up with a cold-wash.

Skipping down the stairs, she felt like a young girl again. As she walked into the panelled dining-room,

Chantelle noticed there were only four people eating. Honey came over with a steaming plate of breakfast and whispered in a low voice "They come here all the time, practically live 'ere they do.... Lovely bunch though, not 'ave a bad word said against them." The other diners looked over and studied the quiet, thoughtful young woman. One turned to her husband and said "She looks as if she's got a lot on her mind, doesn't she Malcolm?"

The husband stared at Chantelle for a few seconds and then turned to his wife and said "Maud, mind you're your business, whatever she's doing is nowt to do with you, get on with your food woman!", and she did. The food was excellent and it didn't take her long to polish off the 'fry-up'.

Chantelle popped her head round the kitchen door and called to Honey. "I'm off now Honey; hopefully if all goes well today and I get some work done, I'll be back around six. Is that too late for dinner?"

"No", the reply came from the open fridge, "I don't serve dinner until near 7.00 pm. It depends on what I decide to cook really, and the older ones don't mind waiting... They're quite happy with a couple of biccy's and a nice cuppa tea to tide them over... Don't forget your lunch Chantelle love it's on the table in the big box... See you later". With that Honey disappeared into the fridge again muttering to herself, about the 'lack of items and 'what on earth' was she going to cook tonight?'

Chantelle smiled to herself. You know, Honey really was a "sweetie", she reminded her of Granny Wilson, her Mum's mum, she was fabulous and she'd helped her a lot over the past five years. Enough of that though, she had a job to do and that was what she was going to focus on now. So with that mental telling-off, she strode forcefully out to her car,

"Oh... Damn", she'd forgotten she had left it in the hedge. Striding off towards the garage, she really hoped,

13

'Old Gedd' as Honey called him, would have a spare run-about until her car was fixed.

"Hello, anyone there?"

She called out, into the open garage. Chantelle walked in and looked for Gedd in the office.

"Hello mi dear, did you sleep alright... I managed to pull your car out of the ditch, it's round the back".

Chantelle walked slowly round the back of the garage, she really didn't want to see 'her little car' in the bad way she knew it would be, but it had to be done.

"Oh God, it's a mess!"... She looked at the 'mess' attached to Gedd's tow truck. It definitely didn't look like her car; it was greener with plant life than silver paint, that's for sure.

"I'll fix her up... A good job it'll be for sure, don't you fret about that ok".

She turned round and saw compassion in his eyes.

"Thank you Gedd... I know you will... Is it possible to borrow a car? I need to get down to the cottage to start work". She thought that meeting 'Glyn' would be interesting too.

The little car trundled down the lane at quite a fair pace. Gedd had definitely come up 'trumps'. The mini was not in its prime, but it did go from A to B and if it continued to do that, then that was a lot better than walking. As Chantelle drove round the last bend, just past the large gap in the hedge – made by her car, she saw a large red Mercedes parked in front of the cottage. It couldn't be 'The car' could it? She could feel her temper beginning to bubble-up. She got out of the car and 'slammed' the door as hard as she could. She could hear a 'cursing and muttering' coming from the cottage.

"Okay... Who's the joker with attitude trying to put me off my work?" The 'lived-in face' appeared at the door and the face looked like thunder.

"Oh... it's the line-cutter in person... what are you doing here?" said Chantelle.

"I'm trying to do some work before my boss turns up!"

"Well," she replied, "she just did... I'm your 'boss', and before we start work let's try to clear the air. YOU were driving too fast, not me, and Mister Bully with the 'lived-in face'. Get off my back, out of my face and start work, OK!"

Glyn looked at the 'nutcase' he'd seen in the hedgerow... It was only yesterday wasn't it...? Why then did it feel that he'd known her for years? "Okay then 'Miss Boss Lady', would you mind coming into the cottage and I'll tell you what I think needs replacing, or adding and then you can tell me what your angle is, OK?" Chantelle agreed and followed Glyn into the living-room.

After four hours, they both decided it would be a good idea to have something to eat. Glyn said he'd go eat in the village and Chantelle didn't stop him. She had some serious thinking to do. What a different man he seemed to be when he was talking about something he really knew about. The beams overhead needed treating, but not replacing. Which was good because she thought it would change the feel of the room if they had to come out. And all the ideas for the upper-rooms were well thought out too... If he could do what he talked about, the decoration she had to do there would be much simpler.

He didn't seem to be such a hot-tempered person when he was working. While Chantelle mused, she decided to eat Honey's well made lunch box. How did Honey know that cottage-cheese and lettuce were one of her favourites? She polished them off and washed them down with flavoured mineral water. To finish she munched her way through a very juicy peach.

"Oh... Now I'm all sticky" she said aloud.

Reviving a Rose

"Well you'd better wash it off then." Said this very deep voice, behind her.

"Eek (she leapt up) you idiot, you made me jump. What am I going to wash the 'sticky' off with brainy?"

"Well you could try the old water butt at the back of the kitchen; it's quite clean… or you could walk down the path and spring clean yourself in the stream." With that Glyn went back into the cottage to do some work. There was a kind of mysteriousness about her… if only he could figure it out what it was. He had tried over dinner, but that just gave him a headache and a strange feeling in the pit of his stomach. Still enough of her, he had some serious work to do.

The beams didn't take long to treat, but when it came to sorting out the fire place, he'd need some muscle power there. He went out to the Mercedes and 'popped' the boot. He grabbed the chimney cleaning stuff and also something that looked a bit like a small pick. It was definitely hard work, he was sweating buckets, so the only thing he could do was to take off his shirt and 'get' stuck in.

Plumes of coal dust seemed to fill the room and all that could be seen of him, was his feet. The digging was well in hand and Glyn was pleased to discover an immaculate Victorian fireplace, well it would be when he'd given it some black-leading. It would certainly be a wonderful centre-piece, and a definite focal point of the room, when everything was finished. He tried to picture the result. No… he never would do that… that needed brain cells and his were already occupied.

4

Chantelle had taken Glyn's second suggestion and forged a path down to the stream she'd seen on her earlier visit. The willows seemed to stretch out their branches to welcome her down the path towards them and to the stream. She shivered, it was freezing, she decided just to dip her hands in and splash her face.

"Oh… damn" she didn't have a towel. As Chantelle stood up, the sun decided to put in an appearance. She returned to the cottage, smiling to herself and pondering what plan of action she'd have for the garden. She let herself into the kitchen, only to be met by a dense cloud of coal dust.

"Oh… Brilliant" said Chantelle as she gingerly made her way into the living-room.

"Oy… watch where you put your feet" a voice said… where did it come from, she couldn't even see her hand in front of her face, Glyn stood up and Chantelle laughed out loud. "You look like you've just finished at the pit face."

"Yeah... well it's gotta be done, otherwise the chimney will catch fire... anyway try looking in the mirror 'Spitfire', you don't look so clean yourself." Chantelle thought for a minute before replying "What do you mean Spitfire?" Glyn laughed and said "small plane... looks tame... hidden depths and fire power... I think that fits you to a tee."

With that, he strolled off out the back door and marched purposely down the garden path towards the willows. She didn't mean to look but her gaze was drawn to the coal covered muscles and sinews, as he started to strip off. God, he wasn't going to dive in was he! Peeping through the little kitchen window, she gasped and stared as the two toned Adonis dived into the stream. She let out a chuckle, betraying the fact that she was watching and enjoying the view, as Glyn surfaced and looked up towards the cottage. He could just see someone at the kitchen window.

"It's freezing, but you're welcome to join me BOSS." He shouted. Quickly Chantelle turned away and she blushed, but you couldn't see it because of the coal dust. She decided the safest option would be to get a hand towel from Gedd's car and use the water butt. I mean, going down to the stream was tempting fate and fate could be a dangerous animal, as well as Glyn Mathews too!

The work in the living room was progressing very well, and it was hard for Chantelle to comprehend, how almost a week had gone by since she'd seen Glyn well muscled coal covered body disappear into the stream. He didn't mention it and she certainly wasn't going to bring the subject up. Mind you, she had some real trouble getting to sleep, talk about colourful dreams. She hadn't realised her imagination was so vivid. I mean, Glyn hadn't even 'touched' her, apart from picking her up when she fell into the remains of the hedge on the day they had met.

Chantelle's Journey

Something to eat she thought, it must be time for lunch. Looking at her watch, she was surprised it was nearly 2 pm. Because Glyn was working so hard inside and she was tackling the garden, all sense of time had vanished. She called through the back door.

"Glyn! Are you hungry? It's nearly 2 pm and I thought you might like to share my lunch... it's far too late to get anything in the village now!"

"OK Boss lady, I'll break bread with you." Glyn came out into the back garden and stood with his hands on his hips, to survey the view. He had to admit it; 'the spitfire' had done some amount of work on the messy garden, that he'd seen when he arrived on the first day. Because his stuff was out the front, he had no need to walk round and see what Chantelle had been up to, not that he'd been tempted though. He perched on the upturned planter and decided that the best plan was to start off with pleasant conversation and see if it led anywhere.

"Are you enjoying your stay at the Briory Bush? I hear it's really nice there." He picked up a sandwich, which was so full of salad it looked as if it might explode, and sank his immaculate set of teeth into it.

"Yes I am" she replied "Honey Graham is such a love; I think she's trying to feed me up. I mean, just look at the size of her sandwiches. Their like a three course meal in themselves aren't they."

She decided it would be easier to eat some of the salad from the sandwich first before tackling the rest. Glyn watched as she picked out bits of lettuce and tomatoes and nibbled on them like a rabbit. Talk about still waters running deep, he thought about his next statement whilst he chewed on his sandwich.

"Were you a rabbit in a previous life or are you practising for the next one?" Chantelle stopped chewing and looked at Glyn properly, fully, for the first time.

"I beg your pardon... am I a what?" she hadn't been listening; she was trying so hard to think of trivial conversation... it was hard work!

"I said... were you thinking of being a rabbit in your next life, you certainly eat like one." He wasn't sure if she was just startled or embarrassed.

"I didn't realise my eating was putting you off," and with that Chantelle stood up so quickly that the box on her lap spilled over.

"Oh..." She bent to pick it up and as she did so, so did Glyn. The bang of their heads seemed to stun the pair of them. Glyn recovered first though. "Well spitfire I didn't think your framework was so thick! I think I may have to retire for maintenance."

"Pardon me... I'm sure," she replied. "Your head must be as thick as the chimney breast in the cottage at least," Then they both rubbed their own heads and laughed. An easy truce seemed to have evolved. Glyn wished he'd bumped her head earlier. She was definitely a hard nut to crack, so to speak!!

Two hours later, after digging out lots of weeds and wearing out one set of gardening gloves, Chantelle stood up and stretched. Putting her hands in the small of her back, she leaned over backwards slightly to get the knots out.

"Ouch" she groaned "I need to exercise more," she said to herself and decided that they had both done enough grafting for one day. "Glyn you can finish for today, I'm all done in anyway, and I don't expect you to work on if I'm going."

Glyn walked out and looked about the garden. "Well 'Boss-Lady' you sure have been busy, I'm doing fine in there and if you don't mind I'd like to work on and finish the fireplace tonight... I'm at a crucial stage and I like to get it done in one go, that's if you don't mind!" Chantelle walked in and the room seemed remarkably clean now. The last time she'd seen it, it was full of soot!

"Yes, you carry on then Mr Mathews."

"Glyn if you please." He said quickly.

"Glyn then; Um ... I'm going back to the hotel... if you'd like to join me for dinner, we could draw up some sketches of what to work on next, and I'd appreciate some input regarding the garden!"

Why had she said that! Surely she didn't want him getting close. No, she thought to herself, it was just work; after all, wasn't it?

5

Chantelle wandered around her room. Just what would she wear, she didn't want to look too 'glamorous' but then she also didn't really want to sit down in jeans either. In the end she settled on a denim dress with a bib and brace top. It looked like a compromise between the two sets of clothes, yeah that would do.

She looked at the little bedside travel clock... it said nearly 7.00 pm. Chantelle rang down to reception to ask Honey what was for dinner. It took quite a few rings before a breathless husky voice asked. "Is that you Chantelle love? I was just in the middle of making the gravy."

"I am sorry I disturbed you Honey, but I've been out all day at the cottage and I wondered what was for dinner. Also, could you feed one more?"

"Hang on a minute, one question at a time love!" Honey said, "Now let me see... there's a nice rib of beef, with three different veg, finishing my half bags you know... 'Em... there's roast taters and Yorkshire pudding, one of me specials that is. Next you got a baked Alaska but I cheated there... I bought some little ones in town last week when I went to whole-sellers"

"Honey" interrupted Chantelle, cor she couldn't half talk. "Is it okay to feed one more?"

"What... Oh course it is love, yeah there's only the four regulars, your self, me and Gedd." Chantelle wondered if Honey was blushing.

"Yeah... I think I can stretch the beef to feed eight love... see you in a minute. Oh by the way, do I know who's coming to dinner?" Honey chuckled to herself and Chantelle replaced the receiver. "Well, here goes." She took a deep breath and went down stairs.

Glyn had taken all of ten minutes to get ready. He had left some gear at Gedd's Garage. Gedd was a nice old bloke and he passed quite a lot of work Glyn's way. Glyn gave Gedd a few quid to store his tools and other stuff in one of his old sheds round the back of the garage. Cold water and a small shaving mirror, that's all he needed. I mean, he wasn't getting all dressed up for the "Boss-Lady" was he. He didn't even know her name either. Glyn decided that the casual look was the best option for this meal at least. Maybe it could be the first of many, who knows.

As Glyn walked over to the Briory Bush he decided to do just a little investigating. Walking into reception he saw a 'mature lady' standing at the desk talking on the phone. What he didn't know was Honey was talking to Chantelle.

"Excuse me Mrs!"

"Graham," said Honey, filling in the pause. "Can I help you love?" She said as she replaced phone, still chuckling as she thought of what she'd just said to Chantelle.

"Yes" Glyn said, "I'm supposed to be meeting a lady here for dinner!"

Reviving a Rose

"Oh you're my extra meal then are you? I 'spect that Miss Adams will be down in a minute, you just go through and sit where you fancy. OK!" Honey said smiling. Well she thought he's a bit of 'nice crackling' and no mistake... a feast for the eyes. "Rats." Glyn said under his breathe; he'd hope Mrs Graham would have told him his boss' first name.

He had just sat down at a small table in a little alcove when Chantelle walked in. Not sure of herself she stepped through into Honey's lovely and comfortable dining room; she saw Glyn in the alcove and walked across to join him.

"Evening "Boss-Lady" or is it Miss Adams," Glyn said as he stood up. Chantelle grimaced and said slightly offishly,

"You can't call me that! Look Glyn, the name is Chantelle okay. If you want to use any other name, please keep that for work!" She sat down. That went well didn't it! Oh, bother, was she going to get on with this man or what!

Glyn grinned and decided to put a light-hearted tone in his manner. After-all he did have to work with her, didn't he.

"So Boss... Chantelle, erm what do you have in mind for the décor then?" He asked just as Honey appeared with some minestrone soup. "Out of a tin." she whispered to Chantelle, as she placed a bowl on the table in front of her. Chantelle stifled a giggle. Honey really was a one-off. Glyn, obviously not in on the catering arrangements looked between the two of them and decided, they'd ganged up on him.

"Well come on girls? What's the joke then?" They both looked at him and burst out laughing.

"Nothing" Chantelle spluttered, "Honestly it's nothing." Glyn wasn't too sure about that. Honey looked to Glyn and said "Do you mind a nice Roast Beef dinner Mr?"

"The names 'Glyn Mathews', and 'yes please' in answer to your questions." Honey blushed.

"Oh... you're the one who's got stuff out at 'old Gedd's' place then. He really thinks well of you... he told me so when he came in just now for his dinner... Oh! I'd better go and save my Yorkshire Pud from the oven." With that she shot off towards the kitchen.

"She likes Gedd a lot." Chantelle said "Honey is really stuck on him."

"Is that her name, its different isn't it?" Glyn said eating his soup.

"It's short for Honeysuckle... her dad named her after all the honeysuckle at the cottage. Apparently, there was lots of it flowering when she was born." Chantelle stopped talking, she thought she was babbling on and she didn't want Glyn to think she was stupid.

While they waited for the main course, Chantelle showed Glyn her sketches of the finished living-room.

"This is what I'm hoping to achieve, but I want to look in the attics upstairs to see what colour-scheme is up there. Glyn thought, now there's a prospect, being up close with 'her' in a small space, but he said nothing.

Honeysuckle Graham and Gedd Williams sat at the old wooden table in Honey's large 'farm-house' style kitchen. Tucking into their dinner Gedd said "that Glyn's a nice boy Honey, I wonder if he's got an eye on 'your' Chantelle then."

"I don't know" Honey replied as she lifted up another fork full."

"But that girl out there sure looks wounded from something in 'er past." Honey munched her beef and then stood up. "They'll 'ave ate their soup by now... and the famous four out there... I'll just serve up the dinners Gedd and be right back okay!" Gedd winked at her and she scurried out into the dining-room with her trolley. Six dinners delivered she went back to her meal with 'old Gedd'... in a while maybe 'her old Gedd'.

Reviving a Rose

Chantelle looked down at her plate, 'how on earth' was she going to eat all that!

"I think Honeysuckle is trying to feed me up." She said

"I don't think you need it, but that's just my opinion," Glyn said through a mouthful of beef.

"Do you really think so?" she replied, though she wasn't fishing for complements, Glyn would sense that. They ate the rest of the meal talking about the main heavy work that Glyn had to do upstairs on the conversion.

"That en-suite bathroom will need extra support beams put in. We don't want 'your Mr. Rodgers' falling through while he's in the bath, do we?" A picture flashed into Chantelle' head, of 'her' boss, falling through the ceiling while in a bath-full of bubbles. She nearly choked on her veg.

"No... we don't" she agreed.

Honey and Gedd were now polishing off their Baked Alaska's and Chantelle and Glyn ears should have been burning because they were the main topic of conversation in the kitchen.

"So Honey, do you think they are going to get together then… I think there is along way to go."

Honey looked up and said, "they do 'ave a long journey but I think after a few false starts, those two 'ave got a definite future. Only trouble is who's going to make the first move." They sat there pondering and Gedd thought that this was quite a comfortable place to be and Honey was a good cook too! Maybe he ought to think about his future as well.

Honey took the dessert out to the diners. The 'famous 4' declined and retired off to their homes in the village. Honey had told Chantelle that it was cheaper to eat here together as 4 than it would be for them to cook in their own homes.

She said, she gave them a bit of a discount on account, they were lovely and did no harm, and she liked cooking any how.

6

Feeling as if she would burst Chantelle stood up.

"Well Glyn, if you ready, we could go up now?" For a second Glyn couldn't remember where they were going, not her room surely. No stupid the attic, remember, he told himself.

"Honey" Chantelle stuck her head round the kitchen door and asked for the attic keys. She stopped in full flight... what she saw was not meant for her eyes. Gedd had pulled Honey into his wiry-but-powerful body and kissed her full on the mouth.

"Well" he said "There's plenty more if you want 'em." Honey blushed like a schoolchild.

"Well I wouldn't mind but slow down a bit Gedd."

"Slow down" he said "we could be six foot under next week girlie, gotta get it while we can. Bits could drop off you know!" Gedd chuckled and let her go.

"Oh... 'Ello love', Honey; stop blushing woman and give the girl that damn key, will you. Then we can carry on where we left off."

Chantelle grabbed the key, garbled a thank you and shot out of the kitchen like a scolded cat.

"What's up Chantelle... seen a ghost," asked Glyn.

"No" she said "Even scarier, Gedd was kissing Honey in there... I've never been so embarrassed!"

"Well don't dwell on it 'Spitfire' we've got some snooping to do... remember!" Glyn said as he headed off towards the stairs.

The nearer they got to the attic, the more nervous Chantelle got. Stop being so silly, she told herself, we're only going to look at the attic not 'ravish' each other. She was glad it was dark, he couldn't see her blush. Glyn opened the door and snapped on the light-switch. A single bulb swung back and forward in the room. As Chantelle walked in she was 'dumb-struck'. The room hadn't been touched. The walls were covered in the original paper. This must have been where the servants slept.

So although it was old, the paper was not the real 'posh' stuff she'd hoped for. Still you couldn't have everything.

"Chantelle, come over here." Glyn said she walked across the dusty floorboards. "Look what I just found."

She was amazed, it was like finding treasure. Glyn had found an old hessian sack with 12 rolls of wall paper. From what she could see, the bright colour red with flecks of gold. It had to be remains of the stuff used to decorate the 'downstairs' when it was first built. God; It must have been up here for, what 120 years at least and no-one had chucked it out. What a find! She was excited she hugged Glyn and kissed his cheek. Just as she realised what she had done, she pulled back, but two strong arms pinned her against his chest.

"Hush, I'm not going to hurt you 'spitfire' trust me!" Glyn said, breathing in the perfume from her hair. She felt wonderful, soft and firm at the same time. Chantelle began to struggle.

"Look... I'm sorry I did that but... I would appreciate you letting go please... you're squashing me!"

He was holding her and she wanted to get away... but she felt safe at the same time. What was wrong with her? Didn't men just want one thing?

"I'm sorry," she said and breaking free she picked up the sack and almost ran for door.

"I'll... em... see you back at the cottage tomorrow." And with that she bolted like a frightened rabbit down stairs to her room.

Glyn looked on "thank you for dinner" he said but she didn't hear him. Well! What a 'spitfire'. Yep, he'd been right about that. But what was this 'freezing' in his arms bit? Someone had hurt her and he felt angry... he had wanted to keep her in his arms and protect her, but from what? He would have to find out.

"Oh well" he said, and locking up the door, he went down stairs to hand in the keys. Maybe Gedd or Honey could shed some light on what was bothering Chantelle.

Glyn 'pinged' the bell, he didn't know if Honey was still in the kitchen, he waited by the desk. A very flustered Honey bustled in and said

"Hello again... you were quick up there... I thought you'd both be pokin' around up there for ages yet!"

"No" Glyn replied. "Chantelle left rather hurriedly, I think I may have upset her, but I don't know why!" Honey studied his grave looking face.

"Well I'm not sure love, but it seems she's been 'urt real bad like by some past boy of hers."

"That's what I thought too." Glyn said "I think she needs careful handling there, sort of 'burnt fingers' syndrome." He said and then Honey asks him to come into the kitchen.

Reviving a Rose

Gedd was still there and the three of them sat down for coffee. They decided to 'sort her out' even though she wasn't actually in the room.

"That girl needs someone special to fetch her round." Honey said, as she poured the hot steaming coffee into 3 mugs.

"Yep" said Gedd. "She's some doll... it's amazing what a drop of ol' romance can do for a person." With that he smacked Honey on the bottom.

"Oh you are a saucy devil. Pack that in, I nearly had the coffee over, you daft old coot." Honey tried to sound angry, but she started to giggle.

"Hold it you two, stop mucking about and let's get back to the topic in hand... the 'Spitfire' upstairs..."

"Spitfire, now there's an unusual nickname," mused Gedd... "Any reason why Glyn?"

"Yeah, but it's kinda hard to explain... Okay." With that the three of them put their heads together and tried to psycho-analyze Chantelle Adams.

Meanwhile the person in question was sitting on her bed deep in thought. What did she run for, she was the one who had cuddled Glyn and kissed him! Oh, did she feel like a prize pillock or what!

Chantelle lifted the hessian sack onto the bed and pulled out one of the rolls. God, this stuff was beautiful. Maybe Honey would let her buy it to use in the cottage. "Forget the rag-rolling," She would do wonders with this stuff. The roll seemed to be quite thick, and as she unravelled some of it, the stunning colour seemed to leap out at her. It was so rich and screamed 'money' at her, who ever had originally built the hotel certainly had a few pounds to his name.

"I wonder who he was." She said aloud, could be interesting to find out, maybe he had built some other bits of the village. Maybe, she was getting excited now; maybe he had built the cottage too. She rolled the paper back up and decided to take the 'bull by the horns' and ask Honey tonight about buying her 'treasure'. After all Glyn would surely have gone home, wherever that was, by now.

Why she almost crept down the stairs, she didn't know. Shaking herself mentally she stopped and thought, don't be so bloody daft, you're not a burglar for heavens sake. Crossing the Dining room she walked straight into the kitchen. The effect was stunning, the three people in the room all stopped talking and looked at her. They looked like naughty school kids caught pinching sweets. She laughed and said,

"What have I walked in on then?" Nobody said anything so she pulled out the spare chair and turned to Glyn. "I thought you'd have gone home by now!"

"What makes you think that then "Boss-Lady"!" Glyn grinned, he liked teasing her, she was like an itch and he needed to scratch badly. She was getting under his skin, that's for sure.

"I'm enjoying Honey and Gedd's very fine company and we were having a very graphic conversation.

"What about" asked Chantelle. Her curiosity was starting to get the better of her.

"Mind your own..." Glyn said tapping the side of his nose.

"Well I don't care anyway; I have other things on my mind." Chantelle sat down at the table and purposely ignored Glyn.

Staring at Honey she asked "You know we found the sack with the original paper in."

"Yes! What about it?" Honey said

"Well" "I was hoping you might sell it to me, to use at the cottage." Chantelle said and then Honey's head came straight up.

"Oh no... I'm sorry Chantelle love... I can't take money for that stuff its priceless." Chantelle looked crestfallen and was about to get up when Honey added.

"But you can have it for nowt... I couldn't take your money love. You use it as you see fit, alright!" Chantelle jumped up and hugged Honey.

"Oh, thank you, it's brilliant... I can't find the words to say thank you."

"I think you just did love!" Honey stated. The two men just looked at each other shrugged their shoulders.

"Women!" they both said.

Honey said "Chantelle love there's just one thing I will ask of you, if you don't mind."

"Fire away Honey" Chantelle replied.

"If you could take some photos of your work for me, I'd like to see the old place done up nice." Honey sat back down and looked at Gedd.

"Ain't it about time you went 'ome yer dirty ol' stop out!?"

Gedd stood up "I know when I'm not wanted. You're coming Glyn?" He said turning to the younger man.

"Sure Gedd, I've got a lot on tomorrow, the bedroom needs working on now, a lot of hard graft." The two men both said goodnight and Gedd sneaked a quick kiss off Honey.

Honey and Chantelle both cleaned up the remnants of the evening meal together quickly as the boys left and went off to Gedd's garage.

Chantelle said "It's time I turned in too. Thanks again Honey... I'll do a good job you'll see and you'll definitely get some cracking photos... Goodnight, sleep well."

"Yeah you too love. See you in the morning." Then the both of them went to their own rooms.

7

The day dawned clear and bright and Chantelle got up and dressed really fast, she had a garden to work on. There were tons of jobs to do and if she was very lucky Glyn would stay upstairs. The man in question was already at work, he hadn't slept too well, his dreams were full of Chantelle, but she didn't run away in them. In fact, the way he dreamed it, she had pulled him down onto the floor and passion unbounded had been there aplenty! The beams and plaster work needed his fullest attention so he stripped to the waist again and set to work.

Chantelle meanwhile, had polished off her cereal and had now arrived at the cottage. She walked round to the back garden and stood still. It was still a beautiful view. Now then, what would she do today? Well she had found the herb plot, it was full of Parsley, Dill and Thyme, and they all smelt so wonderful. Especially as she had cut them back, fresh cut herbs always had a lovely bouquet.

Reviving a Rose

Unlocking the little out-house at the rear of the cottage, Chantelle changed into some dungarees, put on a stout pair of gardening gloves And then, picking up a large shovel and fork, she went to the first flower-bed.

"Ugh... the mud must be bone dry." She said to herself as the fork hit the earth. Maybe if she soaked it a bit she'd be able to do more. And so it was, that half an hour later after soaking as much of the garden as she could she set to work digging. "That's better" Chantelle mumbled to herself and set to work bringing the large flowerbed back to its former glory.

She was surprised to find three rose bushes that looked very sorry for themselves. 'I need some good old fashioned manure and bone meal', she thought as she cleaned the bindweed and other weeds away. She sat back on her sturdy boots and looked at her work. It was thirsty work for sure, so she drank hard from the water bottle Honey had filled to go with her lunch.

Onto the next one, "Up and at it" that's what her Granny would have said. The next bed was a weird shape to say the least. It made its way round a big mound, which was covered in bramble and briar-bush.

This was going to be a challenge. Grabbing a handful of the 'mess', she tugged hard. It was held fast by what ever was underneath. She tramped back to the outhouse and rummaged around to find some clippers.

Back at the 'mess' she hacked away for about 20 minutes and had amassed a pile of brambles. The 'mound in the middle' was slowly being uncovered.

"Wow! Oh wow! It's lovely." Chantelle's face lit up and as she brushed the dusty moss off, she could now see it was a large statue. It seemed to be of an old man and young child. The child was standing at the man's feet looking up. He in turn had something in his hand. She brushed again and revealed a bunch of roses tied up with what looked like ribbons.

"Oh how beautiful." She decided to plough on and clean the rest of the prickly mess away. Chantelle wanted to finish this bit off before having her lunch.

Meanwhile, Glyn was having a hard time of it too. The plasterwork would all need stripping and the beams here didn't look too sound. Clumping down the stairs, he collected a sack of plaster mix and a bucket. He had already taken a mixing board upstairs to mix on and a trowel. It was heavy work and he was sweating well. As he dumped the sack down on the bedroom floor, he looked out of one of the tiny leaded windows. There in the wilderness of the 'garden' he could see Chantelle tugging at some 'prickly stuff'.

"Nah" let her get on with it. She'd only say he was patronising.

Pulling his gaze away he began to bash the dodgy plaster on the walls. It fell like off like icing from a cake. Underneath he could see the original framework by who-ever had built the cottage. What a privilege it was to work here, he would definitely take care on this job. It was almost a sin to take payment, but he had debt-demons to feed, so that thought disappeared quickly.

"Damn," he'd forgotten to bring up some water to mix up his plaster.

"Oh well, better go and ask the 'Spitfire under prickles' if she had a bucket. Conveniently hiding the one he had under the plaster he had knocked off.

Glyn opened one of the tiny windows and called out.

"Chantelle, would you please give me a hand to fetch some water to mix the plaster." He stopped and looked out of the window at the flower bed. There seemed to be a large tangled mess of prickles with legs! What a sight, he hadn't laughed so much for ages. Hearing the laughter Chantelle dropped the bundle and called up.

"If you've got so much energy... then how come you're not giving some help here, especially if you want help yourself matey. So get your butt down here and lend a hand eh!!"

"OK 'Boss-Lady'" Glyn said, retreating inside.

A few clumping noises were heard and then he appeared in the garden next to her. She jumped.

"God... you're like a creeping cat, why didn't you whistle or something?"

"Cos; I didn't know a good tune, that's why." He replied grinning to himself.

"Oh shut up and look at this." Chantelle said as she showed Glyn the statue.

"Wow" he said, "That's a cracker huh!" "Right 'Boss-Lady', what has to be shifted then?" He said

"If you could shift the chopped stuff round to the side of the cottage with the rest of the rubbish and plant life I've cleared. I'm going to make a compost heap when I've finished the garden, to go behind the trellis I'm planning near the bottom."

"OK" he said and grabbed an armful "Ouch... you didn't say the prickles were that sharp!"

"Well that's what prickles do dafty!" She grinned and grabbed some as well. Chantelle was glad she had thick sleeves on. Mind you; it didn't stop her sweating though.

After they had finished shifting all the garden rubbish, Chantelle filled up a bucket with water and went inside. Glyn decided to try to run a hose up outside the cottage and feed it through the window. Because it had a special nozzle he'd be able turn it on and off like a tap.

Walking into the bedroom, Chantelle was surprised too see how much plaster Glyn had actually taken off. "Well, now what?" Chantelle said, as she put the bucket down.

"Can you drop that rope out of the window, and I'll tie it to the hose? Then I can pull it up to the bedroom." Glyn said as he stuck his head in the doorway. With that clumped back down the stairs and back out into the garden.

"Chantelle" he hollered.

"Can you drop the line?"

"Coming down" she called back and flung out the coiled rope making sure she kept hold of the other end.

It didn't take long before he was back in the bedroom. The room seemed really small and dusty now with both of them in there.

"Right "Boss-Lady" a lesson in making plaster. If you just tip some plaster mix onto the board and make a well in the middle... that's right. Then tip in a little water. It's kinda like making a cake!"

Some cake; the plaster seemed to have a life of its own and it didn't want to stay on the board. She scraped and mixed and after a bit, it almost looked like plaster. Looking up she could feel her temper rising,

"I never said I could do this you know... you're the workman... work then!" and with that she stood up. In doing so she managed to kick the bucket 'so to speak' and it tipped over. For a little amount it certainly went along way. What with all the dust, the floor got very slippery and as Chantelle tried to escape she slipped.

"Ouch... help me can't you?" Glyn tried to but he slipped too. Almost landing in her lap he rolled to one side and a very deep rumble from his chest started to grow into a loud throaty laugh. Full bodied it was and he just rolled around clutching his stomach.

"Priceless... that was just priceless. My boss 'kicked the bucket' and still managed to get dirty as well." With that he tried to get onto his knees to help Chantelle get up. But despite her best efforts, she started to laugh too. The pair of them couldn't get up for laughing. If anyone could see them... well what a sight. The whole room was literally 'plastered' in plaster but not in the right place.

"You need a wash 'Boss-Lady'" said Glyn as he tried to stand up.

"Yes... I'll have to go back to the hotel."

"No you won't" came the reply.

"It's hot enough to dry off outside."

"Outside... what the..." With that Glyn scooped up Chantelle and made his way down the stairs. When he was half-way down the path Chantelle realised what was going to happen.

"No... put me down... Glyn; please... No you can't!"

She suddenly realised where he was going, and it wasn't down the side of the cottage towards the car.

"Oh yes I can and I will put you down now!" Glyn said as he jumped into the stream still holding his Boss.

Spluttering and screaming Chantelle surfaced. It was extremely cold in the water even though the day was hot. Glyn, meanwhile, had dunked himself and was rubbing the mess off his chest, Chantelle was transfixed. What a body... if only she could just rub some of the dirt off. Almost as if she was hypnotised she made her way towards Glyn. He in turn was amazed at what she was going to do. Would she have the nerve to do it?

A shaking hand lightly and hesitantly, brushed against the solid muscled wall. Glyn gasped, and it was only one hand. God, she didn't know what she was doing to him. He was so glad the water was cold. Chantelle was now stood in the front of Glyn and the other hand had of its own free will, it seemed, joined its partner in the cleaning of her work-man.

"Can I do the same for you?" Glyn said shakily.

"No... Please don't speak... I... I've never done this sort of thing before." Chantelle couldn't fathom out her body at all. Her hands were working to their own set of rules and her body seemed to be on fire. An aching feeling in her stomach nagged at her and she really wanted to kiss him... God what was she doing. Glyn decided that maybe one kiss was worth a try. He looked deep into her eyes and drew her towards him.

When their lips met, both seemed to forget they were in the water. Chantelle's body was on fire... the heat seemed to be everywhere and her brain was going scatty. Glyn in the meantime was having trouble telling his body to behave. The kiss was definitely getting to him, he broke away and they just both seemed to be dazed.

"Oh... God..." Chantelle suddenly realised where she was. This was too embarrassing, that was twice she'd thrown herself at him. What must he think of her? She waded to the bank and clambered out.

"I'm going to the hotel to change if you want you can finish for the day, I am..."

Glyn didn't speak, he didn't trust himself too. That girl definitely got to him, even the water wasn't working anymore. He got out of the stream slowly and headed back up towards the cottage. "Well, it's hot enough" he said to himself and stripped all his wet clothes off except for his 'boxers'. The day had started off fairly well and when he had jumped in the stream with Chantelle it had gone downhill rapidly. Would he have a job tomorrow? Oh well, he might as well get on with the walls.

Walking back upstairs Glyn stepped back into the bedroom. He could still feel the electric atmosphere. The floor was covered in a kind of slurry, he would leave it to dry and sweep it up later. Turning to the job in hand, Glyn started to mix up some proper plaster on the board and set to work doing the walls. Because the walls were sound behind the old plaster it was quite a straightforward job. He worked on solidly and the room was finally completed in 6 hours.

He hadn't realised how long he had been working and his stomach grumbled noisily. He decided to head off to 'Gedd's' get a wash and hopefully have something to eat, if he grovelled to Honey.

He locked up the cottage and set off to his new 'old truck'. It was much easier to use for working. Besides, using the 'Merc' was not a good idea. Gedd had sold him the old run-about for the price of decorating the living quarters. He couldn't do a job like Chantelle would but then Gedd wasn't going to live in a palace. All Gedd had wanted done was a lick of paint and fill in some holes. Glyn thought he had the best end of the deal.

The truck chugged its way down the lane and into the garage car park round the back. He definitely needed a hot bath, but as Gedd only had a shower that would have to do. He had gathered up all the soggy clothes that he'd stripped off earlier in the day and stuffed them into the washing machine. The shower was cold but Glyn didn't mind, the water cleaned all the soap off his body, but his mind was working overtime. He was transported back to the stream with Chantelle hands running over his chest; he would have let her do more.

Why had she lost her nerve? He decided that he would ask Honey if she knew where Chantelle had come from. There couldn't be too many girls with her name and body around here, could there?

Chantelle had arrived back at the hotel, cold, wet and very angry. Not with Glyn though. He hadn't done anything wrong, she was fuming with herself. What was it about his body that made her brain switch off?

A sort of automatic pilot clicked in and her body did anything it wanted with her brain screaming 'No' and the body saying 'Yes please, more, more'. She went straight up to her room and she hoped she wasn't making the carpet too wet. Chantelle closed her curtains and stripped off completely. She put her wet things in the sink and decided a good soak in a hot bubble-bath was the best plan of action. Steamy plumes soon rose up towards the ceiling. The bathroom smelled of exotic fruits and spices. She sighed as she slipped gently into the bubbles.

"Ah... bliss" She sank down slowly and just soaked for a while letting the water take away the chill from within her bones. What-on earth had possessed her to do that. He must think she was such a tramp, and yet nothing could be further from the truth.

Chantelle had had no boyfriends after her encounter with Ben. "Ugh" even just the thought of him made her cringe and shiver. The bath suddenly felt cold, so she topped it up with hot water until she nearly boiled herself like a lobster. If she had to, she would scrub away to rid herself of the 'dirty feeling'. Would she ever feel clean and rid of 'him'.

"Men" they just weren't worth it! After towelling her body dry and putting on clean clothes, Chantelle rang down to ask Honey what she had for tea!

"Honey... Is that you...?. "Oh hello, it's you Gedd... What are you doing down there?"

"Honey has her 'ead stuck in the oven... it's alright she's just cleaning it love".

"Oh right... could you ask her what's for tea tonight please?" She could hear Gedd speaking to Honey but she couldn't quite make out what out what Honey said in reply.

"Uh, huh... right, I'll tell her... she said to tell you it's omelettes for her 'regulars' and if you fancy it she's going to 'ave a go at a stir-fry job".

Gedd spoke again to Honey and said again. "She said, is that a yes or what?"

"Yes please" Chantelle said "I like stir-fry its one of my favourites actually". With that she put the phone down and picked up a sketch pad.

Chantelle was quite an artist and with the cottage logged in her memory, she drew some sketches of how she wanted the rooms to look. She drew steadily for what seemed ages and then putting down her pen, she massaged her hand. The sketches were very precise and so full of detail that if anyone had seen them, they

Reviving a Rose

would have thought the job was done already and not just a vision in a girls head.

It was just after 5.00 pm that Chantelle woke with a start. For a moment she couldn't remember where she was. She had been curled up in a ball in the foetal position with a 'throw' covering her. She couldn't remember pulling that over herself but she must have, because the door was still locked. Her sketches had dropped to the floor and she scooped them up and closed the book to protect them.

She scrambled off the bed and into the bathroom; cold water was splashed onto her face and it seemed to wake her up. She went back into the bedroom and looked at her sketches. Yes the Living Room would look fantastic when she'd done it up. Chantelle wondered if Glyn had carried on working or gone home like she did. Well it wasn't quite home but she really felt comfortable here. Honey was a smashing woman and Gedd wasn't a bad old bloke either. But Glyn; now something really sparked her body off there; trouble was it kept doing it at the wrong time.

Tidying herself up, she put on a clean pair of slacks and a lacy top over a crop top bra. She felt clean and refreshed but Chantelle wished she hadn't done what she did at the cottage; men weren't to be trusted were they. I mean 'Ben' had proved that for sure, didn't he.

Giving her reflection a smile; in the mirror to cheer herself up. She went down stairs.

"Honey where's that stir-fry then?" she said, as she trooped into the kitchen. She stopped dead in her tracks.

"What are you doing here?" She said to a 'Cheshire Cat looking' Glyn, sitting at Honey's table tucking into a large plateful of 'Stir-Fry'.

"Oh, I see you've dried out then... I've just been telling these two about your dip!"

Chantelle's Journey

Chantelle blushed and sat down hard, surely he hadn't gone into graphic detail.

"Really, and what was that?" She tried to sound curious, but it came out really fast like a challenge.

"Well" Said Gedd. "'E said that you'd been working in the garden and got all hot an' bothered what with all that sun today, and he felt sorry for yer, so he chucked you in the stream".

Glyn stuck a forkful into his mouth and chewed, a twinkle sparkled in his eyes. Chantelle thought that it wasn't far off the mark, but with a certain bit missing.

"Yes, it was really hot today, wasn't it?" She said, not to anyone in particular, just to the room. Honey decided the two men had had enough fun and she came to Chantelle's aid.

"Ere you are love; a nice bowl-full; just out the 'Wok thingy'. It doesn't 'alf jiggle about on the cooker. I think I prefer frying pans me self." Chantelle gratefully took the bowl and head down she really got stuck in. After about four mouthfuls, she began to focus on the taste. This was really fantastic, what had Honey put in it? She would have to get the recipe for when she went home.

"Honey, this is brill' where did you get the recipe from?"

"No where love... out of my old head, I just kind of chucked bits 'n' bobs in and some soy sauce... it's not bad is it?" Honey said; as she sat down to eat with the rest of them in the kitchen.

"Mind you I don't think my 'regulars' would eat this. They'd say it were rabbit food for sure!"

They all laughed and a sense of friendship and comfort descended on the kitchen. Chantelle watched Glyn eat his food. He attacked like a ferocious predator, it didn't last long. He looked up and grinned, Chantelle's stomach flipped over and she could feel her blood beginning to race around her body and straight to her head. She

43

could also feel her cheeks burning, but valiantly looked straight back and smiled gently.

Gedd and Honey exchanged knowing looks but said nothing. They had a kind of telepathy going on, that two kindred spirits did and words weren't needed. He decided he was getting too old to wait months to court her so he'd have to act fast; he didn't want her getting away.

Honey really like Gedd she thought they would make a good team, maybe he'd help her run the hotel. She had been thinking of getting help an anyway. What with all the fetching and carrying she had to do in the busy summer months.

"Well then, you lot want any pudding?" Honey said; after finishing her food. "I'm just going to have a look-see in mi' freezer... Fancy an ice cream or something?"

The three others in the kitchen all said together, "Yes please, that would be brilliant!"

Then Gedd said with a wicked grin on his face,

"Yeah, we need something to un-burn our tongues... they're on fire!" He chuckled and then said 'Ouch' as Honey playfully clonked him on the head with her wooden spatula.

"You cheeky bugger don't insult my cooking or I'll make you eat the leftovers from Sunday my lad!" The two older people in the kitchen decided to wash up so it left the two younger people at a loose end.

They grabbed a coffee each and went into the lounge. Chantelle sat down and nervously sipped her coffee, just what would she talk about. Then she remembered the drawings.

"Oh Glyn... I did some drawings of the cottage; you know how I hope it will turn out when I've finished decorating, I'll just go and get them." Without waiting for a reply she scampered upstairs to her room to get them.

Glyn flopped down into a chair. What had he done this time, nothing he could think of? Just as he was mulling this over, she re-appeared. This time though, she had a sketchbook under her arm.

"Glyn, here's the book, would you mind looking through the sketches and give me your honest opinion!" Chantelle passed her work over to Glyn. He flipped the pad open and studied the sketches. She was good; he could really see the cottage finished. Maybe he'd still be around when it was.

"They're really good 'Boss Lady', really good. I wish I had an imagination like yours, I can almost see the finished product. You really do know your stuff don't you?"

"Well I did study for my degree, although it took a bit longer than most courses do."

"Why?" Glyn said; although as he said it, he noticed that her eyes had now gone very dark and hooded. She seemed to be retreating into a shell, like a scared little hermit crab.

"I had to take a break for a while," she paused and said almost too herself. "It took a while to get over it!" Why has she said anything, Chantelle was really angry with herself. But there was something about Glyn that made her feel safe enough to talk.

"Over what?" He said softly. He wanted to help her, he liked Chantelle an awful lot and something about her made him want to protect her and keep her safe.

Chantelle took a deep breath and in a quiet voice, almost a whisper, told Glyn exactly what 'Ben' had done to her, and how with help from her family, especially her gran, she tried to get on with her life. By the time she had finished she was crying, as she spoke and it tore at Glyn's heart. He didn't like seeing her cry; if he could get his hands on that excuse of a man he wouldn't be responsible for his actions.

"Please Glyn," Chantelle said after wiping her eyes, "don't tell anyone please... I'm trying to get on with my life and I don't want the pitying looks, I had enough of it in my own town. I don't know how people found out but I had to get away."

"Of course I won't" he said "I won't say a word if you don't want me too!" Glyn passed Chantelle her coffee, it was cold but she drank it anyway.

"Er... would you like a fresh one?" Glyn said as he headed for the kitchen. His head was filled with her 'trauma', how on earth would he be able to help her.

Well that was it; he would be gone now... why on earth had she told him all the stuff from her past. She hadn't told people outside her family. But some of them had told 'their' friends, which was obvious after awhile so she had to leave town.

"Here's your fresh coffee!" The sound of Glyn's voice made her jump, she looked up into a pair of very concerned eyes. Chantelle didn't see pity, for a change, but what she did see gave her hope.

"Thanks Glyn. Look, I'm sorry for off-loading on you like that; I didn't mean too, I don't normally tell people about my past."

"That's okay Boss... Chantelle" This wasn't the time for nicknames.

"My shoulders are big enough, I can handle it." Glyn hoped this was true for both their sakes.

Meanwhile back in the kitchen, Honey and Gedd had finished all the dishes, and after talking on their own, they decided to 'just have a peek' at the 'young-uns' to see how they were getting on. To say they were 'shocked', to see that Chantelle had been crying, was an under-statement.

"Well then," Gedd said trying to ease the tension in the room. "What you two been up to, you'll soak Honey's carpet, you will, she'll not be very pleased." Glyn sat up and nodded very slightly in recognition and beckoned the pair over.

"What's up love? My cooking's not that bad is it?" Said Honey. Sniffing loudly and wiping her eyes Chantelle said in a watery voice.

"No Honey, it wasn't your cooking I've just been getting something off my chest, that's all."

"Ere, that Glyn there hasn't been upsetting you as e?"

"No Honey, actually Glyn has been really nice honest!"

"Look I'm feeling a bit 'wrung-out' so I'll just go up to bed okay." With that Chantelle got up and bid them all good night and with lead-filled legs she slowly climbed the stairs to her room.

Gedd, Glyn and Honey went back into the kitchen. Honey put on a new pot of coffee and turned to ask Glyn.

"Well then what's upset 'my Chantelle' then? It wasn't you was it?" Glyn shook his head.

"Who's gone and hurt 'the girl' then?" Honey fired off a rapid sortie of questions.

"Hold on, hold on there. No, and I am not allowed to tell you."

"Why not, and what's wrong?" Honey asked as she poured out 3 steaming mugs of coffee. Gedd replied before Glyn.

"You can't ask 'im to break a confidence if he's promised ol' girl, he said he promised, so you'll have to wait and see if the young 'un will tell you herself, drink you coffee woman!" He shoved Honey's mug towards her. The three sat in silence apart from the odd slurping sound as Gedd drank his coffee.

"Well," said Glyn. "I think I'll head off to bed too, there's a lot more plastering to do and I want to start on the bathroom tomorrow as well if I can."

Reviving a Rose

Glyn lay on his bed re-running all the evening through his mind. No wonder she was all chop-n-change. She was hurting very bad inside and he decided that he would try to help her as much as he could. Mind you he'd have to tread carefully; he didn't want to scare her off.

When he did finally get to sleep his dreams were very vivid and actually made him sit up. One in particular had him punching lumps out of 'Ben', but it was like the camera was behind the one being punched because Glyn couldn't see 'Ben's' face. He had sat up with a jerk, covered in sweat and shaking his hands in the air. Maybe he'd been strangling the toe-rag. Glyn hoped for Ben's sake he didn't ever meet him, because Ben would definitely come off worst.

Glyn looked at the clock it showed 6.30 am, he switched the radio on low so that he didn't wake up Gedd. Plodding off to the washroom he decided to play very carefully with Chantelle. She was damaged and he didn't want to hurt her accidentally.

"Gedd." He shouted, after having a wash and shave.

"Do you want a mug of tea?" Having got no reply he stuck his head round Gedd's bedroom door and grinned. The crafty beggar wasn't in his own bed. Well best of luck to him, Glyn thought to himself as he chuckled and got dressed.

Honey was a lovely woman and a very good cook too! Gedd would do well to land her. Glyn decided to take a snack to the cottage rather than stick around and sort out breakfast.

He packed a picnic basket, well a big plastic box, with enough food to last all day. Then he found three large bottles, two of which had still water in and the third one cherry pop, he wanted to finish the bathroom and the less time he needed to stop the better. Within half hour Glyn had arrived at the cottage and he set off upstairs to tackle the bathroom.

The subject of last night's dreams was herself awake early. After escaping the previous evening, Chantelle had filled her bath up as much as possible with bubbles, and it was as hot as she could possibly stand it. She had soaked in the bath for a long time and had a good cry. By the time Chantelle had dried off and crawled into bed she felt almost calmer. She felt like a great weight had been lifted off her shoulders, talking to Glyn at the time had been really hard, she'd definitely been through the 'wringer' but the after effects had outweighed the first painful steps. He seemed so calm, and strong. She would like to get to know him but it would take time and patience. When she had woken up in the morning Chantelle felt really light and happy, she had slept like a log and her body and mind both seemed to be very, very refreshed.

She too unbeknown to Glyn had decided to go to work early and 'get stuck in'. It was about 7.00 am when she almost skipped down the stairs and she walked into the kitchen. Funnily enough, it didn't feel like a hotel, it felt like a really comfortable home. Maybe it had something to do with Honey, she was definitely an 'Earth Mother' and Chantelle, felt really happy staying there at 'The Briory Bush Inn'.

8

All sane and happy thoughts disappeared from her head as she saw Gedd's face contorted in pain and shock; he was trying to lift Honey off the kitchen floor.

"I just came down from upstairs. "He said

"And there she was, just lyin' on the floor. I think she banged her head on the table as she fell down, there's some blood on it." He said almost crying as he half carried, and half pulled Honey's limp body into the lounge.

"She asked me to stay over, cos we had been gettin on so well like, and I was going to ask her er to wed me an all!" Gedd said in a broken voice.

Between the two of them they managed to get Honey onto a sofa. Chantelle was stunned for a minute or two, but then a sort of automatic pilot clicked in.

"Gedd, go and ring for the doctor and whilst you're there call an ambulance too! And please try not to worry OK!"

Gedd almost ran, off towards the reception area to phone, and Chantelle put Honey into the recovery position. She sat on the floor next to the sofa and watched 'her patient' like a hawk. Satisfied that Honey was breathing OK and not about to peg out on her she nipped quickly into the kitchen for a cold compress for Honey's head. Just as she got back to the sofa; Gedd came back through.

"Dr. McArdle said he'd be 'ere as quickly as he could, he said to ring for an ambulance, I told 'im I did and he said OK."

"How's my love doing kid?" asked Gedd.

"Well, she's breathing OK and I've got something cold on her head wound but I'm not a doctor Gedd, lets wait and see uh?"

It seemed to take hours but in fact it was only about ten minutes. They both heard a car pull up, followed almost immediately by the sirens of an ambulance arriving too. Dr. McArdle bustled in and set straight to work. Putting a cuff on Honey's arm and listening to her chest, he smiled slightly as she began to moan softly.

"Well," he said "the patient seems to be coming round."

Gedd sat down on the adjoining sofa and held Honey's hand tightly; this resulted in Honey saying in a low but recognisable voice "Oy what you trying to do dafty, you'll be breaking my fingers... what am I doing on 'ere." She tried to get up and said "Ow... it feels like someone's been trying to crack my 'ead open like a boiled egg!"

Dr. McArdle smiled at her and said

"Honey, whit have you been playin' at woman, trying to dent your kitchen table... can you remember the last thing you did?"

"Um... sort of," she said "I think I was sorting out the dinner for me 'n Gedd, and the regulars too!"

Reviving a Rose

"Well, you won't be cooking anymore today madam, yer blood pressure is way up and I need some tests done on yer, to check up on yer ticker OK."

So saying he put a needle into her arm and drew off three vials of blood.

"Scotty, leave some for me will you, I need it at my age." Said Honey; rubbing her arm.

"Oh! By the way, let me introduce you to Chantelle Adams. Chantelle this is Scotty McArdle local physician and nag and very good friend." The Doctor and Chantelle shook hands and she sensed that he too had been worried until Honey had come too. Gedd in the meantime was a different man. Now his woman was awake, and gabbing away, he looked his normal placid self.

"I woz worried about you," he said

"Don't do that again. I don't know about your flipping 'heart but mine sure did go on a race or two."

He kissed her and cuddled her up into his strong arms to hide the tears shining in his eyes. He didn't want her thinking he was too soft.

"Honey" Scotty said "You need your bed now... no more stairs with you."

Turning to Chantelle, "She'll not need the ambulance I'll send it away." "Mind you watch her... she's libel to sneak away into her kitchen. If you have to, 'staple that one t' the bed', she's t' stay there for the next few days okay."

"But!" said Honey "What about my 'regulars' I can't let them down?" She tried to get up groaned and lay back on the sofa.

"Now you listen t' me woman." Said Scotty

"When I say rest, its rest you will or you'll be leaving in a box. <u>Now</u> do you get me? Look Honey I dinnae want to scare ya', but if you won't listen you've to be telled proper. Now behave and you'll be fine okay!" With that he lifted her chin and kissed Honey's cheek.

Chantelle's Journey

"I like you, your one of ma' oldest friends, stay that way a wee while longer alright!" Scotty said as he peered into her worried face.

He turned to Chantelle and Gedd and beckoned them both outside into the reception area.

"Look you two, you're not to worry cos' she'll get wind of it, make sure she gets the rest and I'll come back tomorrow." Gedd looked at the kindly face and shook his hand firmly.

"Don't you worry on that count Doc, I'll stick 'er down with super glue if I have too, I want 'er well enough to wed 'er not bury 'er." He finished all choked up and blew his nose to hide the tear trickling down his cheek.

"Gedd, what are we going to do? I mean about Honeys 'regulars' I'm a lousy cook... I can make tea 'n' coffee and snacks but the kind of stuff Honey does is well above me." Chantelle shrugged hopelessly.

"Don't you worry love" said Gedd kindly. "When I get all cleaned up... I'm not a bad chef you know... mind you I aren't done it for a while cos' someone (pointing to the lounge) won't let me near 'er cooker. Well time to get cooking I say."

So Gedd went off to investigate the freezer and pantry and Chantelle and Scotty both went to Honey and half-carried her off upstairs to her room. Once the Doctor and Chantelle had made Honey comfortable, they both kissed her on her cheek and quietly left the room. Honey sighed softly and went to sleep. She hated to admit it, but she was really tired, she drifted off to sleep. Honey was relieved, now that 'her' kitchen and hotel were in safe hands.

Meanwhile, downstairs the two people she thought very highly of were listing all the contents. Chantelle picked out an un-labelled bag and frowned.

"What on earth is this then?" She said, as she twirled it around.

"Well, it looks like a bag to me," said Gedd with a smile, "why don't you open it and have a look-see."

"Ugh... it looks like a load of chicken livers, they look really disgusting." Gedd had a look and chuckled.

"Well they don't look to hot, now do they?" He went across the kitchen and picked up a cookbook. Flipping through the pages he found what he was looking for. "Here we are Chantelle, a recipe for 'Chicken Pate Royal', I think we can rescue the 'little blighters' and turn them into something really tasty."

Chantelle pulled a funny face and said "Well it might be tasty, but I think I'll pass thank you."

The two of them plodded on and finally after two hours, they had listed all of the contents of the pantry, fridge and freezer.

"Phew, I could do with a cuppa, I don't know about you young lady. Do you want one?" Gedd filled up the kettle and looked at Chantelle with a questioning gaze.

"Ooh... yes please Gedd, my mouth feels like a sandpit... I suppose we'd better start on the food for the 'regulars' and something light for Honey... Do you think she'd like some tea and a bowl of light soup?" As she was saying this, she filled a small bowl and heated it up in the microwave whilst Gedd made Honey a cup of sweet tea.

A gentle knock on the bedroom door roused Honey from a much needed sleep. "Come in who-ever, I'm awake... and decent." Chantelle laughed and came in.

"Honey... I see you must be feeling much better.... how are you?" Honey sipped her tea and looked at Chantelle.

"Well... I do have a right good headache, and I do feel a bit wobbly too... it's a good job I'm lying down."

Honey finished her tea and made a valiant attempt at the soup, but she only managed half and then she felt really tired. So she called out to Chantelle, who was reading a magazine by the window.

Chantelle's Journey

"Chantelle love... could you be a dear and take the plate of soup down for me... I'm a bit tired now... I think I'll have a sleep for a bit." Chantelle removed the tray, kissed Honey on the cheek and closed the door gently, hoping she wouldn't wake Honey up, who at that moment was snoring softly.

As she walked into the kitchen she sniffed long and hard.

"Hmm... something smells really good."

Gedd looked up and grinned. "Not bad eh... something for dinner tonight Chantelle, come and have a look-see!"

He beckoned her over and she was really impressed, mind you she wasn't quite sure what it was.

"Okay... I Give in... What exactly is it Gedd?" She said peering in and sniffing deeply.

"Well" Gedd said "It's not the livers, though I was tempted to let you taste 'em. No it's another chicken recipe, a sort of casserole-type thing. I'm just about to make some suet dumplings."

The door of the kitchen burst open with such force that both Gedd and Chantelle jumped.

"Where is she... is she really hurt bad... why didn't you let me know?" Glyn said all in one breathe, as he stood in the doorway puffing and he looked really worried too!

"Calm down lad... if yer on about Honey, she's sleeping, an' apart from a bang on the 'nut' she's gonna be fine... Sit down lad and 'ave a mug of coffee, we'll fill you in whilst I do mi' dumplings."

Gedd pushed Glyn down into a chair and Chantelle gave him a mug of coffee with extra sugar in it, and no milk, just right for shock. Actually, Glyn was just as shocked to see Gedd cooking and with a 'pinny' on too! He just had to grin at Gedd and decided that a floral apron was definitely a total change from Gedd's overalls.

Reviving a Rose

"So come on, tell me then... what happened to Honey." Glyn said as his frown returned, so he propped his head on his hands and leaned on the table.

"All I know so far is that the 'Doc' came by the cottage and said that if I needed you for anything," pointing at Gedd, "I was to look for you at 'Honey's Place' 'cos she'd had an accident." He looked between the pair of them like a spectator at a tennis match.

"Well now" said Gedd. "I came down this morning and found my Honey on the floor in 'ere. Was a shock I can tell you...? Anyway just as I was looking at 'er and getting in a bit of a tizzy, young Chantelle there cum in and we got her into the lounge and called the ambulance and the 'Doc'." He finished in a rush and thumped his suet mix for good measure.

"The Doc arrived just as 'My Ol' Honey' started to wake up and did she 'ave a bad temper on her, or what?"

Glyn could just picture Honey with her hackles up, she could be very impressive in full flight. He'd seen 'it' first hand last season when Honey had, had some stroppy customers in the restaurant. Boy did she send them packing, and dripping in soup if he remembered rightly.

"So, are you sure she'll be okay," he said looking at Chantelle "I mean there are no lasting effects or anything?" He sat down, Chantelle was quite impressed at the concern shown on his face, but she didn't answer Gedd did.

"She'll be fine, don't worry, honest Scotty said all she needs is rest. Me' an' the young 'un 'ere," pointing to Chantelle, "will make sure she does." Gedd attacked his dumpling mix one more time for good measure.

"Right 'en lets get these 'ere dumplings into my stew or the 'regulars' will be sending out for pizza." Chantelle scuttled into the pantry for some more flour and just as she reached the table she tripped over Glyn's foot. Although it wasn't deliberate Chantelle flew at him.

"You idiot, we've already had one accident in here today are you trying to make me another statistic." As she said it the flour bag decided to leave her hands and deposit itself all over Glyn's face and shoulders. Despite her temper, Chantelle couldn't help herself and she doubled-up in a fit of hysterics. Even Gedd started to laugh, apart from easing the tension of the day; Glyn really did look funny with all the flour over him.

"Oy..!" Glyn spluttered and coughed, shaking the flour in plumes, and filling up the kitchen.

"Stop it you two... come and help me dust off will you?"

Gedd just stood there laughing and shaking poor old Chantelle couldn't even get up off the floor.

"Right then" said Glyn, and stood up and walked over to a crumpled giggling mess, who was Chantelle. He then proceeded to shake all over her just like a wet dog does, Chantelle looked up and a blanket of flour descended down on her like feathers escaping from a burst pillow.

"Stop it." She said still laughing.

"Stop it you idiot... you're covering me in flour too."

She stood up and grabbing what was left of the flour bag she jammed it down on Glyn's head. The bag exploded, what was left flew around the room and down the back of Glyn's clothes. Gedd sat down hard on one of the kitchen chairs and just looked at the scene evolving in the kitchen.

"Right, you witch!" Glyn said as he grabbed a handful of suet-mix. "Come here if you think you're so brave."

"No...No... Glyn. Come on I was only playing."

Chantelle backed away slowly. Gedd continued to watch, but stealthily he leaned across the table and rescued what was left of his dumpling mix.

"Now, you two," he said "If you're going to play, do it in the yard... I've got to do dinner in 'ere and I need my space." As he said this he slowly guided the two, who were facing each other, out the back-door. Glyn looked at Chantelle and he grinned sneakily as he saw a slight spark of fear in her eyes.

"Now then 'Boss-Lady', if you can dish it out, I think you should be able to take it.... don't you?" Quick as a snake he grabbed her arm and with the other hand he rubbed the handful of suet mix all over her face, and as she tried to protest, he also got some in her mouth too! Glyn let go and studied his work.

"Well, Miss Flour-Mix, I don't think you'll try that again... huh?"

Chantelle stood there seething, just what could she use on him? And then she spied it, a water-butt with a saucepan in it. With a sudden turn of speed she ran across the yard and grabbed the saucepan. Dunking it in deeply and quickly she spun round ready to soak Glyn. He was right there in front of her and he grabbed her wrists firmly.

"Ouch," she said, "you're hurting me... ooh you bully."

Glyn just laughed and then very slowly he tilted her right-arm. Slosh!! He tipped the contents of the saucepan right over her head, not forgetting to dribble some down her neck.

"Now... 'Boss-Lady', we're even I think." As he turned to go, thinking he'd won, she dipped the saucepan again and boy, did she slosh him one.

"Ha, see how you like it, buster!" Chantelle said as the water ploshed down on Glyn's head. She squealed out loud, as Glyn turned on his heel and pinned her arms to her sides, he marched her backwards slowly and deliberately.

"Sit on it lady, and cool off!" He said as he SAT her in the water-butt. Chantelle screamed as the ice-cold water soaked through her clothes.

"You pig, you rotten pig... just you wait!" Then Chantelle realised that she couldn't get out of the butt. Her legs had folded and she was in up to her knees.

"Glyn... Please?" She called.

"Glyn, please, what?" He said as he turned round, "you, just called me a pig ... twice I recall... what do you want wet-lady?" Chantelle just sat there looking hopeless and very wet.

"Will you please get me out...? I'm supposed to be helping Gedd, remember?"

Glyn decided to lift her out, and as he did he couldn't help but laugh as a very... very wet Chantelle emerged from the water-but. She stood there shaking, half in temper and half because she was absolutely soaked.

"I suppose I should say thank you... well, thank you for nothing... You stuck me in there in the first place." She looked down at the floor and under her breath, she said, "Just don't."

"Did you say something 'Boss-Lady', only I thought I heard you mumble... maybe it's your teeth chattering? I'm sure you don't want to go back in?"

"No... No... I'm just cold, that's all." She said, "I just need some warm, dry clean clothes, that's all."

Glyn decided that a lot more of her needed warming, she looked really sexy wet. Just as she did at the stream; but he didn't want to rush her.

Mind you Chantelle had similar thoughts, she was impressed with the way Glyn's muscles showed through his work clothes. She stretched out her hand without really knowing what she was doing. Her body seemed to go into automatic pilot again, just like it did in the attic.

Slowly and steadily she stroked her had down Glyn's wet back, feeling the muscles tense and tightening. Glyn could feel his body tense up at Chantelle's touch. He turned around slowly and looked into Chantelle's eyes.

Reviving a Rose

She seemed to be transfixed. Her arms slid around his neck.

Glyn in turn slid his hands around her very neat waist. Chantelle walked into his arms and as she put her head onto his chest, she sighed. Why did this feel so right when she knew in her head that all men were trouble?

Glyn just held her, waiting to see if she would do anything else. He was really enjoying this clinch but his body was also beginning to show it. What would she do? Would it spook her, make her back off?

Chantelle had never felt safer in her life she just wanted to stay there. But hang on a minute, there was something moving below and it registered in her brain (Watch out dummy he's aroused). She tried to spring back, but Glyn held her firm.

"Sh... still... be... still... I won't hurt you... you just get to me that's all." Glyn tipped her chin up and looked at her, (She had green eyes that he wanted to drown in.) "Look Chantelle, I'm not going to hurt you, okay. I just really like where you are, you feel wonderful. Hasn't anyone told you how beautiful and sexy you are?"

Chantelle looked at him and said, "No... not that anyone's meant it anyway!" She looked down.

"I don't feel very beautiful, in fact, I don't think about it. I don't think I am." She sounded so sad. Glyn wished he could have got hold of 'Ben'. He really could have killed him for this.

"Look Chantelle,' Glyn said as he tipped her chin again, 'I really do like you but I won't push myself on you. If you want anything, we'll go at your speed okay!"

With that he kissed her gently on the lips, his brain went BANG and all sorts of weird and wonderful feelings flowed all through him.

The same effect seemed to have happened to Chantelle, her legs seemed to have gone all wobbly, so she clung to Glyn and gulped a few deep breaths.

Glyn held her firmly and she reached up again, her hands under their own steam, stroked his cheeks and just kissed him. (Oh, it felt like lots of waves rushed all over her.) It felt so good, her lips tingled and she kissed him again to see if it happened again.

Glyn's brain was turning into mush. Did she know what she was doing to him? His body screamed to be pressed against her, she was gorgeous and he really, really liked her... he did and that surprised him. He thought he was immune to the woman's charms.

It seemed to last for ages but it was only a couple of minutes. Glyn decided to kiss her back 'his' way and see what she did. He kissed her and very slowly he pulled her tight into him. Showing her just how much she affected him. He kissed her deeply and slid his tongue into her mouth and ran it along her teeth.

If Chantelle thought the first lot of 'fireworks' were something, she was WRONG! Her brain was doing its own special firework display, which also seemed to be travelling throughout her body.

Glyn deepened his kiss and teased her tongue, and nibbled her lips. He moved off of her mouth and across her cheek and off down her neck. He half sucked and half kissed her. Chantelle moaned softly. Then just as suddenly as all this had started, Glyn held her away, making her feel lost.

"Why... you stopped?" She said with startled eyes and swollen lips from just being kissed.

"Why?" Glyn tried to regulate his ragged breathing. "Don't you know? If I don't stop now... I might not be able to if we carried on. Besides, you don't want to be ravished right here in the yard, do you?"

Chantelle seemed to come out of her trance-like state. She looked around and shivered. What was she doing?

"Er... I'll go and erm... help Gedd with dinner... em after I've changed... yes, that's what I'll do, then yes... erm, see you later at dinner then!"

And with that she shot off, in the direction of the kitchen door. Glyn watched her go and sighed deeply.

Maybe this was going too fast but she was setting the pace, wasn't she? (I mean,) he thought (I'm only human… I don't think she realises just how much she affecting me). He shook his head and walked off in the direction of Gedd's Garage to have a VERY COLD shower.

Meanwhile, safely in her room and in a stinging shower of her own, Chantelle tried to sort out her body and her brain. The 'body part' was easy; she thought as she scrubbed away at herself with the loofah, the 'Brain Part' was going to take longer.

She felt so safe in Glyn's arms, but weren't all men 'bad'? And if so, why was she letting herself be hurt again? Towelling herself off she dressed quickly, deep in thought she set off downstairs for the kitchen.

Pushing open the kitchen door she sniffed deeply, something definitely smelled 'good'.

"Oh… you're back are you then?' said Gedd. "I thought you'd got lost. Has Glyn gone off somewhere then?" He said with a wink and a sly grin.

"Yes." Said a very; embarrassed Chantelle. "He said to tell you he's going to do something in the garage…he'll be over for dinner later."

With that Chantelle looked for a distraction and got stuck into sorting out the plates for the 'regulars'.

"Right then, madam!" Gedd said as he opened the oven door, "Let's get the 'old 'uns' fed and watered." He put some soup into the four dainty bowls he had found in the cupboard.

"Chantelle, love," he said "could you take the soup through and sort out the 'regulars'." As an afterthought he said "Oh… If they ask about Honey tell 'em she's fine and resting, okay?"

Chantelle did as she was asked, and as she was setting the bowls the 'regulars' all requested the full story on Honey.

"Well," she said "Gedd found her in the kitchen this morning." Chantelle didn't think they needed to know he'd walked down from upstairs, she continued.

"Honey was on the floor unconscious,' the 'regulars' all gasped, 'don't worry." Chantelle said, "She soon regained consciousness and 'the Doc' said that apart from a nasty bang on the head and a brilliant headache, she'd be fine. Honey just needs to rest and have a few tests run on her, that's all."

Maud, the one who had watched Chantelle's arrival asked, "Who's cooking then? I mean if Honey's upstairs, then who's feeding us lot?"

"Well,' said Chantelle with a smile and a chuckle, 'you'll never guess, but it's Gedd!"

The 'regulars' looked stunned, and Malcolm, Maud's long suffering other half said with a grin.

"Will it be edible then? We've never had a sample of 'his' cooking." Chantelle laughed softly and they all thought she looked much nicer than when she first arrived.

"Gedd's never been allowed in the kitchen before. It takes a bang on her head for Honey to let Gedd anywhere near her cooking utensils."

Chantelle chuckled again and unknown to her, her whole face lit up and her eyes sparkled.

"Chantelle!"

Said a muffled voice from the kitchen.

"Can you take up something for Honey, I got mi' hands full with the stew."

Gedd looked up as she walked into the kitchen.

"A 'nice' cup of tea and a very light omelette should 'do' Honey just fine."

A few moments later Chantelle knocked gently on the bedroom door.

"Come in who-ever, I'm not asleep." Honey's voice said through the crack in the opening in the door.

"Hello," said Chantelle, "How's the headache then?"

Reviving a Rose

"Oh... not too bad, only six blacksmith's banging around, instead of the twelve earlier." Chantelle put the food across Honey's lap.

"I hope your appetite is better than the last meal... still do you best eh... I'll be up later for your tray. Have you had your painkillers?"

"No, I was waiting for something solid to take them with."

Honey said Chantelle left her to it and went downstairs to report to Gedd in the kitchen.

"How is the invalid then?" He said as soon as she walked into the room.

"Fine, she's had a good sleep and is a little hungry, she said she'd try and eat as much as she could. Why don't you go up and see her after you've finished here?"

"Yeah," Gedd said, "I'll just do that."

He dished up the food for 'the regulars' and Chantelle transported it into the lounge. A chorus of voice all at once said in unison,

"How's our chief doing? Is she alright?"

"Yes, yes, she's fine. Honey's resting upstairs and we are all looking after her. Now, please eat your food. Gedd took a lot of time over it."

The Oldies tucked in and Chantelle returned to the kitchen.

"Well, is there enough left for us?" Chantelle asked Gedd as she walked back into the kitchen, "Or are we on the egg diet too!"

"No, we're having stew as well, Oh, I called Glyn and he's coming over for some 'scoff' too! He's not a cook like me!"

Chantelle chuckled to herself as a visual picture of Glyn trying to cook and failing miserably. He was covered in dough of some description and swearing.

"What are you sniggering at 'Boss-Lady?" said Glyn as he stepped into the welcoming kitchen.

"I just came round to update you on the work I've got done today."

He sat down at the table and Gedd placed a large plateful of stew 'n' dumplings in front of him.

"Are you 'ungry Glyn, I thought you might have worked up a bit of an appetite down at the cottage?"

Chantelle and Gedd joined Glyn at the table and tucked in. Not much talking was done until the plates were empty.

"So" Chantelle said, as she cleaned her bowl with bread, "You promised an update on the work." She looked up from the plate and into his eyes, the tummy was flipping a bit but she swallowed hard and made her brain behave itself.

Glyn returned her gaze and grinned. "Well, the bedroom is finished and awaits your expert touch. As to the en-suite bathroom/shower there is a little more tiling to do and then it's all yours as well."

Chantelle was impressed but didn't let on to much. "OK... well that means you can help-out here. I'm sure Gedd will teach you if you asked him nicely."

She smiled an impish grin and Glyn had a feeling he'd been set up!

Gedd watched the pair of them and decided he would report the very early stages of the romance to 'his-girl' upstairs. He stood up and said

"I'm just going to check on my lady, I won't be long, please try and entertain your selves till I get back."

With that he walked out of the room grinning. Chantelle and Glyn just looked at each other and smirked.

"Well I" they both said at the same time, "No you first, I was just going to say that if you had anything else to do, don't let me stop you. I'm going to clean up in here for Gedd." Chantelle said and set to work putting all the dishes in the sink.

Glyn sat on the edge of the table.

Reviving a Rose

"I think I'll just sit here awhile and enjoy the view," he said and ducked as Chantelle threw a wet cloth at his head.

"So!" Glyn said "How is Honey doing really? I didn't want to ask whilst Gedd was still here?"

Chantelle put down the retrieved cloth and turned to Glyn saying

"Well Scotty is happy with the way she's behaving so far, but he still wants to take some more bloods for testing, just to make sure that there isn't a serious reason for the fainting episode.

So it looks like the cottage will have to wait for a while until Honey's better.

I think I'll go up now and send Mr. Rodgers a letter of explanation, as to why completion will be a bit late. I'm sure he won't mind, he likes it here and he may be worried about Honey himself." So with that she finished the dishes.

"Leave that" said Glyn. "I'll finish drying-up and let myself out. Oh... and don't worry about your deadlines, I'll do as much as I can and I might even clear a bit more of the garden. But I won't do your important stuff I promise!" And with that Glyn kissed Chantelle on the cheek and pushed her gently out of the way and picked up the tea-towel.

Chantelle blushed and 'scooted' up to her room. As she did so, she could hear a deep throaty chuckle coming from the kitchen.

She let herself into room No. 7 which felt so much like a special place to her now. Chantelle felt safe here, like her old bedroom back home.

Sitting on the bed she began to write the letter to Mr. Rodgers;

> *I hope you liked the first set of photos sent to you recently. The cottage is a dream and hopefully I will do it justice. There is a slight problem with our agreed finishing date.*
>
> *I am at present living in the 'Briory Bush Inn', which I have been informed that you stayed in whilst looking for a 'new home'. The lady who runs this establishment as you may or may not know is called 'Honeysuckle Graham' and she is not well at all. In fact, not wanting to distress you, she was found on the floor in her kitchen with a 'gash' on her head and unconscious. I must stress that although she is awake, she needs a few tests to check her over. Until they have been done, I have offered my limited services in assisting Gedd Williams (the owner of the garage) to look after the hotel.*
>
> *I do apologise and will write again soon to keep you informed.*
>
> *Yours respectfully*
C. Adams

By the time Chantelle had finished it was after 10.00 pm. She decided to just 'pop' her head 'round Honey's door. Just to check on her. Chantelle opened the door very quietly. As she peeked around the door she held back a gasp.

Gedd was kneeling on the carpet by the bed, and although she couldn't see Honey's face, she felt sure that she knew what was going on. She closed the door as quietly as possible, so that the two people wrapped up in their own little world wouldn't be disturbed.

Maybe by tomorrow Gedd would have an extremely huge grin plastered all over his face. She closed the door gently and returned to her room.

9

The following morning Chantelle woke up and decided to 'try' and sort out breakfast for the 'regulars' and her two favourite people at the moment.

She washed quickly and put a freshly pressed cotton T-shirt on and a comfortable pair of jogging bottoms. Anyway! – Who was going to stare at her? She wasn't 'that' pretty, was she?

She pushed open the kitchen door and to, to say she was amazed was one hell of an understatement. Glyn was standing by the cooker 'sorting out a fry-up!'

"Honey can't eat that! She'll have a heart attack if you feed that to her." Chantelle said with her hands on her slight hips. Framed in the doorway she didn't realize how provocative she looked and Glyn was definitely enjoying the pose!

"I wasn't cooking it for Honey; it's for the 'oldies', Gedd and Me. I know you're a cereal freak!"

"No I'm not... I like a fry-up every now and again... it's just that I'm trying to look after my body" she retorted.

"Looks fine to me" Glyn said as he returned his gaze to the cooker. "Hmmm"

"Well what is on the menu for Honey then?" Chantelle said as she started to get the dishes ready.

"And how did you get in here?"

"A few scrambled eggs for the first question and Gedd gave me the spare key last night, just for today! He said he had an important question for a certain lady and he did say that hopefully he would be staying over."

The breakfast all ready, it only took a couple of minutes to serve the 'oldies' next door in the lounge.

"Right then, do you want to take Honey's food up, or shall I, just in case she's not alone?" Glyn said with a cheeky grin and conspiratorial wink!

"I think I will take it up thank you very much, I'm not a prude you know!" Chantelle picked up the tray with Honey's breakfast on it.

"If Gedd is there he'll be down those stairs quick smart for his own breakfast Okay!" And with that she made for the stairs.

A gentle tap on the door and Chantelle called softly.

"Honey, are you awake in there... I've got some light breakfast for you?" She couldn't hear any noise, so very quietly she opened the door and walked in.

What met her eyes made her glow inside. Gedd was sitting in a chair by the bed and his arm was resting on the coverlet holding Honey's hand. He had a bedspread draped around his shoulders and his feet were resting on a kind of 'pouffe'.

Chantelle felt very privileged to have seen the beautiful 'picture' before her. As she walked across the room, to place the tray on the small window table, Honey stirred and woke up. She was smiling and her whole face seemed to be glowing.

"Morning" said Chantelle "How are you feeling today, or is that a daft question?"

Reviving a Rose

"Well" Honey replied as she wriggled up the bed a bit. "I'm not sure how I feel; I've never been engaged this early in the morning before."

With that she squeezed Gedd's hand and he also woke up. The smile on his face matched Honey's and Chantelle put the tray down, she darted across the room to give them both a kiss and cuddle.

"I'll 'ave to get engaged more often" said Gedd "If pretty girls is gonna come running and giving us a cuddle."

"Oy" said Honey "Behave you old bugger, your mine now just you mind and remember that right?"

Gedd saluted as he stood up.

"Right then my woman, I'm off down stairs to wash and brush up and tell Glyn how I got on. You behave an' all madam, and I'll see you in a bit."

He left the room and both women waited until he had clumped down the stairs before both 'squealing' with delight.

"It's about time, Honey!" Chantelle said as she sat on the edge of the bed.

"Well I 'ad to make sure of 'im and make 'im realise it was all his idea!" Honey chuckled, she paused slightly… "How do I look really" she said, her eyes clouding over

"Do I really look better?" Chantelle could see that Honey was quite worried.

"What's up? All you did was 'bang' your head, there's a nice dent in the kitchen too! Look to be honest, you look 100% better than when I found you with Gedd. Talk about unusual ways of making your man make his mind up! Honestly." Chantelle said, holding Honey's hand.

"You look positively 'glowing'. How's the head?"

"Well now, it's still bashing my eyeballs from the inside, but I must admit that the sleep has 'elped… What time is it; I've got breakfast to get on the go?"

"No you haven't, remember what Scotty said you had to rest for a while, and so far you've only spent one night off duty!"

As she climbed off the bed to fetch the breakfast tray Chantelle said

"Do you remember what happened, or did you faint?"

"Well I was going into the kitchen to start sorting out the dinner like I always do and then I was on the sofa looking into Gedd's ugly mug" Honey said

"So the answer is <u>no</u> then! Never mind it was probably nothing." Chantelle said

"Maybe you over did it the night before?" She mused.

"No I never" honey said on the defensive. But a wicked smile played around the edges of her mouth.

"Well" said Chantelle. "Do you remember Scotty saying that you had to have some blood test, just in case?" As she finished saying that Honey looked worried, Chantelle gave her a quick hug.

"Look." She continued. "Scotty said it's just a formality... don't worry. I'll come with you if you want."

"Will you?" Honey gripped Chantelle's hand.

"I know Gedd loves me but I'd rather have you with me, in case it's 'women's troubles', you know!"

"Of course I will now stop worrying. Try and eat some of your food, Glyn cooked it for you 'specially. I didn't even know he could cook until this morning."

Chantelle hoped that she had re-assured Honey a bit and as she got up to go she grinned again.

"Where's the ring then?" Honey smiled and said

"He didn't want to buy it in case I said no. Well that's what I think anyway. Gedd said he needed to know how big!! Cheeky sod put a 'lastic band on look!"

She pulled out her left hand from under the covers and sure enough, on the 3rd finger was a bright yellow elastic band. Chantelle laughed and said

Reviving a Rose

"Mind it's not on too tight, we don't want your finger to fall off. I'll see you after okay." She headed off towards the door and Honey called out.

"Thanks Chantelle, you and Glyn have been a godsend to me and my Gedd. Thanks again."

"No need" said Chantelle, "It's an absolute pleasure, and I'd do it again. You're the tops Honey. I would rate you as good if not better than my Granny and she's the best." So saying, Chantelle left the room and went to find 'the boys' downstairs.

"So how do you think she really is then?" Said the boys?

"Look, I've just had this conversation upstairs. Honey looks fine to me. Let's just wait and see what Scotty has to say when he comes over alright!.. Oh, and by the way Gedd... I love the ring, it's very original." Turning to Glyn, Chantelle added.

"So where's my cereal then? I'm starving." She sat at the table with an empty bowl in front of her and spoon in hand ready for action.

"There you go 'Boss-Lady'" he said as he lobbed a box of muesli over to her. "Dig in."

Gedd was by now also sitting at the table and he seemed to have found his appetite as well, because he managed to polish off his 'fry-up' and eat some extra toast too!

There was a slight tap at the back door, and in came Scotty.

"Morning folks? Is there any tea going?" He pulled out a chair and dumped his black bag on the floor next to him.

"I've been round aboot the place doin' ma rounds and I thought 'two birds wi' one stone yer ken! Anyhoo how's ma wee girl up the stairs then?"

Chantelle answered before the boys had a chance.

"She seemed to have slept so comfortably last night that she discovered an engagement ring on her finger this morning 'made of elastic'."

Scotty turned to Gedd, who by now had turned beetroot red. "Well man, I take it yon 'lasticity' thing is yours then!"

"I didn't have the real one, cos I don't know 'ow blasted big 'er fingers are did I!" Gedd said talking into his tea cup.

"Och away... I'm only messin' ya' dafty. I'm that well pleased for yer man, 'onestly I am. Honey's a wonderful woman you're well lucky."

Scotty shook Gedd's hand in both of his, pumping it up and down.

"Steady on" said Glyn, "You'll be having water flowing out of his nose in a minute." The two men laughed and Gedd finished his tea.

"Will you be takin' some stuff off of 'my lady' this morning, and didn't you say summit about tests up at t'ospital?"

"Yes and yes" said Scotty.

"I'm no' too concerned aboot Honey up there, but just for piece o' mind, I'd like to check on the red stuff ok wi' you there Gedd?"

"Well yes" said Gedd. "I need 'er well enough to wed 'er and maybe a few years extra an' all if that's not too greedy."

"Och I think she'll manage that alright." Scotty said

"I'm away up I see you'se before I leave OK you lot."

As Scotty left the kitchen the atmosphere seemed to calm down a bit.

"Come on Gedd, don't worry so much." Said Glyn, "She's got one of the best looking after her and there's us lot too!"

Scotty tapped gently on the bedroom door and a gentle voice called out.

73

"Come in... ooh ever you are, I'm decent and pleasantly full of omelette!"

Scotty walked and smiled at Honey.

"Mornin' to ya, how's the bump on the heed, this morning. I'm going to take a wee bit more of your red stuff, just for my piece o' mind okay madam."

Honey wriggled up in the bed a little more and put both arms out straight so Scotty could chose which one to attack.

"Very nice 'lastic ring you've got there, but is it too tight?" Scotty said as he started hunting for a vein.

"Interesting yellow isn't it... the old dafty said 'e didn't have a ring cos 'e weren't sure just 'ow big mi' fingers were. Ouch... steady on." The doctor had filled three vials up and was pressing a little wad of cotton wool onto the back of Honey's hand.

"Sorry 'darlin', now then, I would like ya to pop down to the local hospital and have a wee trace done of your ticker. I don't think it will show anything but I like to be sure. In fact maybe it might just be a little anaemia and all you'll be needin', is some iron tablets and vitamins to set you right."

Scotty packed up his stethoscope and bottles and as he went to leave the room he turned to Honey and said

"I'm away to the hospital myself this afternoon, so if you like I'll take you over there?"

"Thanks" said Honey. "If it's alright, could Chantelle come with me, to keep me company?" Scotty smiled.

"Of course darlin' I've a wee bit o' room in ma car, and yon Chantelle isn't too big, she'll no tak up much room in the back there wi' you." So saying he left Honey's room and went down stairs to update the three people in the kitchen.

As Scotty sat down at the table he relayed all that he had said to Honey. "So as I said, she's to just have a trace of her ticker and just a couple of other tests this afternoon and I'll bring her back as well."

Chantelle's Journey

"Thank you" Chantelle said "I am very grateful to you, Honey's a lovely lady and I just want to reassure myself and for those two as well that she's going to be fine."

Glyn and Gedd looked at her shining eyes and both felt that Honey would be well looked after. Chantelle left the kitchen and went up stairs to see what Honey wanted to wear, when she went to the hospital.

"Oh, just a nice tidy skirt and blouse and mebbie a cardy in case it gets chilly that'll do me." Honey said, as she attempted to get off the bed.

"Oh I do feel a little spaced out, think the bump on mi noggin' 'as let some fresh air in." She said as she stood up and got her bearings.

"Steady now, there's no need to rush." Chantelle said as she helped Honey to the bathroom. "Now you sit on the chair by the sink in case you feel wobbly and I'll fill up the sink and let you have a little wash."

"Thank you darlin', I do appreciate all you and Glyn is doing, to help Gedd and me."

"Nonsense, it's not a problem! I'm pleased to be able to help in some way, I'm just going to pop next door and check my e-mails while you freshen up."

Chantelle logged on and to her relief was a reply from Mr. Rodgers waiting to be read:

Dear Chantelle (it read)

Have just read your message, most upset for Honey but glad she's in good hands. Don't worry in the slightest about Rose Cottage. Quite understand will be down to see you all at half-term. Regards to Honey & Gedd.

Yours
Geoffrey Michael Rodgers.

Reviving a Rose

Well, thought Chantelle, half-term wasn't too far away, and it would be very nice to meet Mr. Rodgers again. Yes he did look like a Geoffrey and it suited him to a tee.

She closed the lap-top and scooted back next door. Honey had not only had a wash but she'd managed to get dressed too. "Ee but I'm whacked out now... just get mi down the stairs for a cuppa and we'll wait for Scotty in the kitchen shall we?"

Chantelle agreed and they took it very slowly going down to meet the two men in the kitchen.

"Honey wouldn't a lift make a difference. I mean if it were tastefully hidden behind one of your lovely oak doors."

"Yes darlin' it would, and before I had mi funny turn I was thinking of putting one in. Look like I'll have to now, still it'll be good for trade though, eh!"

They made their way down the rest of the stairs and across the hall, past the reception desk and into the kitchen.

Gedd shot up out of his seat and said "Are you supposed to be outta bed love, what with yer bump an' all?"

Honey smiled. "Well ow do yer think I'll get to hospital, I'm not walking there on me 'head am I."

Gedd just smiled. His Honey was back on form. He pulled her into his arms and just held her tight. "God you didn't 'alf scare me, 'at I'm off down to town to get yer ring. It'll be waiting for yer wen you get back love... God I really love you woman!"

He said as he wiped his eyes, and sat Honey down at the table. She looked up and smiled. He'd do and she was glad she nabbed him. Gedd made his apologies to the others and went off to buy a 'right nice ring' for his lady.

Glyn and Chantelle looked at each other and smiled. They both thought the same thing, Gedd and Honey made a lovely couple.

Chantelle sat in the back of Dr. McArdle's car and watched the world go by. The Old Cottage Hospital was a beautiful building. Victorian and grand, it was lovely to look at. Even if the reason for coming wasn't pleasant the view certainly was.

"Right, now madam," said Dr. McArdle "Just you go off doon to the Medical Assessment Unit and get all the tests done, that have been ordered by me, and I'll catch up wi' you later on okay Honey."

Scotty said as he pulled up by the large front door with planters filled with flowers and smelling gorgeous. After leaving the car, Honey and Chantelle walked into the hospital and then slowly down the pristine corridor in the direction of M.A.U. Honey gripped Chantelle's arm tightly and sighed.

"God I 'ope all the tests are okay... Gedd'll have a fit if owts wrong wi' me."

"You'll be fine, you'll see." Said Chantelle, hoping she sounded more confident than she felt. She didn't like hospitals much, too antiseptic smelling. It reminded her of the many baths she'd had, to try and 'clean' her self after 'Ben' had done what he did. Mentally shaking herself she pulled herself together, and reminding her muddled brain, that she was here for Honey and to sort her self out.

"Ere we are then." Honey said, with more pep than she felt as she felt Chantelle tense up slightly. I'll have to find out what that's all about she said to herself. With that they both went into the unit together.

"Good afternoon Mrs Graham" The Staff Nurse on duty said

"If you'll just come through here and slip this gown on. It's just so you don't get your nice clothes dirty. Just put your things on there and we'll be back in a while alright?" The Staff Nurse assured as she, Chantelle and Honey, walked into a little room just off of the reception area. Chantelle looked at Honey and got her to sit down, she looked a little scared.

"It's just I've not bin in 'ospital apart from childbirth, and it's a bit scary." Honey said as she sat on the bed.

Chantelle squeezed Honey's hand and smiled, "It's only tests remember... not major surgery...they'll soon be finished and we'll all be in your kitchen admiring your new engagement ring, minus the elastic."

Honey smiled despite herself; yes she was lucky to have Gedd. Get a grip woman she thought. Get these tests done, get home to Gedd and then start thinking about the wedding. She smiled and Chantelle did too she hoped that the wedding would be soon, so that she would be able to go. Mind you, Honey had said that she wanted Chantelle there on 'her' side, so to speak.

The Staff Nurse came back in, and smiling at Honey said

"Oh good, you're ready then. Right oh Mrs. Graham."

"Honey please" said Honey from the bed.

"Pardon, sorry, yes okay Honey it is, what a pretty name."

"Yes," said Honey "its short for Honeysuckle, mi dad said there were a lot blooming when I was born." She felt that she was rambling a bit but it seemed to calm her down slightly.

"Certainly Honey" said Staff "and you may call me Susan. Now then lets get you all wired up and see if we can get Classic FM on your read-out shall we?"

The afternoon passed quite quickly; what with all the comings and goings in Honey's room. The ECG lady came in and stuck, what seemed to Honey, hundreds of stickers on her chest.

"How many of these sticky things 'ave I got on mi chest love." She said

"Not many, about twelve I think." said Chantelle counting. The test took no more than five minutes and ECG lady smiled ripped the result off and said okay. With that she un-plugged her machine and went off to find her next patient.

"Chantelle love," said Honey. When the lady; had left. "Could you take these sticky's off love. It'll scare the life out of Gedd. Not that e'll see 'em but all the same." She tailed off.

Chantelle grinned "of course, just a mo'." She pulled them off as gently as she could but some did pinch a bit. "Sorry, they're really sticky aren't they?" She said as the last one came off and Honey winced abit..

"S' alright darling I've had worse" Honey said as she pulled the gown down.

After having numerous tests done, checking her eyes, ears, chest, blood pressure, legs, head and everywhere else in between, Dr McArdle finally appeared. "Well Honey... I can definitely say... you're no' pregnant."

Honey and Chantelle laughed and both felt much better. If the Doc was joking things couldn't be that bad could they.

"You've got low blood pressure" he continued... "Which; is not un-common in ladies of a certain age."

"Oy" Said Honey.

"Anyway, to continue... a wee tablet a day should sort that and your iron level is a wee bit low as well... so you'll need an iron supplement. I'll give you the liquid one... it doesn't block up the tubes so to speak. We don't want to make trouble lower down do we?" He said smiling at them both. "You're done girl... it's time I took you away back hame."

"Oh thank you Scotty I'm that grateful... it's such a load off my mind..." Honey said

The Staff Nurse came back into the room and looked at Dr. McArdle with Honey. What a lovely man he was, and Honey saw the look on Susan's face too. Hmm, she thought, another guest for the wedding reception I think.

"Doctor!" said Staff Susan Walker.

"Here are the take homes you asked for." She blushed ever-so slightly, as her hand touched his and he looked straight into her eyes. Fancy that, he'd never noticed the grey flecks before, absolutely stunning. How long had she worked here... he'd have to find out.

"Thank you" he said finally. "I'm away to fetch the car to the front. Could you arrange a wheelchair for ma patient here, she's a wee bit tired. Thank you again for your help Staff, looking after Honey, she's one of my special ladies from the village and I'm glad you looked after her... Sorry Staff I don't know your name?" God did he say that out loud.

"You're welcome doctor, Honey is now a new friend of mine, she's invited me to her forthcoming wedding so maybe I'll see you there... it's Susan Walker by the way." She said over her shoulder as she left the room. Scotty! That's a nice name; Honey had called him that, it suited him a lot. Maybe he'd be 'her Scotty'. She laughed to herself, silly woman get on with your work and stop day-dreaming there was a wheelchair to find.

Back in the room Chantelle and Honey both digested the information and body language of Susan and Scotty.

"Well girls" said Scotty clearing his throat, "I'll meet you at the front, like a well trained chauffer." And so saying he escaped rather quickly and slightly pink.

What had he said to Staff (no Susan) he'd not noticed her until today, and she was going to Honey and Gedd's wedding, well this could be interesting.

Susan returned with the porter and wheelchair and they managed to get Honey comfortably seated. "I know it wasn't the best reasons to meet somebody but I'm so glad you came here today Honey." She said as she walked alongside the wheelchair. Chantelle and Honey both smiled.

Honey said "It's nice to meet new folk like yourself and Chantelle here. She's been a god-send to me, like a daughter."

Chantelle blushed. "Anyone would do the same for you Honey."

"No" Honey said "my own family are all far away and most people don't do owt for nowt these days Susan." She said looking at the slim nurse next to her "I'm right glad I asked you to my wedding, we don't want Scotty stood on 'is own do we?" Susan looked down and her slight smile and twinkle in her eyes said more than words could. The porter digested all this information; oh it would definitely get him a pint at the club tonight. Staff-Nurse Walker and Dr. McArdle... Well why not? They were both single and seemed well matched.

Scotty opened the car door and he and the porter helped Honey to get in the front seat. He closed the door and just before he got in he spoke to Susan. "I'm off then Staff... rounds on Tuesday and thanks again for your help."

"You're welcome" she said softly, so that the porter couldn't hear. Dr. McArdle was a sweetie; he gave her a quick wink which Chantelle and Susan saw, but not the porter and as Chantelle got in he said again as if not wanting to go, "well... yes, see you on Tuesday, and if you need to know anything about Mrs. Graham of course, then just call me."

With that, he got into his 'wee car' and whisked Honey and Chantelle back to the Inn where Gedd was nervously pacing the kitchen.

Glyn put on some coffee and said to Gedd "Isn't time we fed the regulars you can always tell them the good news."

"No" said Gedd "not till the rings on 'er finger and I've 'eared she's well, but I s'pose we'd best feed 'em as

Reviving a Rose

you say." They rummaged in the pantry and decided on Shepherd's Pie with fresh veg and Apple pie and Custard for dessert.

Just as the mince was frying in the pan they heard a car pull up outside. Gedd nearly dropped his wooden spoon in his hurry to get outside. "Steady on Gedd, she'll be in, in a minute and the ring is still in your coat, remember?"

"Oh God, oh eye it is; isn't it, Bugger... oh can you help 'er in Glyn while I get the box out mi' pocket... otherwise I'll lose mi' nerve."

Honey was slightly surprised that Gedd hadn't come out to meet her, but Glyn allayed her fears, he confided that Gedd was looking for a certain box. Dr. McArdle and Glyn fetched Honey through into the kitchen and sat her down.

"Just you sit" said Scotty "and take the weight off yer legs madam." He turned round to the others in the room and said "The patient is tired and has a few pin holes aboot the arm but she, Honey I should say," as he rested his arm on her shoulder, "is fine. Apart from patient confidentiality I can say, cos Honey wants me too, that all she needs is some iron and vitamins and general TLC in vast quantities, well the last bit any road."

Honey grinned and said "See I'm just a bit worn out, just need to look after mi-self... "

"No you don't," said Gedd coming into the kitchen. "It's going to be my job to do that my girl... and before you say owt..." Gedd knelt very carefully on one bended knee in front of Honey "I'd like to know as would you do me the 'onor and pleasure of wedding me ... cos I love you Honeysuckle Graham and I want to spend what's left of my life wi' you... If you'll have mi?" Gedd stayed on the floor and carefully opened the little silk box in his hand. He took out a beautiful 3 stone engagement ring (which looked Victorian) and placed it Honey's outstretched hand.

"Oh God... it's bootiful and it fits and all..." "Yes, but will yer wed me woman?" said Gedd.

"Corse I will, yer daft bugger, I'll have yer and wed yer, so get up off the cold floor before rheumatics set in!" Honey said smiling through tears.

Gedd grinned like a school boy, he didn't look 65 at all, he looked much younger, must be love thought Chantelle.

Everyone cheered; hugging Honey and Gedd in turn and shook hands. Chantelle hugged Scotty and Glyn, but as soon as she touched Glyn her stomach did the 'flipping' thing again and her breath seemed to disappear.

"Isn't it great" she said "Yes" said Glyn, but he was thinking about her being in his arms as he replied.

Scotty said his farewell and told Honey to get an early night as all this excitement would not do her BP any good. She'd not taken a tablet yet. They all laughed and said goodbye. He said he check back in a week or so.

And so when the dinner was finally served about an hour later, the regulars heard the good news.

10

Malcolm and his wife Maud Pennington said they would be delighted to come to the wedding and sit on Honey's side. As her family lived and worked away spread about the country and she wasn't sure if they could make it. The other couple, the quiet ones, were called Tim and Renee Pike. They had known Honey since school, although they were a few years older. In a village school like theirs, everyone knew everyone from 5 years to the ones leaving to work at 13 or 14.

Mr. Pike stood up and made a little toast, which was a big thing for him as he was quite shy. "Eh... hem." He said clearing his throat "It is with great pleasure that I call on you all, to raise your glasses and drink a toast on this very special day. It's not often that I speak... Renee normally does." He received a chuckle from everyone and a wink off Renee.

"Cheeky ol' buffer!" She said and cuffed him gently on the elbow.

"Anyway as I was saying" continued Tim "raise your glasses and drink to the health and happiness of our old friends Gedd and a lovely school pal Honey, on their forthcoming wedding." And so saying he lifted his glass with everyone. "Honey and Gedd; Cheers, your future health and happiness." Everyone else said "Honey and Gedd" and they all had a good slug of wine.

"Thanks all 'o yer fer that" said Gedd "I'd just like to thank yer all for the kind words and to this lovely lady fer exceptin' mi." He held Honey's hand and lifted it up to his mouth and kissed it, very gently.

"Away yer daft sod" said Honey "you know yer mean the world to me so stop slobberin' over mi hand and get the pudding will yer." Everyone laughed and Gedd scooted off to the kitchen to get the 'Pie'.

Much later, when the four regulars had gone home, Chantelle hugged Honey and Gedd again. "Congratulations, and now I think it's time you got to your bed Honey."

"Don't you worry lass...?" Said Gedd "I'll get 'er off to bed and she'll sleep an all... if she knows what's good for 'er." And so saying he helped the now tired and very happy Honey out of her chair and away up to her room.

He wasn't going to stay with her though unless she asked him. He was still after all a gentleman.

Chantelle started to clear away all the dinner things and then she realised that Glyn was still there and he was watching her intently. "What?" she said "Look if you're still here, how about a hand with the dishes. You can wash if you like?"

Glyn stood up and smiled "Of course I'll help you 'Cinderella' and you can wipe. We'd better leave a clean kitchen for Gedd in the morning or he'll skin us alive." They both collected all the dishes and made their way into the kitchen.

Glyn found a rather fetching floral pinny and put it on. "Well I don't want to get my trousers wet, do I?" he said Chantelle smiled and picked up a tea-towel. She watched Glyn as he concentrated on the dishes. He had very firm muscular arms and still he managed to wash the plates with such a delicate touch. God, he really was a fine specimen. He turned round, almost as if he had felt her eyes on him.

"What?" he said, "haven't you seen a man so close to a sink before?"

"No" she replied "It's just you have such a gentle touch... and now you'll have lovely soft hands too." She blushed as she realised what she had just said and Glyn, eyebrows raised as he tilted his head to one side, said

"I'm flattered that you noticed." He stepped towards her and asked, "Would you like to check for yourself?"

Chantelle felt like she was drugged but not like before with 'him'. It was a nice kind of fluffy feeling, she felt warm and her arms lifted automatically and stroked Glyn's hands. It was a soft caress and Glyn's heart thudded and his body tightened. God she really didn't have a clue what she was doing to him.

He let her carry on and her hands started to travel up his arms. Chantelle began to feel heat coursing through the body. It was almost like someone had lit a fire in the pit of her abdomen and it was radiating outwards to all of her extremities. She was sure that if she looked into a mirror she would be glowing.

Glyn watched her face, it was alive and allsorts of expressions were appearing and changing on it. Her green eyes were looking smoky and hooded. He could also see the fear that was just ever-so-slightly hanging around the edges.

Chantelle's breathing was starting to get shallow and fast, the pulse in her nape showed Glyn that she was as affected by this as he was. He was glad he had the pinny on now. Although he was really aroused, he still didn't want to scare her off. Whatever demons she had to fight, he had to let her start on her own. He didn't want to spook her and lose the moment.

Chantelle felt as if she were floating slightly above herself and was watching her body and Glyn's. Her arms travelled up his arms and onto his muscular shoulders. Glyn's blood was coming to the boil he really wanted to crush her body to him, and feel the closeness of her hips against his ever hardening maleness.

He still just stood passively, let her lead. His brain was screaming. Stay in control let her lead, let her lead.

Chantelle had now just started to push her fingers into Glyn's hair at his nape and to do so she stepped a little closer. God it felt so good, his hair was quite course but still it claimed her fingers. She wanted to... what... pull his head over and taste his lips again. Her stomach was doing overtime now and the butterflies had turned into a tumble-dryer, turning first one way and then the next.

Nearly there thought Glyn, she'll be kissing me any second and then what... I hope I can hold it together. Oh... God as she kissed his mouth.

Chantelle head seemed to be exploding, stars, fireworks, cannons were all going off. She felt like she was lifted off the floor, and yet she was still there.

His mouth was strong and sensual; Chantelle moved closer, she needed to taste more. Slowly she pressed harder, her tongue, of its own will. Flicked across Glyn's lips... Slowly he opened them, like an awakened rose.

'Wow' thought Glyn, she is dynamite, and she didn't know what power she had. That excited him even more. He had so many things to discover and also to teach her that he opened mouth slowly and his brain exploded too! Yes, even the seasoned Glyn had found the fireworks himself.

Reviving a Rose

    Pressing closer Chantelle seemed to need Glyn's kisses like oxygen. He, in turn, put his arms around her and drew her into his embrace. She felt so good; she was snuggling into his arms and holding on for grim death.

11

When they both came up for air, they gasped and grinned at the same time. Glyn rather shakier than he'd admit turned towards the sink and said, "I think the waters gone cold... we'd better finish up here."

Chantelle awoke from her trance like state and felt abandoned. She wanted his arms around her again, it felt so safe. They continued the washing and drying up in silence, both wrapped up in their own thoughts. Glyn was blown away, his firecracker, his spitfire certainly had hidden depths, and boy did he want to plunge into them. Whoever had scared her into hiding them behind that wall of hers had really done a job on her and he wanted to find out more about this 'Ben'.

Little did he know that it would be sooner rather than later? When they had finished the dishes, they both just stood and looked at each other.

"Well..." "I just..." "No you first..." They both spoke at the same time. Chantelle took a breath and said softly, "I don't know what that was; I've never felt anything like

Reviving a Rose

that before, but..." She added blushing slightly, "I'd like to taste some more please."

And with that Glyn crushed her into his chest and kissed her hungrily. He felt as if he hadn't held her for hours. Yet it was only 10 minutes since they had kissed before. God she felt so good in his arms and all the same heat seemed to flood his body again. If she hadn't been hurt in the first place he felt as if he could have taken her there and then on the kitchen table.

They continued to kiss and discover each others bodies. The clothes, to Chantelle, were in the way. She tentatively undid Glyn's shirt buttons and gazed at his chest. Her own chest seemed to have the oxygen forced out of it and as her hands ran over his bronzed chest wall she sucked in a breath and seemed to sigh and relax a little.

This was what Glyn had been hoping for, but what now? Oh he knew what he wanted to do, but he still had to let Chantelle take control. If he took over all her fears could come rushing back and spoil it all and he definitely didn't want that.

It was Chantelle who made the next move and although it surprised Glyn, he was more than willing to follow her. "Glyn... I've never... I mean I have but not like... will you come with me before I lose my nerve..." She knew she was rambling but if she didn't do this soon, well what would she do!

She knew she wanted Glyn that surprised her. She didn't think she needed any man after 'Ben'. No stupid, don't think about him, think about Glyn, about the stream and plaster all over his body. Oh God... he made her feel things she'd never dreamed she would ever feel. They walked up the big wide oak stairs, Chantelle led Glyn and he followed meekly but full of expectations. What a mixed bag she was, he couldn't wait to heal her wounds.

Chantelle's Journey

They stopped outside room 7; it was Chantelle's call now. Did she have the courage for the next step? Swallowing the lump in her throat she opened the door and led Glyn inside.

Softly the door closed and Glyn leaned against it, he looked at the scared, yet obviously aroused woman before him. Chantelle walked over to the curtains, "Leave them" said Glyn "I want to look at you."

Chantelle stopped what she was doing and turned to look at Glyn. "I don't know what to do... I've never been in this position before... I'm not sure..." she trailed off.

Glyn stepped forwards and just enveloped her into his arms. He wanted to take away her fear and hesitance. As soon as he had her in his arms, she melted against him and rested her head on his chest. He let her rest there a minute and then he slowly lifted her chin up.

"Let me show you just how lovely you are, you hypnotise me, d'you know that?" He said

"No... I... you make me feel so safe." She said... gazing straight into his eyes.

Glyn felt his heart swell, as did another part of his body. This woman had 'bewitched' him and he liked it! Strange, he thought, he had always stayed in control. But with 'his spitfire' he just wanted to fly away with her where-ever she wanted to take him. He held her until she felt ready to continue exploring. Chantelle looked up into his face and she could see all the passion too! It could be hers if she wanted it; all she had to do was carry on.

So, taking her courage in both hands, she reached up and cupped his face between her trembling fingers and drew him down to her for a kiss. The same waves of emotion that she had felt downstairs in the kitchen enveloped her body and she pushed her fingers into Glyn's hair to pull him closer.

Glyn himself was filled with emotion and he was just about hanging onto his sanity, the woman in his arms

Reviving a Rose

was turning his bones to mush. He would have to sit down before he fell down. So very slowly he edged his way towards the bed. It was still a little rumpled from her previous nights sleep. As he sat down, he still held Chantelle but his arms slid down to her waist and caressed her very slowly and gently.

Chantelle moaned softly in spite of herself. So many emotions were coursing through her body that she didn't know what she was doing. She pressed Glyn head to her breasts and he breathed her scent in.

Glyn slowly ran his hands up Chantelle's back and slipped his roaming fingers under her T-shirt up and gazed at her pert breasts in their perfectly comfortable but sporty bra. It had no clasp, so he ran his fingers around the bottom and breathed in her scent as he lifted it up to free what was straining against the fabric.

Chantelle ran her fingers through Glyn's hair and moaned. This was so exquisite it was almost painful. What was he doing to her? Oh... her legs nearly gave way as he suckled one of her pert breasts. They tasted of honey. She must use some lotion with it in, he thought. Chantelle put her hand under his chin and lifted it up so she could again lose herself in his kiss. A heat was burning deep within her and she didn't know what to do to soothe it.

"Glyn... what do I do next... please show me?" She said in between kisses.

Glyn groaned as she caressed his body. "You're doing fine 'spitfire'... you're doing fine." He took her hand and drew it down to his lap. She flinched slightly, a little scared of what she had touched. Had she done that to him, did her body excite him that much? What was this... this, these emotions she was feeling... whatever it was she didn't want it to stop?

Glyn hardened as her hand stayed where he had left it. He undid his trousers to free what was now straining against the zip. Chantelle gasped as Glyn's hardened male shaft touched her, only the thin fabric of his boxer shorts stopped skin touching skin.

He undid the little lace on her jogging bottoms and slid them down to her knees. Very carefully she stepped out of them and also took her t-shirt off with her bra. They were too restrictive; she wanted to feel his skin on hers. Glyn stood up and let his trousers fall, to the floor along with his shirt, to join Chantelle's jogging bottoms just as he hoped their bodies would as well.

And so they stood face to face, all that stood between them was Glyn's boxers.

"Take them off for me Chantelle." Glyn said, he gasped with pleasure as she slowly slid them down his buttocks and helped the now throbbing pinnacle of his manhood free from all bondage.

Chantelle was transfixed by it; she just stroked it, because she didn't know what else to do.

"God... that is fantastic... you really don't know what you're doing do you?" he said holding her arms.

"Am I doing it wrong?" she said as she let go.

"No... don't stop... it's amazing, just trust your instincts... just explore where ever you want. Glyn said as his arms brushed her taught nipples.

"Oh... that's... Oh so... um..." Chantelle just quivered in his arms.

Glyn gently led Chantelle onto the bed; his boxers had by now joined with all the other clothes on the floor. Chantelle shivered slightly. "Are you cold?" Glyn said as he kissed her neck, slowly working his way south.

"No... I don't think so... I feel like I'm on fire... its lovely." She gasped.

Chantelle didn't feel dirty now, just consumed with desire and all she wanted was Glyn to hold her and remove the bad memories that had haunted her for years.

"Touch me!" He said as he nibbled and teased her swelling nipples. He placed her hand on his own swelling.

Reviving a Rose

Chantelle gripped him gently and moved her hand in some primeval trance. Glyn could stand it no more, he was being driven insane. He laid Chantelle alongside him and caressed her quivering body everywhere he could think of. She arched and bucked under is touch; her very limbs were turning to liquid. Even her most feminine place seemed to be turning to an inferno which was about to explode.

"Not yet my love." Glyn said without even realising he'd said the word 'love'. He parted her thighs and teased her moist hub gently. Chantelle squirmed under his touch. It was so good but she wanted more.

"Now please Glyn now!" She said and moved his hand away from the place that was sending her into orbit. Chantelle looked straight into his eyes. "Fill me please... make me whole... take away the bad memories and heal me... give me new dreams please. "

Glyn stopped her with a firm kiss. "Yes my little 'spitfire', yes I will, I'll try and be gently but I can't promise, you're burning me up and I need quenching." So saying; he pushed into her core and suddenly he felt as if he were home.

Chantelle eyes flew open and she pulled Glyn closer by wrapping her legs around him.

Glyn almost came right there and then, but managed to stop himself. He must please Chantelle first, make her feel whole. He moved slowly at first, pushing in and drawing back. Chantelle gasped as waves of heat soared through her body. Her very female Inner most places seemed to be contorting and convulsing with pleasure. Glyn rolled onto his back and Chantelle found herself on top. She gasped again and he too could feel himself losing the battle within.

He rocked her backwards and forwards on his solid male shaft and he could feel her Inner muscles gripping him so he wouldn't leave her. Faster and faster he pushed, Chantelle rocked and squeezed and soon they were both gasping and crying out each others names as they finally both erupted together into space and wave upon wave shattered their hold onto reality. Both spent, they just lay there in the moonlight and sighed.

"Don't speak" said Chantelle "just hold me and make me feel safe." Glyn did as he was told and in doing so pulled the coverlet over them both, and they both slept a dreamless but satisfied sleep.

Chantelle woke next morning and stretched like a cat. She then realised that Glyn wasn't beside her anymore. She felt bereft! Where had he gone, did he now regret sleeping with her, did he not want to see her? A myriad of thoughts ran through her head. They still had to work together as well. Oh God, this was going to be hard. As if as an after thought she suddenly realised that they hadn't used any protection.

She sat up! "God, oh God, oh blast..." she hadn't ever been on the pill either. After Ben, she hadn't seen the need; no one could ever want her in that way, would they? Well, that theory had been well and truly blown out of the water hadn't it.

Then her other senses kicked in. Sniffing the air she grinned, she smelled bacon cooking. It permeated her bedroom and she began salivate. Diving into the bathroom, she washed quickly, and brushed her teeth. Then she pulled on a clean pair of panties and jogging bottoms; a colourful crop-top, finished off her outfit.

She almost skipped down the stairs feeling incredibly light and rested. It felt like all the weight, on her shoulders for the past 4 years, had been finally lifted.

"Morning," said Glyn over his shoulder. "I decided we all needed a good solid breakfast to build us up. Well to replace some energy anyway. I slept right through." He turned round and smiled at Chantelle. She returned it and took in the jaunty picture of Glyn in 'that pinny' again but clean clothes this time. As if reading her mind

Reviving a Rose

he said "I nipped back to Gedd's'... he's not there by the way... and put my stuff in the wash."

"How did you know it was me? It could have been Honey or Gedd coming through the door?"

"No sweetheart!" Her heart leapt in her chest, he'd called me sweetheart "they don't smell as sweet as you. You smell like a garden full of flowers this morning. What have you got on then? Chantelle started to blush a little and replied "Just soap and a little body spray, that's all."

"Well whatever it is, you smell lovely... come and give this hard working 'Chef' a kiss and cuddle for all the grafting I'm doing." She did as she was asked and slid her hands around his waist. She would never have thought a pinny could be such a turn on, but visions of the last evening made her smile wickedly.

"What are you thinking about?" Glyn asked as he kissed the top of her head.

"Oh...just things..." She said "....just very special things"

"You know I'd kiss you but breakfast won't get done if I do..., so make yourself useful and make the coffee will you. I'll just finish the scrambled eggs and then I'll call the two love-birds okay? She nodded and got to work with the peculator. Well at least she could do coffee, even if her food wasn't up to much.

Glyn disappeared from the kitchen to call Gedd and Honey. Apparently they had slept really well 'in separate rooms', Honey said as she held Gedd's arm and led him into the kitchen. Chantelle turned from the coffee making and smiled at them both. They, in turn, looked at her luminous face and then each other, and nodded as if to answer a question not yet asked.

"Sit down you two and dig in, you both need feeding up," Glyn said as he started to dish up. "Oh..." said Honey "I might have to trade you in Gedd... these eggs are lovely."

Chantelle's Journey

Gedd looked up and squeezed her hand. "Ey but he can't warm yer heart up like I can though, can he, eh?" She returned his grasp and smiled with slightly shiny eyes. "Ey love, mebbie you're right... except for you're sharp toe-nails ...oh I shouldn't have said that should I?"

Everyone laughed and Glyn looked at Chantelle and squeezed her leg gently under the table. Even that slight touch, was enough to turn her stomach over and send her pulse soaring.

"Well!" said Glyn. "No rest for the wicked... I've got a cottage to finish and you 'Boss-Lady' have a date with some herbs don't you?"

Chantelle had complete forgotten the cottage, how could she forget that... she was supposed to be finishing the garden so that Mr. Rodgers could see exactly what a gem he had. She didn't think he'd looked at the garden at all when he bought the cottage. So hopefully it would be a lovely surprise.

Much later in the garden Chantelle sat back on her heels and admired her handy work. The garden looked fabulous, even if she said so herself. The statue, she had revealed, looked beautiful in the afternoon sun and as she stretched she realised she was hungry.

"Glyn!" she called out as she went into the little kitchen. "Do you want some food?"

"Eh?"... Was the muffled reply from upstairs? She heard him come across the landing and start to clump down the stairs. "What did you say?" Glyn said as he appeared in the front room.

Chantelle smiled and her heart lifted "I said... do want some food?" She was holding a large Tupperware box filled with sandwiches and fruit and other goodies. It seemed that Gedd and Honey decided that only one box was needed now.

"Sure" he said... "Where are we going to eat?"

97

Chantelle glanced out of the little window. "Come and see what I've been up to and then we can share our food in the garden." They both walked outside and Glyn was pleasantly surprised at the amount of work Chantelle had put in, in doing up the garden.

"Are you sure you don't do landscaping as well as interior design? It's absolutely lovely." She blushed, the compliment made her heart swell with pride. He made her feel very special.

"Come here and let me give you a special hug for all your hard work." Glyn said she stepped into his arms and laid her head on his solid chest. He just held her, even though he wanted more, they had still work to do.

The garden was stunning. The path had now been properly cleared; it looked very neat as it weaved its way down to the stream. If you stood in the cottage the statue was on the right side of the garden and as the sun shone down lit it up. It must have looked lovely in the summers gone by.

"Where did the statue come from?" Glyn asked "did you buy it, it certainly looks the part."

"No" Chantelle said as she pulled up two empty planters big enough to sit on. "It was hidden under all the prickles. I don't know who it is supposed to be, or who carved it, but yes I agree it certainly fits this garden doesn't it?"

They ate in a comfortable silence apart from the obvious munching noises. Once all the food and drink had been demolished Glyn looked at Chantelle and said

"Do you know that even when you've covered in dirt and cobwebs and things, you're still really beautiful?" He really meant it too; she had definitely got under his skin.

"Thank you" she replied "You're not so bad yourself, sweat makes your muscles stand out, and if we didn't have work to do I would gladly kiss you all over, the rest of the afternoon at least!"

Glyn grinned "Why thank you "Boss-Lady. I'll sure picture that whilst I'm working" He said standing up... "But I settle for just one real one just for now, to keep me going."

Chantelle stood up and walked into his arms. Turning her face up to his, she tasted the orange juice, still lingering on his lips. "Mmm you taste lovely." She kissed him again, but she made a slight moue though, when he held her away.

"No... if I don't stop now I'll have to ravish you in the herb bed and that 'although tempting' wouldn't be a good idea, now..." he said smacking her jean-clad bottom... "Get back to work woman."

She looked at him and thought, hang on who's the boss here.

"OK you win, but I'm still the boss you know... I'm paying your wages. .. So get to it." And so saying she packed all the rubbish back into the box and finished her sweeping and tidying. She was happy, the garden was finished... Well as finished as she could do anyway.

If Mr. Rodgers wanted to change anything he would have to get a proper gardener in. She went into the cottage to check on the work Glyn had done.

Downstairs was now ready for her to begin decorating. The small kitchen had been transformed. Glyn had re-plastered and tiled it and new tasteful cupboards had been fitted. A small range, which had been hidden under rubbish and years of dust, now gleamed. Glyn had 'black-leaded' it too! The work surfaces were quite pale as if to bring in more light.

Chantelle wanted to ask Mr. Rodgers if he wanted a window in the lean-to ceiling. That would increase the light and airy feel and also make it look much bigger. The sitting room looked just as good. All new plaster and fireplace looked lovely, she could imagine a lovely log-fire crackling in the winter, with snow outside on

Reviving a Rose

the garden. The view down to the stream would look lovely.

As she climbed the stairs, Chantelle had a thought, maybe a rope handrail instead of the usual one. It would be really different but somehow in keeping with the cottage. It would also be more practical as the stairs swept around the chimney breast. She walked into the larger room, which now looked much more like a bedroom, although it had no furniture as yet. That was another thing she had to check on. Did Mr. Rodgers want her to furnish it too?

"In here "Boss-Lady""... said a disjointed voice. Glyn was sitting in the bath tiling the wall above it. "What d'you think, then... is the colour okay? I went with my gut instinct and picked a pale blue... you know, to kind of bring the garden into the cottage?" Glyn said as he stepped out of the bath.

"I think... "She said pausing for effect... "It's lovely and your instinct is very sound... and I'm not just saying that cos I fancy you either!" Suddenly the bathroom felt much smaller than it already was. There was so much static electricity that Chantelle was certain she could have lit up a whole street.

Glyn smiled and held her close "Much as I would love to do more... I must get this done before the grout goes off! Tiling is an art you know!"

"Yes" she said breathlessly "I'm sure it is... umm... I've finished out there." She said as she gestured out to the garden. "I'm off back to the Inn to check on Honey and e-mail 'My Boss', just to update him... do you fancy dinner out somewhere tonight?"

What had made her say that? Mind you, lovely as Honey and Gedd were, Chantelle wanted to see if Glyn and she would actually enjoy an evening on their own and not run out of things to say. And so much later that day; she found herself telling Honey that there were two less for dinner.

"Aw! Said Honey. "An' I were going to do a lovely steak, still I'm sure what ever you eat will taste lovely pet!"

Chantelle went upstairs to change, she had e-mailed Mr. Rodgers with the photos she'd taken of the cottage, along with some 'before' pictures and asked if he wanted it finished.

She slipped into lovely smoky grey dress which clung to her like shimmering water in the moonlight. She decided to put her hair up and wear some funky drop earrings and just one necklace. Chantelle couldn't see the point of wearing too many, they just got tangled and snagged things. So giving herself one more look in the full view mirror she thought 'that'll do, can't expect miracles' and went downstairs to find Glyn. The man in question had scrubbed up well and was wearing a dark shirt and tie.

"I thought, seeing as how my boss is going to be very generous when the job is finished, I'd treat us to a cracking meal, all posh stuff, no beans." Glyn said smiling and looking very dashing.

Chantelle and Glyn set off for the restaurant in the nearby town. All thoughts of 'Ben' now banished from her head. Unknown to her they would soon be coming back to haunt her and with interest too!

Honey and Gedd were sitting in the kitchen, after a very cosy steak dinner; all the regulars had long since gone home.

"I've started to think on all the people I'd like to see mi wed yer!" Gedd said as he stood up to make the coffee.

"Ave you now... well I've a few an all mind." Said Honey, smiling.

"Mind you..." Gedd replied "not that there'll be that many... I mean we won't after bookin' a great big 'tent thingy'... you know Marquette thing."

"Marquee love, that's wot yer mean. No make more sense to 'ave it 'ere... you know get someone in t' cook 'n that. Save my energy for the day."

Reviving a Rose

"You make sure you bloody do!" Gedd said, sitting down with two steaming cups of milky coffee. "I don't want you falling down at me knees... well not till later any road..."

"You cheeky bugger... at your age an all" So the list was duly compiled.

Gedd would call his sister in Dorset and see if she wanted to come. She had been a widow for over 10 years and had one son Ben, so maybe he'd like to come along to his mother company. Frank Locke, her dead husband, hadn't been a wealthy fellow but she'd done alright out of him after he'd passed on.

"My sides going to be pretty empty." Gedd said looking pretty grim.

"Don't be daft; the entire village will sit on your side... Scotty and Nurse Susan... They'll not need asking (the villagers lot) free food 'ull see to that... not that they don't like you... you're a good mechanic Gedd and you charge really fair too!" Honey replied, giving his hand a squeeze on the table.

"Oy," he grinned "mind your blood pressure woman." But he didn't move his hand away.

Honey had asked her family down to come, she hoped they would. She'd been lonely along time and hoped that they would be pleased for her. She didn't see as much of them as she'd like, still it would be nice if they came though.

12

And so in early September the invites were sent out. Gedd also stuck a few posters in the Inn, Post Office, the local Pub, the Church Hall and his Garage so that everyone in the village knew about the forthcoming wedding;

> To All Our Dear Friends In
> Chettle Village.
>
> Let it be known that
>
> HONEYSUCKLE GRAHAM
>
> Is to marry
>
> GEDD WILLIAMS
>
> At 11.00 am
> Briory Bush Inn
>
> Reception to follow (Same place)
>
> All friends are welcome to toast the
> Happy couple.

Honey sent the invitations to both her children and families and also to Gedd's sister and her son. She hoped they would all come and wish them well.

The cottage was now well and truly finished the difference between before and after was stunning. Even Chantelle, her own worst critic, was pleased with the finished result. Gedd and Honey had come out to have a look-see.

"Oh... Chantelle love, it's beautiful, you've done a grand job. Mi old dad would be weepin' buckets to look at it..." Honey said as she sniffed into a hanky.

"Yep" said Gedd "Crackin' job an' no mistake... I know 'oo ter come to if |I need owt decorated."

"Just wait till you see the garden then" said a voice from behind. Glyn had joined them after parking the car. And so they all walked into the cottage to get through to the garden. Mind you it was a bit of a struggle, as Honey kept stopping to admire everything and she nearly didn't get out the back door when she saw the kitchen.

"God I thought outside was bloody good... but in 'ere... well it takes yer breath away..."

"Well get a lungful and get through the door woman... yer blocking mi way..." Said Gedd, as he gently pushed her out the door into the garden.

"Ohh... love it's stunning... oh look the 'erbs... the roses... ohh... ohh, look Gedd the statue... look... look at the view." Honey didn't draw breath and so Gedd led her to a little bench under the window and got her to sit down for a minute. Chantelle had put it there; it seemed to be the best place for it. You could see right the way down to the stream and admire all the roses, herbs, honeysuckle and of course the statue in the flower bed.

"Where d'ya gets that from love?" said Gedd, Honey was still catching her breath.

"It was buried under a load of brambles..."

"Yes, and she hacked them all out by herself." Said Glyn. He felt so proud of her; his heart was full for her and of her. Did that mean he loved her... he was sure he'd never felt like this before. He knew he didn't want to leave her. Maybe he would find a job for them to work on, through his contacts. Glyn was hiding a secret from all of them, but he didn't want to say anything just yet. After all it wasn't a bad secret; he'd just got sick of women going out with him for his money.

Surely Chantelle liked him for himself, as far as she knew he was just a builder who worked whenever he was given a contract.

"Yes" said Chantelle perching on the arm of the bench "it was hard work but definitely worth it; I think someone local did the sculpting but I haven't found out whom yet, I'm still searching the web."

"D'yer knows I think mi dad mentioned the statue to me as a nipper." Honey said "He said it always made 'im smile, I can see why now!"

Gedd and Honey stood up slowly and walked over to it. The man looked much older close to, sort of grandfather type, he was holding a bunch of roses; they were tied with a beautifully sculptured ribbon. The bow and ribbon edges looked as if they were just about to blow in the wind. The little boy was gazing up at the older man, whilst sitting at his feet.

"Mebbie he's takin' the flowers to the boys gran... yer never know..." Gedd said

"Your absolutely right you know!" They all turned around to look at the very tall distinguished man who was striding towards them all, his hand out-stretched.

"You must be Chantelle, so pleased to meet you, in the flesh so to speak."

Chantelle felt her hand being firmly shaken and she smiled in response. "Mr. Rodgers, I presume... you're most welcome but you didn't say you were coming today... I hope..."

Reviving a Rose

"No my dear," he cut in "I don't mind at all, in fact I have been listening to all the well deserved praise from the kitchen. I must admit, this place has surpassed even my wildest dreams. When I bought 'her', I always refer to my cottage in the feminine, I had high hopes and you my dear have fulfilled each and everyone." So saying Mr. Rodgers did a thing he didn't often do, he hugged Chantelle and she returned it.

Everyone laughed and applauded Mr. Rodgers who broke away blushing.

"Awfully sorry... I don't go around hugging people, but it just seemed the right response to convey my gratitude and pleasure for all the work you must have put in.

"Please, you making me blush," Chantelle said "... and please you must also thank Glyn here for all his hard work inside."

"Yes indeed sir." Mr. Rodgers said "Praise where it is due, a pleasure sir to make your acquaintance. Would you do me the honour of introducing these two lovely people?"

"Oh come on... you know the both of us... stop yer messing Mr. R." Said Honey and she grasped his hand in both of hers. You know Gedd too... he's tinkered under your car bonnet before now... remember?"

"Oh... of course, yes last summer wasn't it old chap?"

"Yep... it was Mr. R. and right glad of it too yer fan belt did snap clean through."

"Oh yes... I was nearly late back to school... yes... Oh I must apologise... its old age you see and not seeing you in your normal surroundings."

"Not so much of the old if yer please... yer younger than us to fer a start!" said Honey laughing.

"I'm so glad you both like 'my cottage', I'm sorry my dear you did say it was finished didn't you?" he said turning to Chantelle.

"Yes Mr. Rodgers, apart from a few minor things we need to discuss."

"Please... Geoffrey... I'm sure what ever needs doing will be just right, so I'll leave it to you my dear, seeing as you have done such a sterling job so far."

"... Er yes Mr... Geoffrey it's all nearly done now and ready for you to move in."

As she said it Chantelle felt a little sad, she'd put a lot of time and effort into it, she'd be leaving after the wedding. Where to... she didn't yet know? Then a thought struck her, what about Glyn, what would happen next. Did she want to lose him, did she ... the more she thought the more she felt, and her future was with Glyn, if he'd have her?

"What you thinkin' so 'ard about then missy?" Gedd said, bringing her out of the trance like state. Glyn was watching her with a slight smile on his face. Quick change the subject she thought. Honey must have read her mind too because she said

"Ere Mr. R... sorry Geoffrey... Ooh it's to posh for me... it'll have ter be Geoff, sorry."

"Geoff is fine Honey absolutely fine; I'm not a school master here am I!" He said laughing at himself, he felt very relaxed here, just the tonic after school.

".. Would you like ter come to Gedd 'n mi's wedding... it's not long away an' we'd love yer to come, wouldn't we Gedd?" She said turning to the man she was to marry.

"Corse he can, if he wants, the more the merrier and I'm sure e'll bring a bit a' class to the day!"

"I would be honoured to attend but please let me know when so that I'm not stuck in school with the boys. Yes that sounds most delightful."

Chantelle and Glyn were locking up the cottage with Mr. Rodgers. "Please call me Geoffrey my dear" he said again as they locked the front door. "You have done a cracking job and I shan't hesitate in giving you a glowing reference for your outstanding work!"

Reviving a Rose

"Thank you... Geoffrey. I really appreciate it... and also on Glyn's behalf ... he's been an absolute gem." She replied blushing ever so slightly. Glyn just touched her arm in support. Mr. Rodgers thought they looked absolutely right together. Glyn was pleased she had paid him a compliment, she didn't have to. He was after all only the hired muscle and manual work. It meant she really had no idea who he really was; she must think he needed more referrals.

The trip back to the Inn was made in Glyn's Mercedes. She wondered how he could afford such a big car. Funny that, she'd never even thought about it before. Maybe he borrowed 'the boss's car for this one.

"Glyn? Is this your car, or are you borrowing it?" Chantelle said as they glided down the lanes.

"Actually it's mine." Glyn said thinking quickly on his feet. "I got it as a bonus off my previous boss." He didn't say he'd given it to himself as one. "The work was finished ahead of schedule so all the workforce had something, as a thank you!"

"He must be very generous then, are you going back to work with him, after the wedding. Chantelle heart lurched in her chest. Maybe Glyn wouldn't come back. She was stunned to find that she really didn't want him to go. She had never thought she would feel like that about any man, after being crushed mentally and physically by Ben.

13

The preparations for the wedding seemed to fly past and Honey had done an awful lot of baking, even though she'd said that there would be caterers. Gedd asked her why she was making so many fancy cakes.

"Well, it's just I love t' an' it calms m' down. All this rushing t' do… its windin' mi up a bit!"

"Well I'll 'ave t' tell the Doc then, won't I!" He replied.

"No you don't!!" Honey screamed, "E'll stop mi weddin."

"No 'e won't yer daft woman e'll just up your pills a bit, so yer won't have a funny turn." So saying, he left her to her baking and went off to have a word with Dr. McArdle, on the phone.

"What's the problem Gedd is she not behaving her self?" Said Scotty; with a slight smile on his face.

"Well she's a bit het up an' that!" explained Gedd.

"I'll just away an' see her for ma self" said Scotty. It would be nice to see her looking well, rather than the last time he'd seen her. Maybe he'd tell Susan how

Reviving a Rose

Honey was. Yes, that would be a good reason to talk to her and it was medical after all.

Gedd felt much better after he'd replaced the receiver in its cradle. Then he noticed someone standing in the foyer.

"Enid... My god yer gave mi a turn, oh I'm right glad you could come... and this must be Ben. Well look at you... you're a fine specimen an' no mistake." Gedd scooted round the desk and hugged his sister tightly.

"Ooh! Don't break m' bones lad... I'm glad t' see yer too... where's yer Honey lass then?"

"In t' kitchen baking for whole village if I'm not wrong... She wants to keep busy does mi lady." He said with pride and shiny eyes.

The lady in question came through the door and took in the scene. Gedd still had his arm around his sister and he was grinning fit to bust.

"Just talkin' 'bout you pet... let me introduce mi little sister an' 'er boy. Enid love this is mi other 'arf soon t' be mi wife... Honey Graham. This 'ere fine specimen; is Enid's boy Ben."

"Welcome both" said Honey. "The Inn's shut for paying guests, but not for my guests... I'm letting yer have rooms 9 & 10. I hope you'll like 'em?"

"I'm sure we will" said Enid, The 'otel's lovely an' all... my Frank would 'ave liked it... its pretty. 'Ow old is it?"

"I think the original bits 'a good few 'undred years old mebbie, not right sure I'll t'ave to find out for yer!"

So in a companionable muffle of greetings they all went up stairs to show Ben & Enid their rooms.

"Ow long till the wedding, Gedd?"

"Next weekend, we thought yer'd like to t'ave a poke about and see the village and garage. You know I've no kids so I'm thinkin' on leavin' it to yer Ben... if 'e wants it like!"

Chantelle's Journey

"Uncle Gedd... I've trained as a mechanic for 4 years so far... to have a share or own a garage would be brilliant." Ben said

"Ooh yer edges t'ave been polished off a bit 'ain't they lad. Said Gedd chuckling.

Enid opted to have a little rest; her son's driving was a little fast for her.

So it was decided that Gedd would show Ben around and Honey would rest a little while and make some tea later. The 'regulars' would be in for their tea about 5, so Honey thought it would be nice to introduce them all to Gedd's family. It didn't take long to walk to the garage, and Gedd stood there with pride and asked Ben what he thought of his business.

"Well lad, wot d'ya make of mi garage then?" Gedd said again, as he led Ben around the workshop.

"It's abit like being in a sweetshop to a kiddy. I can't wait to work in it uncle Gedd. Mind you... I think some of your prices are mild... to say the very least!"

Gedd looked at Ben sideways and narrowed his eyes slightly. The boy liked money eh! Well if he were to work here before Gedd popped his clogs, he would not allow him to con his friends out of their money.

"Shall we walk back lad?" Gedd asked Ben poked about in the cupboards and on the desks. He seemed to be costing the tools up thought Gedd. Maybe leaving him the garage wasn't such a good idea. He'd have to have a talk with Honey about it later.

Back at the Inn, Honey was nicely refreshed and calm after her nap. The kitchen was warming up a treat and she had 'tea' on the cooker already.

"Alright love!" Asked Gedd, as he walked in. "Ey love" Honey replied. Ben looked on, maybe the old girl would wear his uncle out and the garage would come to him sooner rather than later. Mind you, play it sweet he thought, get your feet under this tasty table and he'd get free board and lodgings and a business too!

Reviving a Rose

"Yer mums up love" Said Honey "She's reading in the lounge next door d'yer want t' take a cuppa through?"

"Sure, she would enjoy that, set her up lovely for tea. I hear you're a wonderful cook!" He crooned sweetly.

"I don't know what 'e's been telling yer but thanks any road. Get yourself along and take the tea through."

As Ben went into the lounge Gedd looked at Honey quizzically "What d'yer make on 'im then mi love?" Honey put her spoon down and looked into Gedd's face and said

"I'm not right sure yet... there's summit 'n' nowt... but I can't place it... I think I'll reserve mi judgement." Honey said; turning back to the cooker. Tea turned out to be a stick-to-the-rib stew, topped with dumplings the size of footballs.

Honey and Gedd decided to eat in the dining area with the 'regulars' and his sister Enid and nephew Ben. Malcolm Pennington introduced the four regulars to Enid and Ben and invited them over to 'their' large table for after meal coffee.

Gedd had nipped into the kitchen and brought out the coffees. Mr. Rodgers appeared from upstairs.

"Oh hello all, I've been so busy checking dates on my laptop. Wonderful invention isn't it..." he garbled on "Just checking to make sure I'm off school so to speak, so I can attend the forthcoming nuptials."

"Corse you're comin' Mr. R... I mean Geoff... an' most welcome to... in fact," said Honey blushing a little "I was wondering if you would do me the 'onor of givin' mi away, in the big room?"

"I would be totally and absolutely honoured to do so." Geoffrey Rodgers said as he embraced Honey and then shook Gedd's outstretched hand.

"What's all this...?" As Chantelle's words got caught in her throat, all thoughts of Gedd and Honey were banished. She saw a face she never thought she would ever see again, and all her colour drained from her and she had to sit down.

Everyone turned round to look at her and she tried to hide her utter shock.

"Sorry came down the stairs too fast... I haven't eaten yet... sorry," she tailed off, feeling very miserable.

Glyn came in from the kitchen and immediately saw Chantelle's stricken expression. What had upset her, whatever it was it had managed to rip away the happiness at the cottage when she had handed over the keys to Mr. Rodgers.

"Chantelle love" said Honey "You look a bit peaky... you sure you're alright pet?"

"Yes..." she squeaked. "I think the day has caught up with me... I'll just go and get a glass of..."

"No!" Glyn said stepping forward into the room. "I'll get it, you might faint." Just as he said that 'Scotty' came in.

"Hello all just on mi way home and I thought ter kill 2 birds so to speak. Looks like mebbie 3."He said, taking in Chantelle's grey pallor. "Honey just dropping off some more tablets, fer you to take and keep you well fer the weddin' on Saturday... now then Missy..." Scotty said turning to look at Chantelle. "Wot's the matter hen?"

To Chantelle's utter shame she felt her eyes fill up with tears and she frantically tried to gulp in some air. Her throat had gone bone dry. Where was her water?

"I think she's over-done it." Glyn said re-appearing with the water from the kitchen. "Here "Boss-Lady" get this down you but try sipping it eh!!"

Chantelle didn't try to speak; she just took the glass with shaking hands and tried to sip it. Dr McArdle recognised shock when he saw it, and she was definitely in shock.

"Well Missy..." He said again, "I think the best place for you is yer bed young lady."

Reviving a Rose

"I say…" Mr. Rodgers chipped in "I hope doing the cottage hasn't done this to you my dear, sterling job too!" He said looking pained.

"No" said Glyn "She's just been…" Been what? Think fast man.

"I'm just tired…" Chantelle managed at last… "Its all kind of crept up on me… you know Honey's collapse and me actually trying to cook…" She said trying to lighten the mood.

"Well love," said Honey. "Best do as Scotty said; you looked after me so now I'll return it in kind. Gedd love" she said turning round "can you fetch a drop of stew and a cuppa up after us pet?"

"Corse I will love." Gedd looked worried, he had grown fond of Chantelle, as had Honey, she was a lovely lass but what had made her nearly pass out like that?

14

The thing (or should it be person?) in question was also looking stunned, but no-one had noticed. What on earth was "Chelly" doing here in Chettle Village? He hadn't given her a thought after what he'd done in college; in fact he hadn't lost any sleep over her at all. Now though he was going to revise that. She had definitely scrubbed up in the 4-ish years since attending college at Poole.

Maybe he might just be able to get some more honey off of her, he was after all good looking, and she'd be stupid to pass up his attention. He smiled smugly to himself and mentally made a 'note to self', check her out over the weekend. If Honey liked Chelly and he won over Honey and Gedd, surely he'd get into Chelly's bed again.

He tactfully forgot that the last time he had been to bed with Chelly he had drugged and raped her. Well he thought, she'd asked for it, cold bitch, maybe she'd thawed out now. This could be interesting.

Reviving a Rose

Glyn had by now sat down with the regulars, but for some reason had been drawn to watch 'Ben'. Of course he didn't know that this was 'the Ben'.

Gedd suddenly remembered his manners and turned to Glyn. "Glyn... sorry about that; I'll just take some food up... I'd like you to meet my sister Enid and her son Ben,"

"Enid, this is Glyn Mathews, he's been working on the cottage for Mr. Rodgers 'ere. The young lady who's not well has been in charge of the project... Chantelle; 'er name is and she's a lovely lass."

Enid said hello and shook Glyn's hand softly "Glyn, pleased t' meet ya. Any friend of Gedd's one of mine."

Glyn smiled and turned to look at Ben. "Hello you must be Ben... Are you staying for the wedding too?"

"Yes I am." Ben replied shaking Glyn's hand "I came to keep my mother company and to see Uncle Gedd's place, I mean Gedd and Honey. You see my uncle said he might leave it to me..."

"It's not carved in stone yet laddo..." Gedd said slapping his nephews shoulder. "Got to see 'ow you going to shape up lad." Gedd didn't see the scowl on Bens face as he had already left the room, but Glyn did.

Hmm the thoughts were ticking away in Glyn's head. Just what was that boy up to? One to watch I think.

Meanwhile Honey, Chantelle and Dr. McArdle had gone up to Chantelle's room. "Now madam, in tay yer bed lassie and tell me what's the matter?" Scotty sat down on the bed and Honey fussed around, closing curtains and switching on the bedside lights.

"Honestly... it's nothing... just the low after the high that's all..." Chantelle said warily.

"Come on hen even I know more 'an that, it's no just tired is it?"

Honey said sitting down on the other side of the bed. "Please..." Chantelle said, "...it's complicated... I'd rather not say..." Honey looked at Scotty and winked and gestured with her head 'outside'.

"Won't be a minute pet!" said Honey "Just goin' t' see where Gedd is." Outside the room Scotty and Honey huddled together.

"What do you think Honey, something isnae right is it?"

"No... but I'm sure I don't know what it is that's bothering the girl, I do know she's right upset though."

Gedd was puffing up the stairs and he joined the two in the hallway. "Wot's wrong wi 'er the doc?" he said

"I don't know what has caused it, but the young lassie has had a shock. My advice is to leave her eat a wee bite and let her sleep. I'll just give her a bit o' something to calm her down and help her sleep." The Doc said digging in his bag of tricks. The door opened softly, and Honey almost crept in to find Chantelle weeping silently almost hidden under the covers.

"Aww Chantelle... what's upset you love?" She said sitting down and taking Chantelle into her arms. Chantelle cried openly, sniffed, hiccupped and tried to smile.

"It's just that I thought I saw someone downstairs, someone that I never in a million years ever wanted to clap eyes on again." She rubbed her eyes sniffed again, blowing her nose loudly on some tissues.

"Well who love?" But as Honey asked, she realised the only person down there that Chantelle didn't know was Enid and... Ben. Well, what had that young man been up to then?

"It's Ben" Chantelle sniffed "I... he... I knew him in college... Do you remember when I was upset and Glyn was consoling me... well it's to do with Ben..." Chantelle blew her nose and sniffed again.

The door was knocked softly and Gedd's voice from the other side called out. "Is it alright if we come in?"

Reviving a Rose

"Just 'ang on a minute love." Said Honey, turning to Chantelle she said to her softly. "We'll talk after you an' mi pet, and try to sort it out alright... try and eat a bite before you have what Scotty's goin' ter give yer'... it'll settle you down okay."

Chantelle gave a watery smile and sniffed yet again. "I'll take that as a yes then." Said Honey... "Come in Gedd love, you too Scotty she's decent now."

The Doctor and Gedd came into the room, they both looked at Chantelle's crushed expression, what was up, she always looked so in control.

"You two just drop off wot you're to leave and Scotty tell Chantelle how to take 'er medicine, then both out, its women's talk okay."

Both men seemed relieved at that, women were so complicated sometimes. "Now then lassie, just eat a wee bit and then put this in some water and drink it doon okay?" said Scotty.

"Yes" Chantelle said almost childlike.

"An' don't forget yer food" said Gedd.

"She knows that dafty, Scotty already said... now scoot." Honey scolded.

Glyn was downstairs trying to figure out what was wrong with his Chantelle? Was this Ben 'the Ben'? No... it was too much of a coincidence wasn't it! He decided to call it a night and he bid as much to everyone in the room and left. His thoughts much troubled him as he walked to the garage.

15

The person in Glyn's thoughts was tucked up in bed and slowly telling Honey what had happened to her all those years ago.

"Aw love... how awful... and you thought Ben was... are you sure it was him love... I mean it was quite dark down there... not that I don't believe you love!" Honey said, she was shocked that Enid's boy, Honey's future nephew could have done such a thing.

"I have NEVER forgotten 'that' face and yes I believe it's him... I'm so sorry Honey... I'll leave tomorrow." Chantelle said

"No you bloody won't... you're my friend, you're like a daughter to me, and I told' you that before. If it is him, he'll go before you love, don't you fret on that score..." Honey replied.

"I don't want to cause trouble and he's Gedd's family." Chantelle said staring at the covers on the bed.

"You just sleep pet and it'll all wash out in the mornin' you'll see." Said Honey; softly getting up off the bed.

Reviving a Rose

The sleeping draft was starting to work and Chantelle could feel herself relaxing into the mattress. She thought she heard the door shut and click. Honey must have taken the snip off. Well, at least she was safe tonight... With that Chantelle drifted off to sleep the worry lines slowly disappearing off her face as she slipped deeper into slumber.

Gedd, Honey and Scotty all went downstairs together.

"We'll talk later" said Honey to Gedd under her breath.

By the time the three had reached the bottom of the stairs they had decided to say as little as possible. Mind you Dr. McArdle wouldn't be saying much at all anyway, Doctor/Patient confidentiality. He also had another place to be.

He had contacted Susan Walker, just to update her on Honey's wellbeing, in his position as her doctor. But if he were truthful he also wanted to see if she, 'Sue' would do him the honour of being his escort to Gedd and Honey's wedding. Scotty found himself enjoying the process, of getting to know Nurse Susan Walker, very much indeed.

So as the three re-entered the dining room, a lot of eager faces looked up. Enid stood up, as did the regulars and Ben.

"Is the lass okay... Oh she didn't look well Gedd... is she alright?"

"Yes Enid love, don't fret on, she's a tough cookie an' she's just a bit emotional... (Honey nudged Gedd in the ribs)... Just finishing 'er grand project you know sort of release of pressure like." (He whispered to Honey under his breath.) "I told yer, I know what I'm at woman... I'll not embarrass the girl... give me some credit eh!"

"Sorry... I thought you were..." then Honey realised only 'she' knew the real reason, she had to tell Gedd later. "Sorry... she's just a lovely lass that's all..."

Chantelle's Journey

The cause of the problem in the first place had by now, sat back down. He was watching everybody very carefully.

"Well... well... well" he said, to himself. "Chelly's got her feet under some tables here... this could do with looking into." Ben decided that Chelly, which is how he thought of Chantelle, could do with some more of his expertise. Not the 'rape' bit, he didn't even acknowledge that as rape to himself. As far as he was concerned, she had 'asked for it'! I mean hadn't she strung him along for months, little teaser. The longest he'd waited before her, was a week. He didn't put anything in that girls drink, 'what was her name' Sharmaine, or something posh like that; she had been literally gagging for it at the end of the seven days.

Yes he thought Chelly had potential and he intended to try some more of it. Ben hadn't expected to enjoy this trip with his mother, but he did get to check out the garage. His garage would be a good little earner, once the prices were fixed at a rate he thought was profitable.

The others in the room had been listening to Gedd and Honey's version of the 'faint'. They seemed to believe it, so Gedd said it was about time to get off to bed. The regulars bid everyone else goodnight and went on their way. Enid gave Honey a hug and Gedd escorted her to her room. Honey set about clearing-up, and then she noticed Ben sitting in the chair.

"Oh 'ello love... fancy givin' mi a hand then?"

"I don't do dishes... mum does all that stuff." Ben replied, and then thought better of it. "Only kidding... of course I'll help you... anything to oblige." He bowed like an old courtier, very gallantly. Honey arched one eyebrow but said nothing.

The cleared up in near silence, Ben realized found he'd nothing to say... I mean what on earth; could someone like him have to talk about to an old biddy like her.

Granted she would soon be his 'Aunt' but he'd cross that bridge when he got to it.

Honey was also in deep thought; she just wasn't sure about Gedd's 'Ben'. The old saying 'still waters' and 'running deep' sprang to mind. She was sure there was something not quite right about Ben, but she couldn't put her finger on it maybe Chantelle was right.

Ben said goodnight and stomped sullenly up to his room. He didn't realise it, but he was in room 8, next to the object of his newly formulated plan. The lady in question was by now fast asleep but very troubled.

Something was trying to fight its way through the sleeping draft she had been given. Whatever it was she didn't like it. Something was pressing her down, she was fighting back and it felt like she was crying.

"Get off... Get off me... no... I don't want this..."

"Chantelle... love its Honey darling; come on sweetheart... its Honey... shh..." Honey was finding it hard to hold Chantelle down; she wasn't as young as she used to be. She had heard something as she came up the stairs. Softly she had let herself into Chantelle's room with her master key.

What she had seen proved to her that her young friend hadn't been lying? Chantelle had been writhing around fighting off an invisible attacker and not winning. Honey had seen enough, she sat on the edge of the bed and tried to fetch Chantelle out of her nightmare.

Gedd came into the room and asked "What's t' do lass... is she alright?"

"No... give us a 'and and stop her 'urting 'erself." Honey said Gedd scooted around the other side and gently but firmly held the frightened girl. He slowly managed to lift her into his arms. God she could fight though and he thought he was strong. Whoever done this must have been brutal, she was not giving in.

"Chantelle…" he said softly along with Honey. "It's us two love… come on pet you're safe… it's me and Honey… we're both 'ere love… come on wake up…"

Slowly the fog in Chantelle's head began to lift, and she realised, she wasn't fighting off Ben anymore. Honey was holding her hand and Gedd had her in a firm 'bear-hug'.

"By 'eck… You can't 'alf fight love." Gedd said a little raggedly, you're not bloody soft are yer?" He released her and sat back a bit. He was shocked at how hard she had fought him, well, not him but who ever the 'other' person was.

"Gedd love" said Honey "Go an' make a brew… fetch 3 cups up… I think we could all use one."

"Eye love… I think I need somethin' in mine an' all…" He said, as he went of down stairs.

Honey pulled Chantelle into her arms, now it was safe to do so. God she was shaking like a leaf. "Come on love, come over 'ere t' me… were it 'im again?"

"Yes" Chantelle said "He was… he was trying to…"

"Yer don't need to tell mi love, I could see you fightin' 'im off. Was it the one you told me about? Were it Gedd's Boy?"

"Yes." Chantelle said quietly, "Does Gedd know?"

"Do I know what?" A voice said carrying a tea tray into the room. "What should I know?" Gedd passed Honey a cup of strong tea and then got one for himself and the still scared looking creature in the bed.

"You're not goin' to like it much?" Honey said, taking a sip of her tea.

"Well the sooner you say it, the quicker it's out." Gedd said perching on the end of the bed.

Chantelle couldn't speak; her mouth had gone bone dry. Honey looked at her and said gently. "I'll tell 'im shall I?"… Chantelle nodded. "Well then my love "Honey said as she turned to Gedd. "It seems as yer Enid's boy… Ben…"

Reviving a Rose

Even his name spoken out loud made Chantelle flinch.

"...was the one who hurt our young friend here?"

"What Ben?" Gedd said, not quite trusting his hearing.

"Yes," Honey continued. "He did something awful to 'our Chantelle ere, when they were both at college... Where were it love? Poole I think you said didn't you?"

Chantelle nodded again, and her eyes filled with silent tears. "Please..." she mumbled. "Please don't say anything... he might not even remember me... it was awhile ago... I've change a lot since then..."

"Ey... I'll bet" chipped in Honey.

Gedd looked at the distraught but stunning young woman before him; he would definitely be having words with 'mi laddo' about Chantelle. God to think that someone he was related to could do something like that made him feel physically sick. Excusing himself as he stood up Gedd said; "I'll leave you to 'try' and sleep love we'll mebbie talk in the morning okay?"

He nodded at Honey and kissed the top of Chantelle's head. "I believe you pet, don't you fret on that score... but it's a lot to tek in..." as he passed Honey he put both hands on her cheeks and kissed her too.

"See yer in a bit love... we need to talk you an' me... night love." He said to Chantelle as he left the room.

"He doesn't believe me does he?" Chantelle said shakily. "I mean... Ben is his nephew."

"Nothing excuses 'that' boy...nothing!" said Honey firmly. "I'm going t' watch 'im like a hawk. You're not t' worry sweetheart, we'll sort this out alright."

Honey took the cup off Chantelle; she hadn't drunk much anyway, and placed it on the tray. "I'll get that in the morning. You stay in yer bed 'till I come for yer! Don't open yer door to anyone but me and Gedd... or Glyn." She said as an after thought, he'd protect her, Honey was sure of that.

The door 'clicked' shut and Chantelle heard Honey making sure it was locked

"It's locked love. See yer in the morning." Honey walked along the landing to her room, deep in thought. As she went in she looked back along just to make sure Chantelle's door was shut.

"Close the door love..." Gedd said "... I've been thinkin' a bit..." "Well then!" Honey said as she got into her nightie "What d'yer make on all that then?"

"To be honest love... I'm stunned... to think someone from my family could do such a thing... I mean we haven't 'eard 'is side, 'ave we?" Gedd said scratching the side of his head. "I'm not saying I don't believe or nowt... but god Honey its rough stuff an' no mistake!"

"I agree with yer... "Honey said, patting Gedd's arm "... but why would she mek it up... if she's never seen Ben before... why accuse a stranger?"

"Don't know... but we need to sort it out before the wedding, anyway cuddle up old girl."

"Less of the old you" Honey replied nudging Gedd in the ribs... "Let's try an' get a bit 'o sleep." So saying Gedd and Honey went to sleep in each others arms.

Ben was oblivious to all that had gone on; he slept the sleep of an Innocent child. After all he had no conscience to bother him. Ben always looked after Ben, first and foremost every time.

16

The morning arrived with brilliant sunshine, and Chantelle stood in the bathroom looking at her reflection in the mirror. God she thought, I look rough. Better put some make-up on and try to look a little like normal. Mind you, Chantelle never normally wore make-up, but she thought that today she had better. The bags under her eyes looked black and they cancelled any colour she had straight away.

Twenty minutes later there was a tap at the door, she jumped like a scalded cat.

"Chantelle ... it's me Glyn... can I come in?" The door had opened even before he'd finished speaking. What he saw shocked him, 'his' girl looked like a ghost. Honey and Gedd had filled him in, when he appeared in the kitchen half hour earlier.

Glyn didn't sleep much after he'd gone to the garage. If Gedd's Ben was 'the one' who'd hurt his 'little spitfire' he would kill him. Well that's what he felt like doing, so Glyn had thought it better to sleep away from the 'Inn', rather than knock Ben's door down and his teeth in too! Which was what his initial reaction had been?

After the update he felt even more angry but more concerned for Chantelle. He needed to see if she was okay.

"Come here you" he said softly. Chantelle flew into his arms just to be held, made her feel better; it was like being surrounded by a safety barrier. "You look rough 'spitfire', someone put out your engines?" Glyn said as he tipped her chin up and kissed her forehead.

Chantelle cuddled Glyn in tighter, she needed Glyn's strength. Glyn in turn felt an overwhelming wave of tenderness. His 'spitfire' needed him, and he was definitely there for her. God that stunned him but it also felt so right. He wasn't going to let her get hurt again. He would pin Ben to the wall if he had to, as far as Glyn was concerned, Ben wasn't going to get anywhere near her.

Chantelle slowly let Glyn go a little, but held his hand tightly. "You know don't you?" she said looking into his face. "It's Ben... I knew it as soon as I saw him. I feel awful for Gedd and Honey but they want me to stay..."

"And so you bloody well should..." Glyn broke in "...if anyone should be going it's him... I could kill him for hurting you."

"Maybe I led him on some how..."

"Don't try and excuse him the scumbag!" Glyn cut in.

"He doesn't seem bothered at all... I watched him after you were taken up here last night. He didn't look worried at all."

"But I don't want to cause trouble... I like Gedd and Honey too much." Chantelle said, her eyes glistening.

"Don't worry you." Glyn said, as he kissed her nose.

"Gedd, Honey and me..."He said patting his chest defiantly... "We are all here for you; even the 'regulars' and Mr. Rodgers, if it comes to it!"

Reviving a Rose

This made Chantelle smile a little, the thought of Mr. Rodgers coming to her rescue, like an old knight with his school cape flapping about him. She told Glyn as much and he smiled to.

"See, you have many champions 'm'lady' and we will defend you. Do you feel up to some breakfast?"

"I'll try" Chantelle said "I must fetch this tray downstairs."

"Go and blow your nose first and we'll go down together okay. Present a united front alright." Glyn said, just let that little scumbag try anything, just once; just the excuse Glyn would need to punch Ben's lights out.

"Ready?" He said, "Let's go then 'Boss-Lady'!" Glyn and Chantelle walked downstairs together and Chantelle was pleased that the place seemed empty. She didn't know what she would have said if anyone had asked her about last night.

They both walked into the kitchen and were met with a beautiful aroma and two grinning people.

"Hi ya both... I'm just makin' the scoff for us all... how did you sleep love?" Gedd asked, as he came over and enveloped Chantelle in a bear hug.

"Fine; thank you... a little shaken if the truth be told... I'm sorry about last night Gedd..."

"Don't you say sorry..." interrupted Honey. "We both support you love and you 'ARE' coming to the wedding right!" She said standing next to the cooker with her hands on her very ample hips.

Chantelle was about to reply but Glyn got in first. "I'll be escorting 'Madame' to your wedding 'guys and she will be well protected I assure you!" He looked straight at Chantelle to see if she was going to contradict him. He was pleased however when she smiled slightly looking very relieved.

"Come on then..." said Honey... "Let's get this breakfast out."

Chantelle opted to stay in the kitchen and made the coffee. If the 'regulars' were in the restaurant, they might ask questions she didn't want to answer. Chantelle had not said anything about her birthday; in fact it had been the last thing on her mind. Good God, she was 26 today and no-one here knew. She didn't feel like telling them either. Maybe she'd say something after the wedding guests had left. Yes, that seemed a much better idea.

"Do you want to eat in the kitchen 'Cinders'..." Glyn said, as he came back in. "Everyone is out there tucking in... including Ben."

Just the thought of seeing 'his' face again put Chantelle off of her food... "I'll just have a piece of toast I don't feel up to a 'Gedd and Honey Special' this morning."

She put two slices in the toaster and sipped her coffee. Glyn gave her a quick hug and took the rest of the coffee out to the others.

Chantelle had her back to the door and assumed it was Glyn, Honey or Gedd coming back into the kitchen, but she froze as soon as she heard Ben's voice.

"Well... well... Chelly, you've been hiding a nice view for a few years haven't you?" Ben said walking towards her. "Turn around; lets see if the front matches the back!"

Chantelle couldn't move, she had solid ice blocks for legs and her hands were trembling as she tried to hold onto the mug of coffee.

"Oy!" Another voice said, "what are you doin' in mi kitchen? ...scoot out mi way, I've got more cooking to do." Honey was watching Chantelle and she, was angry with Ben for being in 'her' kitchen. "I said OUT" Honey raised her voice and Ben looked sheepish.

"Sorry... took a wrong turning to the loo..." He left and Honey went straight to Chantelle and stood behind her and hugged her tightly.

129

"Alright pet... he's gone... bloody cheek comin' in 'ere an all..." She said holding the trembling girl in her arms.

Ben was annoyed, Gedd's old biddy had ruined his come back. He was stupid and selfish enough to think she was trembling in anticipation of his caresses... well he'd get her alone again some how and show her what she'd been missing all those years. He had a couple of days to do it, but Ben conceitedly thought that it would be time aplenty. Yes, she definitely deserved some more training from 'the master'.

Honey had finally managed to turn Chantelle around and get her to sit down at the table. "I can't do it Honey... I can't keep bumping into him... he makes me feel sick and scared..." She could feel her eyes filling up.

"Well..." said Honey sitting down and taking Chantelle's hand in hers. "... We'll have to see what's to be done then, but you are coming to the wedding."

The phone rang in reception and at first Honey wasn't going to answer it. "Go on I'll be fine... honest!" said Chantelle, as if she had read Honey's mind... "Really I'll try and finish this toast." She didn't really want it now, it was cold, but felt that she'd have to eat something. Anything would have tasted like cardboard so she might as well eat the toast.

"Glyn" Honey shouted through the kitchen door "Can you watch the coffee whilst I get the phone love!"

As Glyn came in one door, Honey slipped out the other to answer the still ringing phone.

"Hello... Briory Bush Inn reception... how can I help you?" Honey said

"Mam, oh you sound fab... how's it going?" A female voice called out.

"Sonia... baby... oh it's that good t' ear yer voice... honest... things are going lovely... when you coming down pet?"

Chantelle's Journey

"T'morrow if Stephen can finish early... is it okay to fetch the grand 'uns?"

"Corse it is pet... got the big family room set for yer all... cot an' all for little Rees."

"I'm that excited about for you and Gedd, Mam. Stephen said its brill that you've got a fella... but can you still make him those smashing cakes?" Sonia said laughing.

"Aw love... tells 'im corse I will, you know I love cooking." Honey replied grinning. She loved her daughter's hubby almost as much as she loved Sonia. What a great team they made. Best of all he was in a well paid job. Three beautiful kiddies; God, she thought, Alan must be at least 6 yrs old by now. Cherry the only girl was 4 and a real beauty, then there was little Rees, what was he... must be nearly 10 months old now.

"Mam..." Sonia asked, cutting into Honey's train of thoughts. "You still there... or are you daydreaming... I just said I got to go and take the kids to school. I'll ring later with the decision off of the 'Boss'." Sonia always called Stephen that, it was like a pet name, but meant and said with respect. She loved him so much and he was a fabulous daddy too!

"Okay pet... speak to you later on then!" Said Honey and she hung up and went back through to Chantelle.

Glyn had sat down next to Chantelle and turned her into his arms. "Come here you... you need a good cuddle." He held her firmly but gently, just in case she needed some space. She didn't, Chantelle pushed right into Glyn's arms and shivered. "What's up you? I left you here cooking your toast... what's up?"

"He came in..." Chantelle started to say "What?" said Glyn bristling up like an angry hedgehog "Ben came in here?"

"Yes!" Chantelle carried on "...He spoke to me... but I didn't turn round... and then... and then Honey came

Reviving a Rose

in and told him to leave... he said he'd got the wrong room..." she tailed off.

"I'll give him wrong bloody room." Glyn went to stand up, putting Chantelle of his lap, but she held onto his arms.

"Please stay here... please... I don't want to cause a scene ... Glyn please stay with me." She looked into his face, willing him to stay and comfort her.

"Okay spitfire, but only because you asked me to." Glyn said huffing and puffing up like an angry adder.

Honey looked at them both and said "I didn't like that young man in my kitchen... he'll turn my custard off..."

Chantelle smiled weakly "I think I'll go for a walk around the village."

"I'll come to" said Glyn "how do you fancy checking up on your little car at Gedd's? It looks a lot better than when you last saw it!" He said picking up his jacket.

"If I remember rightly it's your fault my 'little car' is there in the first place!" said Chantelle trying to smile. "I'll just go and get my coat." She walked through the reception door and ran up to her room. She had just reached it when a hand touched hers.

"Chantelle?" She jumped and span round like a scolded cat.

"God you scared me."

"Sorry" said Glyn "I didn't want him cornering you up here on your own!"

"Why is he here?" She said looking around nervously. "No... he's still downstairs with Enid. It's a shame... she seems like such a nice lady."

"Maybe he takes after his dad." Chantelle said spitefully. "I haven't met his mum yet... if you come with me I'll brave it out!"

"Are you sure?" Glyn said, God she was brave.

"Yes, then we can go for that walk to Gedd's place okay?" Chantelle didn't feel particularly brave but she felt she owed it to Gedd and his sister.

Back downstairs she took a deep breath and walked into the restaurant. Everyone looked up from their plates. Even Ben stopped eating, he was curious to see Chelly come towards him. However she stopped by his mother instead. "Mrs. Locke... I'm very pleased to meet you." She stuck her hand out to Enid, who shook it firmly and warmly.

"Like wise, you must be Chantelle, such a pretty name too. Honey's been telling me about you doing up the old cottage. She said it's lovely.

Chantelle found herself warming to Gedd's sister. After all it wasn't her fault her son was a waster.

"And what about me" said Ben sticking his hand out "do I get the same treatment?"

"I'm sorry..." Chantelle said "but I don't wish to speak to you... if your lovely mother wants to know why not, you could always enlighten her about POOLE!!"

Chantelle wasn't going to say anything but Ben had looked so smug; she had wanted to wipe that off his face. She turned on her heel and walked away head held high. That had felt good; maybe she was getting over him at last. Glyn definitely helped there... He made her feel special.

Enid just stood there with her mouth open... what was that all about?

"Ben... what did she mean, tell me about Poole?" Enid said as she turned to look at her son, who was red with contained anger.

"She's just someone from college who I gave the brush-off too... she stalked me if you must know!" He lied, Ben could certainly think on his feet.

"Well she didn't look like a stalker to me... she looked like an angry woman with un-resolved issues?" Enid hit back.

133

Reviving a Rose

"Just leave it mum… the girl wanted what she couldn't have… ME." Ben said sitting down. "I can't help it if I'm good looking, you'd be surprised at just how many girls used to fight it out, to go out on a date with me!" He said the smug expression back on his face.

Enid saw her Frank sitting there, plastered all over Ben's face. Yes, he was a good looking boy, but he had a mean pinched edge to him, just like his dad had. What had her boy done to that young lass, she was going to find out, but somehow Enid knew that it might not be very pleasant.

Glyn had followed Chantelle out; he was being watched by Ben. "Who was he?" mused Ben. Surely the hired brickie didn't fancy himself with the ice-maiden. Well Ben was determined to be bloody first though, and he excused himself to follow brickie-boy and Chelly outside.

"Not so fast" said Enid "You and me got stuff to do for the wedding son… come on… that's why yer 'ere to 'elp me!" Enid said, she could think on her feet too! Best keep Ben close she thought, give the girl some room. Blast thought Ben, how was he; going to watch her now. He painted on a smile

"Of course Mother dearest, I'm always here for you, you know that surely?" he simpered.

"Get on with yer… silly sod… come on lets find Gedd and Honey." She said heading towards the kitchen. Ben sent her a stinking look but she wasn't looking at him.

17

Glyn put on his jacket and slipped his arm around Chantelle's shoulders. She liked that and chivvied into him. They walked amiably down the little lane opposite the Inn, towards Gedd's garage. The sun was still out but it was a little nippy. They came out of the lane at the other end and turned left to cross the road over to Gedd's place.

"I've got some teabags if you fancy a cuppa!" Glyn commented. "Yes" said Chantelle "That sounds lovely but my car first please."

Glyn grinned and escorted 'his spitfire' around the back of the garage.

It was quite open plan with two pumps on the forecourt and a tyre pressure/air check machine to one side. The building was quite large and oblong shaped. It reminded Chantelle of a large yellow shoebox with two smaller grey ones on top. As she and Glyn walked around the back, she could see that one of the grey boxes extended

Reviving a Rose

back and down like an up-turned 'L'. Glyn watched her and said;

"That's Gedd's flat, the 'L' shaped box, and the other one is the office. You can only get into that one from the garage itself." Then Chantelle spotted her 'little car' and a smile lit up her face. Her car looked brand new, it sparkled in the sunlight. Gedd had done a lot of work on it and had re-sprayed it too!

"Oh... it's... lovely. Just wait until I see Gedd... its just..." She trailed off in awe and put her hands up to her face. Chantelle walked over to 'her car' and ran her fingers over the bodywork. What a job Gedd had done, he must be a magician. She was going to find an extra present for Gedd, as well as a wedding present, to say thank you. Mind you, she didn't know how much the repairs would cost. As if he had read her mind.

Glyn said "I'm paying for the repairs; it was my fault after all!"

Chantelle turned around and said, "Can you afford it... I mean couldn't we just go halves or something?" She thought that the money he had earned would all go on the repairs and he'd have worked for nothing.

"Not to worry, the insurance will cover it" Glyn said easily... "Anyway now you've seen the car how about the tea?"

"Yes please... and then maybe have a look for a wedding present... I mean you don't have to shop with me or anything..." she said slightly embarrassed.

"Not a problem "Boss-Lady", I need to buy a present myself, so I might as well have some beautiful company to do it."

Chantelle felt relieved to hear that, she didn't fancy bumping into Ben on her own, he really scared her. Apart from what 'he'd' actually physically done to her, her emotions were all over the place. It was as if she was back at college, the morning after he had attacked her.

Glyn was watching a myriad of emotions course all over her face, he felt angry.

"Hey... come on, tea remember?" He pushed slightly and was not at all amused that she was shaking. "Come on" he took her arm and led her into Gedd's little kitchen "I'll put the kettle on."

Chantelle took off her jacket and put it over the back of a small chair, near the tiny kitchen table. It was one of those drop-leaf ones. She thought that maybe Gedd didn't use it that much as the chair was at the side rather than under it. The drop-leaf was down and if truth be told, a little dusty.

Glyn fetched two mugs and rinsed them in the sink. "Do you want tea or coffee?" he said over his shoulder.

"Tea's fine... not too strong please; just a little milk."

"What about sugar?" Glyn asked.

"No thanks" she replied looking around the room.

"Do you mind if I have a little look-see Gedd's quite a fella isn't he?"

"Help yourself... I'm sure there's nothing here to show he's a part-time axe-murderer!" Glyn commented.

Chantelle grinned "You know what?"

"What?" Glyn replied.

"You're a very special man Glyn Mathews, and I'm glad I met you... even if you did have to run me off the road to do it!" she looked at him slyly.

"You're not so bad yourself, I think what you did with Rose Cottage is fantastic, are you planning to do anymore?" Glyn said He wanted to tell her he loved her, but maybe it was too soon. Stick to neutral topics and let Chantelle take the lead.

"I'm not sure, I hope so... but I haven't got a job lined up just yet. I was thinking of going home to mum for a while and see what turns up. If I get a good reference from Mr. Rodgers, I could put it on my website, it might drum up some more clients."

"Hmm..." Glyn mused. "Are you staying long after the wedding then?" He said as he poured the steaming water into the mugs.

"No... At least I wasn't going to... unless something..." she was thinking some-one close... "Comes up?"

"Would you consider staying on if I asked you to?" He said passing Chantelle her tea.

She looked into her mug and said "I might... we'll see what the weekend brings."

Well it wasn't quite the 'YES' Glyn was after but she hadn't said 'NO' either. They sat down either side of the little table and sipped in relative silence, each one thinking about the other but not saying anything out loud.

Chantelle stood up and moved about the kitchen, she then noticed some small stairs, with a very narrow staircase. "What's up there?"

"It's Gedd's' lounge and bedroom. He likes to see if anyone comes into the garage even if it's shut. There's a big window facing the front of the garage forecourt, want to see?"

"Yes... I mean..."

"I know you don't want to dive into bed, but just have a look-see!" Glyn said covering Chantelle's embarrassment.

Chantelle thought, he must be quite a guy to keep picking up and reading her thoughts like that, plus Glyn wasn't exactly ugly was he? She climbed the stairs and was pleasantly surprised to see that the lounge was spotless. It was totally different to the kitchen.

"Gedd likes to keep his living space clean, the kitchen tends to fetch the dust in from the garage but he makes sure that wherever he is having a time-out, it's clean." Glyn said reading her mind. "Mind you" he said "I've been clearing up too... the couch has been my bed whilst I've been working for you."

Chantelle's Journey

"Couldn't you afford... sorry I shouldn't have asked that... but your car... I thought..." God she was babbling and all she wanted to do was kiss him.

"I'm not totally poor, you know, but I've been helping Gedd as well, so the board and lodge are sort of payment in kind... I'm a bit of a mechanic to, you know!" Glyn said looking quite puffed up.

"Hidden talents then" she said, almost without thinking.

"Yes indeed." Glyn replied and took her mug out of Chantelle's hand. He placed them on the coffee table and then put his hands both side of her face and kissed her. "I've been dying to do that all morning, d'you know that... you are a very special lady." He stopped short of I love you again. She had to lead; he didn't want to scare her off.

Glyn in turn had moved his arms around her waist. He pulled her against his firm chest and breathed in her scent. She was like air to a suffocating man. She filled his lungs, his heart and yes if truth be told, even his soul. Glyn felt bloody wonderful every time 'his spitfire' was in his arms. The kiss deepened but Glyn reluctantly ended it first.

"What..." Chantelle was quite intoxicated.

"Come... come m'lady we must away to the shops... a present or two is needed for the betrothed couple... dost thou not remember?" Glyn said sweeping a bow in front of Chantelle.

"Oh... of course... I'd forgotten... I mean you took my mind off it there!" she said smiling.

Glyn thought she should smile more, Chantelle looked stunning.

"Come on then..." She said "Let's go and hit the shops." She skipped down the stairs and grabbed her jacket and waited outside for 'her' Glyn. When had she started thinking that, mind you she found that she liked it a lot, so what was the harm?

Reviving a Rose

Glyn locked up and slipped his jacket on and also slipped his arm over Chantelle's shoulder. She could feel the weight of it, but strangely it felt really nice. She tucked her arm around his waist and they both strolled into the centre of the village to hunt for presents.

There was quite a few 'little' shops in the square and they looked very 'old fashioned' but really sweet. Just like the nice picture postcard ones you would buy on holiday to say 'Wish you were here!'

They both stopped in front of a lovely little shop called 'Martha's Curio's'. Maybe there would be just the thing in there for Gedd and Honey. The bell tinkled as they walked in and 'Martha' called out from the back of the shop.

"Won't be a tic... just putting something in the oven."

Glyn and Chantelle looked at each other and smiled. They had been thinking along similar lines but in a different place. Still that might happen later who knows?

"Hello there..."Said Martha. "Welcome to my curios... anything take your fancy?"

"We're just having a good look..." said Chantelle "It's so full of wonderful things."

"Yes I know... I do try to find the different stuff you know, out of the ordinary."

Glyn was peering along the shelves and then he spotted 'it'. 'Ah' just what he wanted. At first glance 'it' didn't seem much, but if you studied it carefully you saw so much more. The 'it' was in fact a small angel made of crystal, but she was inside a crystal shell. So the colours of the rainbow shone out in all directions nearly hiding the angel. It was only when you really looked you could see her, and because she was also crystal the colours intensified.

"Wow... that's the one for me!" He said picking the object up very carefully.

"Ohh... let me see..." Chantelle said "Oh Glyn it's beautiful... they'll love it,"

Glyn took his 'prize' over to Martha to be boxed, and hopefully wrapped, like most men he was rubbish at wrapping presents so he smiled at Martha expectantly.

"Sure... I'll wrap it... most of you lot can't do it for toffee." Martha said reading his thoughts.

Chantelle carried on looking... Bingo!! Well didn't that beat all? She had found another one, but as she peered into it she smiled even more. This one had a cheeky looking cherub in it. Well 'he' would be a perfect match for Glyn's 'Angel'.

"Glyn" she said excitedly "look, come and look." At first Glyn thought she had found another 'Angel'. "No it's not... look inside!" She said again, he peered in and also saw the little fat cherub; he seemed to be sitting on a Cushing. What a cracking piece.

"Looks like you've found my 'Angel' perfect partner... I think we must be on the same wave length M'lady."

Martha watched and smiled, don't know about the crystals but those two were definitely well matched. "Are you two going to Honey and Gedd's wedding then?" She asked as she put the finishing touches to Glyn's parcel.

"Yes." They answered almost at the same time, and then they laughed. Glyn spoke first... "We have had the pleasure of knowing them both these last few months, and consider them good friends. Mind you Honey scared us both a bit and Gedd. Confidentially..." he said leaning towards Martha... "I think her little jaunt to hospital made Gedd think on his feet!"

"Oh yes..." said Martha, "those two been friend for years, Gedd and Honey's 'Fred' had been mates since they were at school, here in the village."

"Oh... so that was his first name," Chantelle said "Honey only called him 'My Mr. Graham,"

Reviving a Rose

"Oh that, well that was their joke' y'see, Honey liked to say the 'My' bit, just to remind Fred, not saying he was flirty or anything, in fact the opposite. It just made them feel like they belonged to each other. He called her 'My Mrs. G' back, kind of pet names y'know. She was desolate when he passed... Gedd's certainly put the smile back on her face... and good job too, she's an asset to this village always has been... 'Er there's me rambling on; do you two fancy a cuppa? I'm going to the 'do' on sat'day... I think the whole village is, should be a good turn out."

And with that Martha disappeared into the back, she hadn't even taken any money yet!

"Excuse me... Martha is it? Could we pay first... just in case I forget?" Chantelle said... "I've got a brain like a sieve at the moment and I'd hate to have you chase me down the street, brandishing a teapot."

Martha laughed. "As if I could run after you... still let's get the formal stuff done then as you say." Glyn paid first, as his present was already expertly wrapped by Martha.

"That'll be £80 please" said Martha, not looking up from the till, some things were worth good money and if he had the taste to pick it, surely he had the money to pay. Chantelle looked at Glyn, did he have that much?

"It's okay 'Boss-Lady,'" he said grinning. "I'm not totally skint you know." He pulled out 4 crisp £20 notes and paid Martha. "Your turn now." He turned to Chantelle and waved her forwards.

"I'll just pay for this, but I'm also looking for a thank you present as well, for the work Gedd did on my car!" She said as she pulled a face at Glyn.

"My fault, I'm afraid." He said to Martha... "I sort of forced my boss who I didn't know was going to be my boss, off of the road a couple of months back. We've been working on Rose Cottage." He finished, looking a little sheepish, which quickly turned impish as he grinned at them both in turn.

"Oh it's your little car that Gedd pulled out of the bends... oh that's been the cause of more than a few ditchings that has. Much too narrow;" Martha said seriously. "Well come on then, let's find Gedd a pressie."

She wandered over to the shelves and made a few clucking and sucking noises as if deep in thought.

"Here we are love..." Martha said carefully lifting out a small box... "See what you think of this?" She handed it to Chantelle for closer inspection.

It was little like the angel in some ways. It had hidden depths. The box was about palm size and in-laid with lots of different types of wood.

"What is it?" Chantelle asked turning it over in her hands.

"There's a little secret opener look..." Said Martha, and as she did the box sprang open. "There you are... look at that!"

"Martha your shop definitely has the right name... it's a wonderful 'curio' and is just what a curio is." Chantelle said as she studied it.

"Give us a look!" said Glyn, as he leaned over their shoulders. The open box was lined with green velvet and looked very old. "What was it used for?" Chantelle asked, as she turned it this and that "the workmanship is perfect."

"Well apparently it was given as a keepsake for some one to keep a special something in from their loved ones." Martha replied.

"Should I be giving it to Gedd then?" Chantelle replied.

"Yes love... he'll love it, you never know he might put something in it and pass it on to Honey." Martha said winking conspiratorially at them both.

Reviving a Rose

And so with her two presents picked it was Chantelle's turn to pay. Martha asked with a wicked grin on her face. "Do you want me to wrap them for you?"

"Umm... the wedding gift, yes please but I think I'll wrap Gedd's gift myself if that's okay!" Chantelle said getting her purse out of her bag.

"Not a problem, er... Mr...?" said Martha.

"Glyn... Glyn Mathews" he replied shaking Martha's hand.

"Er... Glyn could you just pop in there" Martha said thumbing over her shoulder "... and take my kettle off the stove ... I'd be grateful..."

"Certainly... not a problem" he said going through to rescue a violently steaming kettle sitting on a gleaming range.

"E's nice... have you two known each other long then?" Martha enquired, as she totted up the bill.

"Not really... I employed Glyn via my website to work on the cottage project for my 'Boss' Mr. Rodgers."

"Oh... Mr. Rodgers who stays here every summer... from the boy's school?"

"Yes that's the one... he's a sweetie, and he gave me my first job. Glyn has been working with me on the building side you know?" Chantelle said, "How much Martha?"

"That's £170 please... not too much I hope... their both worth the money!" She said looking slightly worried.

"Thank you, that's fine and yes they are both worth it and so are Honey and Gedd." Chantelle smiled as she handed over her card. Martha processed it, Chantelle signed and the presents were duly paid for.

"Come on then, cup of tea time. Fancy a piece of cake as well?" Chantelle was surprised at how hungry she felt; mind you the toast she'd tried to eat that morning had tasted awful.

Chantelle followed Martha, through to the back of the shop. The back room was quite small with Glyn in it, it seemed tiny.

"I've made the tea..." he said looking at Martha. "But I couldn't find any cups?"

"Go and sit yourself down. You filling up my room too much, let the dog see the rabbit" She said as she bustled about. "Ah... here we are." Martha produced 3 cups and saucers and also 3 plates. "I was just telling?" She looked towards Chantelle.

"Chantelle... Chantelle Adams... pleased to meet you." Chantelle said quickly shaking Martha's hand.

"As I was saying; I was just telling Chantelle here, I've got a nice cake, would you like a slice with your tea Glyn? Seeing as how you filled up my teapot for me."

"I'd love some... I'm always ready to be fed!" He looked at Chantelle as he said it and raised an eyebrow.

Martha missed it; her head was inside a cupboard. She fetched an enormous cake and placed it on the kitchen table. "I'll just get a knife and put the snip on the shop door. We've earned a little break I think." She said more to herself than anyone in particular.

As Martha went to close the shop for a while, Glyn leaned across the table and kissed Chantelle quickly.

"What was that for?" she said looking a little stunned but pleased.

"Because it's been at least an hour since I last did it!" Glyn said smiling at her. Chantelle smiled back and felt her heart just swell up. She felt warm all over and wished that it was more than just one kiss.

Martha came back through and busied herself looking for a knife to cut some healthy sized slices for them all. "It's my own recipe, off of my mother. Honey and I enter the village fete every year and my fruit cake always wins. Mind you, have you seen the size of her Victoria Sponges, they're massive..." Glyn and Chantelle both had the same naughty thought about Gedd seeing them

Reviving a Rose

but said nothing. "...As if they weren't big enough," Martha continued, "...She then fills them full of cream and jam."

Chantelle nearly choked on her tea. "Sorry it went down the wrong hole," she said coughing and spluttering. Martha tapped her back "Have some cake and soak your tea up." She passed Glyn his piece; he didn't take long to eat it either.

"Umm... this is stunning." He said still with his mouth full of cake. "It's absolutely wonderful."

"Well thank you Glyn; you do say just the right things." Martha said eating her cake in a very lady-like manner. The next half hour or so was pleasantly spent, Chantelle didn't want to go but she had some other things to do.

"I'm awfully sorry Martha," she said standing up "but I have got some other bits and bobs to do... I have really enjoyed your company and especially your cake... we'll see you at the wedding I hope, on Saturday then!"

"You sure will both... I'm making the cake." Martha replied.

"Well it will be lovely I'm sure," said Glyn, as he stood up too. "Thank you Martha," he said kissing her on the cheek "...shall we pass on your good wishes when we get back to the Inn?"

"Yes please do, could you tell Honey the cake's as good as done. It's been a pleasure meeting you two; you make a fine couple you know!" Martha said as she led them back through the shop and unlocked the door. Chantelle hugged Martha and kissed her cheek as Glyn had just done.

"Thank you for your help with Gedd's present and for the tea and cake. See you on Saturday then?" With that they both left the shop holding their goodies carefully.

18

Glyn walked into the kitchen of the Inn and was enveloped in a cloud of icing sugar mist.

"What's up in here?" He said swiping his hand about in front of his face. Chantelle came in too and shut the back door. She bumped into Glyn's back, she couldn't see either.

"Just dusting m' cakes" came Honey's reply, from in the room somewhere.

"We'll leave you to it then and put our goodies upstairs." Chantelle said

"What 'ave yer got?" Honey asked from within a cloud of icing sugar.

"Not telling" Glyn said "you'll have to wait till Saturday."

They both escaped, sneezing as they went and both climbed the stairs to Chantelle's room. Neither of them saw Ben in the corner of the room, he was not impressed; they looked a little too cosy for his liking, that would have to change. He chewed his lip and started planning.

Glyn waited as Chantelle opened her door. "Come in... you haven't got to wait outside." She said standing to one side.

"Thanks." Glyn nodded and walked into the room. The door clicked a definite click. It was locked from the rest of the world. Chantelle put her presents down on the dresser and shook like a dog, icing sugar plumed out from her hair.

"I'll have to wash it, take a seat Glyn, I won't be a minute." Glyn sat down on the bed and listened to Chantelle moving about in the bathroom. She didn't realise it but she began to sing to herself. It wasn't anything amazing but to Glyn it meant she was feeling better, it sounded good to him. He was very tempted to go in and scrub her back but he kept telling himself, let her lead.

The bathroom door opened and Chantelle walked in wrapped in a big fluffy towel. Her hair was in a kind of top-knot. How did women do that? Glyn couldn't take his eyes off of her. Chantelle found herself blushing and suddenly realised she was totally naked under the towels. She had only slept with Glyn the once and she didn't really know how he felt about her. He hadn't professed his love had he!

Glyn for his part felt a lot of emotions flying everywhere. God she was stunning. And what's more she wasn't aware of it, which made her even more special. If he could he would have peeled the big fluffy towels off and made slow, very slow deliberate love to her all afternoon. As it was he just sat there, hoping his manhood didn't betray just how aroused he was.

Chantelle didn't know what to do; she just stood there staring at Glyn. Did she kiss him, as she wanted to or get dressed and go downstairs. She finally after what seemed hours to Glyn! Decided to take her heart in both hands and reach out to him. "Glyn I... I really want you but I'm not sure what to do!"

"Well then," Glyn said standing up. "Come here 'Boss-Lady' and we'll work it out between us shall we?"

She walked into his arms and straight into his heart. Glyn felt 10 feet tall. She trusted him and he felt very humbled after what Chantelle had been through.

"Oh my beautiful spitfire, you just made my heart sing... d'you know that?" He said and held her tightly in his arms as if to prove it.

"You make me feel so safe and I love being held by you, more than anyone else I've ever known." Chantelle said into his chest.

Well thought Glyn, there was a love in there so that's a good start. He held her firmly and rubbed his hands over her back, as if to dry her off. Chantelle in turn was caressing Glyns back. He felt so strong and masculine, she wanted more. Slowly her hands moved all over his back and then they kind of did their own thing. One travelled around the front and up his chest, the other moved up Glyns back to his neck and caressed the soft nape and back of his head. Glyn groaned softly, he pulled her in some more.

He pushed the air out of her and Chantelle sighed. Her face turned up to his and she opened her mouth slightly. Glyn decided that he was going to go for it; she didn't seem scared in his arms at the minute did she. He kissed her mouth and teased her lips with his tongue and teeth. She returned his kisses and was even daring enough to dart her own tongue into his mouth.

Whoa... where did that come from thought Glyn...? I don't know but I bloody love it. She was so dammed sexy and she had absolutely no idea.

The towel by now started to slip down, Chantelle went to grab it, a hand stopped her and Glyn held the towel for her. It was so erotic; she was inside her towel but outside of his clothes. That didn't seem fair to Chantelle who by now was on fire, and Glyn's clothes were stopping her, from what she wasn't sure but she wanted to find

Reviving a Rose

out. Slowly she lifted his shirt out from his trousers. Glyn shrugged off his jacket, still holding the towel, just swapping his hands over to do it.

He pressed in to Chantelle and she held onto him, her hands went under his shirt and up his chest. God he felt good, she felt drugged, and Chantelle needed more. She undid his buttons, ah, that was much better now; she would look at him as well as touch him.

"Chantelle," Glyn said "Are you sure about this, because if you're not we'd better stop now while we can." She looked up and realised he had used her name again. He didn't normally, it was usually the nicknames or pet names he used but she liked the way Glyn said her name.

"I don't want to stop... I might regret it I do... I want to explore you... you are a very special man... and I want you very much... I think I might be in love..."

"What?" Glyn said staring into her eyes... she had said the word at last, he thought his heart would burst. His trousers certainly felt like they did.

"...With you" she finished and then registered the 'what'? "I'm sorry" she said trying to pull away. God she was embarrassed he didn't feel the same.

"Oh! No you don't..." Glyn said as he gathered her back into his arms. "I said 'what,' because I've been waiting so long to hear you say it silly. I've been in love with you for ages but I didn't want to scare you off."

"Oh... Glyn" she said kissing his face, his neck, his eyes even the tip of his nose. "You make me feel as if I could conquer the world; if you were beside me... you make me feel like a complete woman... I never..."

She didn't get to finish the sentence as Glyn kissed her. It was like a drowning man gulping oxygen, Chantelle made him feel whole too... he'd never ever felt that with anyone else before. Glyn loved how it made him feel.

The trousers somehow found their way to the floor and Chantelle could now see just how much she affected

Glyn. Her eyes widened in awe. Good God passion was a wonderful thing and his manhood strained against his boxers.

She felt hot and a deep warm feeling was rushing around her body and sending electric shock waves to her secret place. Something needed to be fixed. Her most female place was pulsing and she wanted it to be freed, healed, and loved.

Glyn let go of the towel, and Chantelle stood there and let him feast his eyes on her. She was a bloody good feast too Glyn thought, he wanted to bury his shaft deep inside her and show her just how much he loved her.

"Come here and undress me then we'll be equal." He took her hand and placed it on his hips.

Chantelle's other hand followed, she slid down the restraining boxers and his pulsing maleness burst out, solid and proud. It quivered slightly, not used to the rush of cool air. Chantelle closed the gap, his skin felt smooth and firm. The chest hair tickled her breasts but she likes it.

Glyn's hands slid down her back and cupped her pert bottom. He pressed her hips into him and she could really feel his arousal. It was nudging her and telling her Inner core what was there to have, if she wanted it? Some how; they ended up on the bed. Glyn pulled the coverlet over them and then began to make love to her, glorious, luxurious, slowly wonderful love to his Chantelle.

They didn't say much, they didn't have to. Their bodies did all the talking. When Glyn finally entered her, she was so ready. Chantelle thought she would explode. She pushed against him and writhed under him. Her body was doing its own thing. It was primeval, animalistic and sensual all at the same time. She felt more alive than she had ever been.

The pressure began to build in both of them and suddenly she found herself on top. The coverlet gone, probably on the floor; Glyn began to rock her gently on his shaft, that had by now pinned her to him. He could feel his own pressure building up too, so he began to rock her a little faster. Chantelle's eyes looked glazed to Glyn but her expressions said more than any words could.

She began to rock herself back and fore and she placed her hands on Glyn's chest to steady herself. Fingers mingled with chest hair, Glyn moved his hands up to her breasts. They felt fantastic, her nipples stood out and strained as if to puncture the air. He had to suckle them; he leaned up and kissed one as his hand caressed the other. Chantelle's gasped, oh that felt amazing. It was like little electrodes were shooting signals straight to her core and building up the fire. She messaged his chest and pushed him back down onto the bed.

"Please Glyn… now please… I want…" Chantelle cried. What did she want? Release and fulfilment!

Glyn flipped her onto her back and her legs lifted up and around his waist holding him in, not wanting him to escape. He was leaning over her, straight arms like pylons and he pushed into her like a piston engine.

"More…" She cried out for fulfilment. "More… fill me… make me feel whole Glyn please!" Glyn could not speak, he just kept pushing and the pressure built up until his seed exploded into her with such force that Chantelle could feel it filling her empty womb.

"Oh my god!" She screamed as her own orgasm started, Glyn kept pushing and he watched her face all the time. She felt like she was climbing up a steep lovely warm hill and the heat was building more and more. Then suddenly she felt as if she had crested the cliff and was now falling… free falling into lots of clouds and it felt so comforting and really soul filling. Her heart felt so full of love for this amazing man that tears glistened in her eyes.

"What are the tears for...? I didn't hurt you did I?" Glyn said rolling off at once.

"No Glyn... you saved me... you have healed me in a way I can never express enough... except to say again I LOVE YOU so much it hurts. Can I have a cuddle now please, I'm getting cold!"

"Of course you can, come here." He pulled up the coverlet off of the floor and they both snuggled up together like spoons, in the foetal position and glowed! "I really love you my spitfire" said Glyn, half asleep. He felt worn out but fantastic. He'd just close his eye for a few minutes he thought! Chantelle wriggled in abit more and did the same. They both slept for nearly 3 hours and didn't even realise it.

19

Somebody else did though, and he was sitting downstairs getting more 'pissed-off' by the minute. Just what the hell were 'they' doing up there, 'Brickie-boy' was going to get it good for treading on Ben's patch. In his twisted mind Chelly belonged to him, to do with as he pleased, and 'Brickie-boy' was not in the equation at all. Ben had to think of a plan and quick-sharp.

"Mam," he said "... do you need anything from your room?"

"No pet... why?"

"No reason" Ben was really pissed off now. How could he go upstairs, without looking as if he were up to something!

It was nearing lunchtime so he suggested a quick walk, breath of fresh air, to build up an appetite for food. He could then look up at the bedroom windows and see if any were drawn.

"You go love... I'm quite happy sitting here... in fact I might give Honey a hand if she wants one." Perfect, thought Ben, I'll have a really good look around, especially if Mam's not with me to get in the way.

"Okay then... see you in a bit?"

With that he slipped out the front entrance and walked across the other side and looked up scanning the rooms. Most of them faced the front; he couldn't see Honey shoving Chelly in a back one.

Unfortunately for Ben, Chantelle had already closed her curtains, just before going into the shower again. This time though, she went in with Glyn. "Don't close the curtains again, open them we'll get dressed in the bathroom, it's much more cosy and warm" Glyn said as he patted her bottom.

"I wasn't going to," she replied. "... But the bathroom isn't very big!"

"That's okay I'll sit on the loo and watch you." Glyn grinned.

"You look like the cat that's got the cream. Mr. Mathews!"

"I have, you!" He said as he kissed the tip of her nose. "You're my lovely jug of cream M'lady and I love it and you."

Ben was still scanning the rooms, blast!! No curtains shut. 'Oh well' he thought, let's go and check out Gedd's garage. After all a couple of years down the line it'll be mine. He set off at a brisk pace and soon reached it, god it looked scruffy. Still if it fetched in the money what did he care.

Ben did a quick walk round and as he was walking round by the workshop end, he peered through the windows. 'Wow' the old boys got a lot of equipment. That must be worth a quid or two. So maybe the morning wasn't totally wasted, after all. He walked slowly back to the Inn. 'I think I'll sit in the lounge so I can see where they come in from,' he mused to himself.

Honey and Enid were in the kitchen sorting out lunch.

"So how long have you been cooking for your regulars, as you call 'em?" Enid queried.

"Oh… must be at least 10 months or more… the meals on wheels thingy had to be cut… save money or summit! Bloody annoying… they paid all their lives… workin' an' that an' now they ain't got a couple of brass ha'pennies; to rub t'gether… it's shocking so it is! So I said one night when they all came in fer dinner… if they wanted good wholesome grub ter come ter me and we'd sort summit out… they been comin' everyday since."

The two women seemed to be on the same wave length and a new friendship was beginning to grow. Enid decided to broach a rather delicate subject.

"Tell me, 'onest like, do you think mi' Ben's done summit to the pretty lass… what's 'er name?" asked Enid out of the blue.

"Chantelle, you mean?" Honey looked up from her cooking. "Well I'm sure she's not makin' it up, if that's; … wot you're saying!"

"No… it's not that Honey love… it's just that I shouldn't think it of 'im, but sometimes 'e's got a lot of 'is Dad in 'im!" Enid looked so sad as she said it, Honey patted her arm in response.

"Well, whatever 'e 'is, you're still Gedd's little sister an' I like you a lot, so lets finish this cooking eh!… and then 'ave a brew." Honey said as she puffed by the table. "I'm not doin' anymore for sat'day; I'm worn out and that's the truth."

She sat down and Enid said softly.

"I'll mak' the brew then? Shall I? Is it alright… you look a bit peeky. Can't 'ave you getting poorly before the do… can we?"

A new bond had formed and with tea on the way the two ladies didn't think anymore about Ben, for the rest of the afternoon. In fact Enid only remembered he was there when they were dishing out dinner.

Chantelle's Journey

The 'man' himself had sat in the lounge the best part of the morning and all bloody afternoon, where were they? Ben didn't realise there was another staircase, right at the back of the Inn; it used to be for the servants of old. The stone steps had worn in the middle from use over the years, but as with the old paper it merely added character.

Chantelle and Glyn didn't know or care that Ben had been sat in the lounge like a lonely sad wallflower. In fact... he only had company when the regulars came in.

The back door open and Glyn walked into the kitchen. The stone stairs had led out into the courtyard at the back, and the two new lovers had, to all intense and purpose looked as if they had just got back from shopping.

"Ave a nice time you two?" asked Enid.

"Oh yes..." grinned Glyn and Chantelle very nice indeed.

"Did you get all you wanted?" Honey asked Innocently...

"More than I would have ever hoped for!" Chantelle said as she began to blush a little. "Oh and I found a darling little thank you present for Gedd, for fixing my little car its fab!"

Dinner was finally served at 5.00pm and because Enid had helped, there was lots of it. Not that Honey was stingy but she was running out of puff a bit.

Ben was surprised that Chantelle had entered from the kitchen, how had she done that? Maybe there was a lift or something; he'd have to ask his 'mum'. She seemed to be getting pally with 'thingy', what was her name? Oh yes Honey. What a stupid name, sticky and sickly like syrup! Then Glyn came out too, and Ben sat up, what the... where did he come from? He would definitely have to see if there was a lift, it might come in handy!!

Reviving a Rose

"Are you all set for Saturday Honey?" asked Maud Pennington.

"Oh I hope so... if it's not done now tough... it's Friday now an' I'm not doing 'owt more, I've cooked 'till mi' arms are about to fall off and the 'ole village should see a good spread, so much for me usin' a caterer. 'Specially as Enid's (she said putting an arm around Enid's shoulder) been 'elping out today."

"You're welcome an' all," said Enid. "Pleased to meet all of you proper like. Honey's been telling me lots about you."

"Not all bad we hope" said Renee Pike "we're all looking forward to Saturday, it's going to lovely." "Hear, hear" said the two gents sitting next to their wives. Tim Pike and Malcolm Pennington didn't always get to say much but when they did they injected a lot of enthusiasm.

"Hello all" Mr. Rodgers said as he came down the stairs "oh... just in time for food too! My tummy must be tuned into your cooking times Mrs. Graham."

"Honey please" she said.

"Wha'... oh sorry... yes of course Honey such a pretty name too!" Geoffrey Rodgers sat down on Ben's table "Hello young man, I don't believe we had had the pleasure of being introduced... My name is Geoffrey Rodgers and you are..?"

"Ben... Ben Locke... I'm Gedd Williams' nephew. His sister Enid is my mother."

"Oh... pleased to meet you." Mr Rodgers replied, as he stuck his hand out.

Ben reluctantly shook it. After all appearances' must be kept up and he didn't want to appear rude, even if the 'old crusty' was boring beyond belief. Ben hoped his mother would sit down soon; at least he'd have someone sort of interesting to talk to, not all these old 'fogies'.

Chantelle spotted Ben as soon as she walked into the lounge, but because Glyn was near by she didn't feel nervous at all. In fact she felt very strong, and extremely calm. Maybe making love had its own special calming effect, as well as the exciting bits that had gone before.

Ben glowered at her and was not happy about its effect. She didn't seem bothered, or flustered, was he losing his touch? Well he'd soon sort that out!

"Excuse me one moment" said Ben "I must go to the bathroom!"

"Of course" Mr. Rodgers said half standing up. Glyn watched and he felt his skin prickle 'that boy's' up to something? What is it?

Ben walked off in the direction of the toilets, but as he went round the corner he veered off to reception. "Ah" he said softly, the register was open on the front desk. "So... Chelly's in room 7 eh! That's handy; it's right next to mine." He grinned rather malevolently to himself and decided to enjoy the rest of the evening. After all he knew where 'she' was going to be sleeping now, didn't he!!

He went back to his seat, after actually going to the loo. Appearances' must be observed, shaking his hand for effect, he resumed his seat. "It's a bit nippy in the ablutions, never mind, I'm sure Honey's food will warm me up." He was very impressed with his 'creeping', Ben thought he did it extremely well.

Chantelle and Glyn both ate with Honey and Gedd. Enid had opted to eat with her son and 'that nice teacher'.

Gedd stood up after food and asked the room in general if they would like to help out with the trimmings and bits 'n' bobs. Of course everyone agreed. Ben did so because he could watch Chelly. Everyone else did because they all liked Gedd and Honey and they wanted the day to go well for them.

"Right then," he said "let's all move int' the posh room an' get a move on 'en!!" He led the way over to some very impressive solid oak doors. Opening them both up he turned back towards his and Honey's friends and said

Reviving a Rose

"Wot d'yer reckon then? Good enough for us two ter' get wed in?"

There were murmurs of agreement; the room was indeed very impressive. It was quite large and all the walls were covered in wooden panels.

"It used to be for the dancing" said Honey as she came up and stood next to Gedd... the 'ole village and from all over came 'ere to dance... 'Specially holidays an' Christmas an' that!"

"Come on everyone" said Chantelle "Let's get busy then... we'll make this room look fantastic for Saturday."

So everyone set to work, trimmings were tacked up carefully, and Chantelle set about draping lots of swathes of bright colours about the room. It seemed to be coming to life on its own. All it needed now were the flowers and people. That would put life back into it.

"After the ceremony on Sat'day we're goin' ter' let yer all go into the lounge for a bit and move the tables away to the side ter' let the band in... We can all 'ave a dance before food... and after if yer' want" Gedd said "the local 'dance band' are gonna blow fer us... gonna be great... we 'aven't 'ad a good waltz... fer ages."

"I didn't know yer could?" said Honey.

"There's lot to find out, and a good few years to find 'em." Gedd said, giving Honey a cuddle; Sat'day couldn't come quickly enough for him. Before everyone knew it, it was 9.00 o'clock in the evening.

"Stop now, put yer' stuff down an' come an' get a drink, you've all worked enough" said Honey.

Well the 'gang' all didn't need telling twice. The regulars all traipsed through to the lounge and sat in 'their' chairs. "Would you like a cuppa or summit a bit stronger?" Honey asked.

"Oh I think we could all make room for a sherry... don't you..." said Malcolm, looking at his three cohorts.

"Oh yes please... Sherry sounds just about right," They all said together.

"Sherry it is then... what about you Enid, Mr. Rodgers?" Honey asked looking at her guests.

"Um... half a lager wouldn't have to struggle down, an' that's fer sure." Said Enid grinning "it's been 'ard graft but worth it eh?" she said looking at both Honey and Mr. Rodgers in turn.

"Most definitely... I think half of your excellent brew for myself too, if you please Honey!" Mr. Rodgers said. He was really enjoying himself; he didn't usually enjoy himself at half term. It was always marking and planning next terms work. Yes this was most definitely more fun! He was feeling fit and proud, he would be giving Honey away, and he felt as if he'd known her for years. She was friendly, and of course Gedd too. His sister was quite interesting too. Not as intellectual as him; but some times a different perspective on life brightened up a dreary day.

Ben was watching Glyn and Chantelle again; 'they' were too close. Not aloud, he thought, he'd fix that. Lots of plans were forming inside that nasty warped mind of his; they all had Chantelle right in the middle of them.

"I'll give you a hand if you like Honey, strong arms and that." God he really was good, she'd be putty in his hands and then he could 'slip' something extra in both 'Brickie-boy' and Chelly's drink.

"What would you two like?" asked Honey looking at Chantelle and Glyn.

"Umm... lagers fine with us too!" They said almost together, Ben scowled, not allowed, to close together.

Honey made her way to the bar, and began to pour four Sherries for the regulars.

"I'll do the lagers for you!" Ben said glass in hand.

Reviving a Rose

"Thanks hon it's over there..." said Honey. Ben quickly poured the four glasses of lager and said "what are you and Uncle Gedd having?"

"A nice brew... I'm just going in the kitchen... won't be a tic."

Ben flicked an eyebrow and grinned to himself 'perfect'. He took two little bottles out of his jacket pocket. One contained a laxative (he sometimes needed to get his mother out of the way, back home in Poole). The other bottle had 'his special' stuff in it; just the stuff for 'Chelly'. He tipped them into two of the glasses and had just popped the bottles back into his pocket as Honey came back through.

"Yer don' yet... their all parched in there... can yer take the Sherries an' all darlin'?" "Of course Honey... my pleasure" he grovelled.

Honey didn't know why, but her hackles were up again, there was something about that boy but she didn't know what.

Ben carried the tray into the lounge like a professional waiter. He made sure, hoped, that the right drinks went where they should. Unfortunately for Ben, pride comes before a fall and he had unwittingly given the 'special stuff' to his mother and the 'laxative' to Mr. Rodgers. Ben had presented the tray, the wrong way round. The 'safe' glasses were in fact given to the two people he had wanted to 'spike'.

The regulars picked up their glasses and Tim toasted the whole room of people on their sterling work. "Here's to Saturday" he said raising his glass. Everyone joined in and Gedd clinked tea-mugs with 'his Honey'.

Enid was thirsty and unusually for her, swallowed half of her drink in one draft. Mr. Rodgers also unusually for him, did the same. He normally didn't drink at all. Ben sat down and waited for the effects he expected.

20

However the effect he desired didn't happen in the right people. It must have been about 20 minutes later that his mother stood up and then slumped back down into her seat.

"Ooh... I do feel a little rough; I think the lager was a bit too strong for me... Ooh I feel..." she didn't finish what she was saying. Enid slid off the chair and straight onto the floor.

"What the..." Gedd said dropping his tea-mug... "Come on you lot give us a hand 'ere."

Glyn came over straight away and lifted Enid up as if she weighed nothing at all. Ben was stupefied, what was going on, was his mother ill... or... Oh God, maybe she'd had the wrong drink. If she did then that meant... Oh shit... the creepy old crusty teacher had swallowed the bloody laxative.

"Erm... if you all don't mind too much... I'll make my way off to bed... it's been a long day hasn't it..." he said as he tailed off.

Reviving a Rose

"Ere ain't you gonna 'elp yer Mam then?" Gedd said

"Well… erm Glyn seems to be coping alright… and I'm sure Mum doesn't want me fussing about!" he finished and scuttled out quickly before anyone could say anymore. All the people in the lounge just stared at him as 'escaped'.

"I'll ring the doc." Said Honey "… Somethin's not right, and it's not anything we've cooked, is it Enid?"

"No its not…" she replied groaning "I think I need my bed though."

Glyn whisked Enid up the stairs as if she weighed no more than a feather. "What's your room number Enid?" Glyn asked when they had reached the top of the stairs.

"Number 9… thanks… I do appreciate this love… don't know where 'My Ben' scarpered off to. Mind you 'e never did like looking after sick people. Once 'is dad got ill, he was always out, it's like 'e's scared of catchin' summit!"

Glyn carefully put Enid down on her bed and placed the coverlet over her. It was very similar to Chantelle's one in her room, but he mustn't be thinking about that now, Gedd's little sister wasn't well.

"Is there anything I can get you?" asked Glyn.

"No ta… I'll just try and sleep a bit if it's all the same t' you." Enid replied.

Glyn softly closed the door and hurried downstairs to the others.

By this time though, the laxative was starting to do its work. Poor Mr. Rodgers sat bolt upright and then clutched his stomach. "Oh my goodness… that doesn't feel right…" he shot off towards the toilets. "Excuse me…" he tailed off as he fled round the corner.

"Well bloody 'ell… what's ter do 'ere then… summat's not ruddy right at all, is it?" Gedd said as he scratched his head. "There's definitely summat fishy goin' on."

Honey and the others all looked at each other. Chantelle stood up and said that she would check on Enid. Honey said she would go and wait out the front for the Doc and Glyn was going to see if Mr. Rodgers was okay. The 'regulars' all thought it would best if they all went home. Mind you they did clear up between before they left.

Glyn went off to the toilets; he had forgotten that he was supposed to be shadowing Chantelle. He heard, rather than found poor old Mr. Rodgers groaning from inside the cubicle.

"Are you okay in there?" Glyn asked.

"Er... I think on the whole my world is falling out of my bottom and not the other way around? ... Maybe something I may have eaten perhaps?"

"I don't think so Geoffrey... everyone else is fine, in fact Gedd, Honey, Chantelle and I think that you and Enid both getting ill is a little suspect... so we have called the doctor in... when you feel a little better... could you come back into the lounge?"

"Certainly dear boy... if the muscles hold out... not far from the ablutions though..." Poor Mr. Rodgers groaned some more and Glyn left to breath some fresh air very deeply outside. Wow... that smell was very potent in there.

Honey meanwhile was waiting by the front door. A small car pulled up and Dr. McArdle got out.

"What's going on then Madam... are you not well again?"

"No two of my guests Scotty and one of 'ems Gedd's sister. She jus' slid right down out of 'er chair and poor Mr. Rodgers who's givin' me away on Sat'day is dying in the loo... 'Aven't got a clue what's goin' on to be straight I 'aven't?"

"Well lead me away to the nearest one then and we'll have a looks see..." The Doc said following Honey inside the Inn. Scotty did not like this at all, a faint for no

Reviving a Rose

reason, also another patient with symptoms of what? They both walked into the lounge and Mr. Rodgers had just made it back himself.

"So sorry I'm awfully sorry… my stomach you know…" he tailed off then stood up again and looked sheepishly around the room before heading back to the toilets.

"'Es been doin' that for about 20 minutes off an' on…" said Gedd "the poor blokes behind must be on fire by now." Gedd tried not to grin, but sometimes laughter can lighten a tense atmosphere. "Shot out of 'ere like a scolded cat and the drinks not been finished either… look here."

Mr. Rodgers glass was indeed still on the table. It was half full and Scotty tipped a little into a sterile pot he had taken out of his 'little black bag'. You have been busy, "does there happen to be any of the other guest's drinks left?" he said as he looked around.

"Yes 'ere it is…" said Honey as she passed the other glass to the doctor. 'Scotty' did the same thing again, and then labelled both pots.

"I'll have these checked 'oot at the lab tomorrow" he said as he placed both pot into identical specimen bags. "These'll go t' the lab and then mebbie we'll have a better idea of what's going on here." Scotty excused himself and said he would just go up to check on Enid.

It was then that Glyn also remembered who else was upstairs Chantelle had said she would check on Gedd's sister but she hadn't come back down yet and didn't Ben leave just before that!

Upstairs Chantelle was blissfully unaware of Ben's presence in the next room. He however knew exactly where she and his mother were. Enid had fallen into a deep sleep, and even quite harsh shaking on Chantelle's part couldn't rouse her. The door was tapped a couple of times and Chantelle wrongly assumed it was Gedd, the Doc or Glyn.

"Come in, she sleeping… she's flat out."

"Don't mind if I do" Ben said closing the door "Nice of you to invite me into your room again!" he sneered "it's not my room..." Chantelle blustered "... and your mother is unwell!"

"So she is... rather fortunate for me then isn't it... I've been dying to do this since you nearly fainted at my feet... so glad I can still affect you Chelly!!" He started across the room and before Chantelle would ay or do anything he grabbed her by the arms. "Come here and let's see if my kisses still make you go weak!"

"No..." she struggled and tried to wrench her arms free "I don't even like you... you're sick in the head... you RAPED ME..." Chantelle was feeling really scared now.

"I... rape you... whatever for... you fell into my arms remember; I only took what was on offer... and I am not sick Chelly... so I think I'll have to taste your honey again."

Ben pressed Chantelle back against the dresser, his mother murmured in the bed. Ben fractionally loosened his grip and in doing so Chantelle managed to wrestle out of his arms and she escaped into the bathroom.

"Let me in..." Ben; seemed to have blocked his mothers presence from his mind "... open up Chelly... don't play hard to get now... I don't need to chase you; I've tasted your goods already... open up you little tease." He banged on the door and tried to barge it open.

Chantelle leaned against the door from her side, with all the strength she had. There was no way 'he' was coming in with her. She thought her legs were going to give in as Ben continued to heaved from his side, but she could suddenly hear voices from the bedroom, and they weren't Ben's or his mothers.

"What are you doing young man... your Mam's away in bed and you're bangin' seven shades oot the door? What are you on man?" Doc McArdle said; he was closely followed into the room by Glyn.

Reviving a Rose

"Um... Chelly seemed to have jammed the door so I was pushing from my side to let her out." Ben replied, it had to be said, the boy could really think fast. Glyn was fuming; he was mentally kicking himself for letting Chantelle come upstairs on her own.

"Anyway... I thought I'd better check on my mother... I think I sounded a little callous downstairs, so I came in to check-up on her. I didn't know Chelly was in here. Then I heard her calling from the bathroom, so I pushed from this side." Ben said looking totally innocent.

"Chantelle" said Glyn "... are you okay in there... are there any problem with the door?"

"No and Yes..." she said as she joined them all around Enid's bed. "The door wasn't jammed... I was leaning against it to stop HIM getting in... you know why Glyn?"

Ben fumed and bristled, she wasn't scared of him anymore. Well she'd bloody pay for that and 'Brickie-boy' as well. Glyn stared at Chantelle ashen face. The Doctor had noticed her reaction to Ben's presence too! Hmm... that cleared up something that had been bothering him. Ever since Honey had phoned about Chantelle's 'collapse', it hadn't felt right. Now Scotty believed he knew the reason for it, and it appeared to be this poor lady's son.

"Right you lot... except you young lady... I need a chaperone... you two OUT! I need to check my patient over."

Ben was about to protest when Gedd appeared, too many people, he didn't like it when he wasn't in control or charge.

"I'll be in my room if you need to ask or tell me anything Doc." He said leaving swiftly and sliding round the door-jam, so as not to come into contact with 'Brickie-boy'.

"Ah Gedd... I was just sayin' you'll all need to get oot whilst I check on yer sister here... Miss..."

"Chantelle please" She said

"Aye... Chantelle is just helping me to do a few checks" Scotty said as he gently pushed Gedd and guided Glyn out the door.

Glyn looked over Scotty's head and mouthed "Are you okay?"

To which Chantelle replied likewise "Yes, I'll speak to you after, okay?"

The door closed and the doctor turned to face Chantelle

"You do realise that anything that happens in here is confidential don't you? I mean, if you need ta' tell me anything at all it'll no leave this room mind?"

"Thank you for that..." she said, "but Honey, Gedd and Glyn know already and I believe you've guessed now why I fainted. It's a long story and I think Enid needs you more!"

Scotty was impressed with this young lady, she had obviously experienced something nasty regarding the young man who'd just left the room, but she still put the boys mother's needs before her own.

"Right then young lady lets get to work." The doctor delved into his black-bag again, just as he had downstairs. This time he took out some vials, and some hypodermic needles that he would draw blood with. "If you hold her arm now... nice and tight and I'll try to get a wee drop o' blood to test along w' the drinks from doon stairs."

Chantelle squeezed Enid's arm tightly. Enid moaned softly and tried to resist. "Well now, that's interestin'..." Scotty said as he filled the vials up. "... She shouldn't be pullin' like that. She should be awake an' sayin' OUCH."

"I think she may have had something in her drink... I felt like that once... someone spiked my drink..." Chantelle commented.

"Was it yon man next door?" Scotty said not looking up, so as he didn't embarrass the girl.

Reviving a Rose

"Yes... I do believe it was..." Chantelle said as she taped some dressing gauze over Enid's Inner elbow. "I knew him a few years ago in college and he assaulted me... but I couldn't prove anything... I was extremely shy and he knew everyone. Ben said I made it up and that I was a frigid ice-maiden, who he wouldn't touch even with a barge pole. He told all his friends I was infatuated with him and that I'd stalked him."

"Now you listen here lassie... you have friends here and they all believe you. If they say you did nothing wrong then I'm inclined to believe them, having seen that young mans performance both in here and down the stairs just now... don't you fret lassie he'll not get near you again."

"Thank you... for your care for Honey and Enid... and for trusting me" Chantelle said in reply.

Scotty just squeezed her hands and patted her on the shoulder. "I'm going to get Gedd and fill him in on his sisters welfare... you okay hen?" Chantelle nodded as he opened the door. Gedd and Glyn virtually fell in. "Not t' worry man, she'll sleep it off., whatever the 'it' is. Mind you Enid won't remember what's gone on t'night so only tell her if she asks okay?"

"Okay Doc, you're the boss" said Gedd stroking his sister's hair away from her face. "Don't forget the wedding t'morrow Doc..." Gedd called out softly, as the doctor left to tell Enid's son what he'd done and how her general health was.

Glyn looked at Chantelle and raised one eyebrow "I'll tell you later" she mouthed across the room, as she tucked Enid back into her bed.

Gedd patted Chantelle's hand. "Thank you sweetheart, fer watchin' over mi 'little sister', we all got tied up downstairs a bit." He said

"What happened down there then?" she asked.

"Well it seems as if 'your poor ole' Mr. Rodgers has got a gippy-tummy an' the Doc put some of 'is drink;'

an' that in a little bottle ter test it or summit." Gedd said getting up and rubbing his knees at the same time. "I'm off to check on Honey, you two be alright in 'ere for a bit?" Gedd disappeared and Glyn was finally able to take Chantelle into his arms.

"It was horrible..." she sniffed "he's actually convinced himself that I fainted because I was glad to see him... God I feel sick..." she said gasping like a fish out of water.

Glyn just held her and he tried to remain calm. God he really wanted to go next door and smash Ben's face in. That 'thing' didn't deserve to be called a man. How the hell could he do that to anyone, Ben must have mixed the drinks up? That meant they had been meant for Chantelle and him. Glyn's eyes closed up as he stared straight ahead, trying to keep a tight rein on his fast and furious temper which was SO ready to pummel a certain person.

"You okay sweetheart?" he finally said when he had got control of his emotions.

"Yes... now you're here..." Chantelle said as she burrowed into his embrace. "He scares me... I don't want to be on my own. I think Ben's got the room next to mine" she shuddered in Glyn's arm and he wrapped his arm around her even more.

If it made her feel secure then he had done his job well.

"Glyn... will you stay with me tonight... I'm not trying to proposition you. I just need..."

"You don't have to ask 'Spitfire'. I'm staying wherever you want me to be and for as long as you need me."

"Thank you Glyn... I'm very grateful." Chantelle whispered.

"I'm here for you... always, that's what people do for the person they love!" Glyn said, and he felt good saying too! Yes he really did love this fragile, yet strong, wilful, yet scared, lovely generous 'Spitfire' in his arms. He tipped her chin up so that he could look into her eyes. "I really love you, you know... in fact I would really like to spend my life loving you and making you feel loved and safe and happy" Then he kissed her deeply that Chantelle felt her toes curling. Every nasty thing that happened before was gone, forgotten in that kiss. He really could wipe away all the hurt and Chantelle felt as if she were on fire. As they both came up for air she managed to gasp a reply.

"I... love you too... you're my knight in shining armour... and I feel like your lady now." She blushed.

Glyn glowed with pride for 'His' lady yep! That suited him just fine.

They broke apart as the door opened but Gedd could tell from the body language, his two young friends were more than friends and he was mighty pleased. He couldn't wait to tell Honey, he was sure she would be just as happy. "Ow's mi' little sister then?"

"She hasn't stirred since the doctor took the bloods Gedd" said Chantelle.

"Well now you two... off to yer beds 'en and I'll keep an eye on mi' sister." As Chantelle passed Gedd, he hugged and said "Thanks again Chantelle, mi' and 'Oney 'preciates what yer done and just ter say, we're on yer side both of us like'"

"Thank you Gedd, that means a lot, coming from you. I mean 'he' is your nephew..."

"Nephew or no', wha' 'e did was wrong and if 'Docs' test's com' back with wot' we all fink 'e'll be sorry 'e come 'ere wiv' 'is Mum, I'll mek' sure of that, an' no mistake!" Gedd said with conviction and he bristled up and hugged Chantelle again, so she knew how he felt about it.

"Night loves... see ya in the mornin'." Gedd settled down in the chair by his sisters' bed. If Ben had done this, by God as his witness he would bloody kill him. The 'little waster' wouldn't be getting the garage for starters and that was certain.

21

The wedding morning was bright and clear. The air was crisp with the on-set of autumn and there was a gentle breeze. All the leaves had started to change colour. A miracle of different arrangements, reds, browns and greens were on display, depending on which tree you happed to be looking at.

It was a small tap on at the door that woke Chantelle up. She had slept safe in Glyn's arms, they hadn't made love but she felt so loved and comforted that she had fallen asleep straight away and slept the Innocent sleep of a child, without a care in the world.

"Chantelle" a quiet voice called "it's me Honey, are yer' awake love?"

"Yes" she replied "just coming." She opened the door and grinned, as she rubbed her sleepy eyes, Honey was standing there with her hair in great big curlers and a very large quilted dressing gown on which the floral print was extremely vivid.

"I know..." she said chuckling "mi' ol' regulars thought one Christmas I needed warming up... so I got this ..." Honey grinned back. "D'yer fancy coming downstairs and givin' mi a 'and with breakfast?"

"You're not cooking today; surely... it's your wedding day Honey?" Chantelle said in surprise tone of voice.

"I know... ain't it exciting... I feel like a little girl at Christmas, just before yer get to open all yer pressies."

Chantelle smiled "I'll just put something on, and meet you down there okay?"

"I'm just doin' a bit of toast an' coffee for Gedd, Enid, Glyn me a' you! Mind ... I'm not feedin' 'it' till I get the results off Scotty... I don't trust 'im anymore."

Even tough Honey hadn't actually said his name Chantelle felt sick. Ben could still have one effect on her. Chantelle closed the door softly and looked at Glyn, still asleep on the bed. He hadn't even got under the cover the night before; he had just held her safe.

Glyn himself hadn't slept for a long while, he had held his Chantelle, his love, his life; in his arms and breathed in her scent. She had slowly relaxed and drifted off to sleep. He watched her expression soften and the furrows disappear from her face. When he was totally convinced she was asleep he tried to relax himself.

It took him a lot longer to unwind, he had awful visions of Ben doing unspeakable things to 'his' girl and that wound him up no-end but eventually he too went to sleep.

Chantelle blew him a kiss as she slipped on some clothes, she didn't want Honey to be doing stuff on her wedding day. With a quick look in the mirror, she put her hair into a ponytail and went off in the direction of the kitchen

As she went down the stairs, Chantelle could smell the toast, it did smell good; but Honey shouldn't be doing any cooking today! On entering the kitchen she grinned

Reviving a Rose

as she saw Gedd in his full glory. Pyjama bottoms on with a very fetching pinny on over the top.

"Wow... don't you look the part?" She said crossing the kitchen.

"Aw go on... yer cheeky thing... come on giv' us a 'and otherwise madam will take over" Gedd said passing the butter knife and board over.

"Chantelle... I'll do it" Honey, said as she went to grab the board.

"No you won't... I told you upstairs, you shouldn't be doing anything today... it's your special day Honey and you will be spoiled so get used to it!!" Chantelle firmly but gently sat Honey down and placed some hot buttered toast and a mug of tea in front of her. "Dig in... you need to build up your strength."

"Umm... s'pose so" Honey said grudgingly and she tucked into the toast with gusto. It was nice to be spoilt a bit every now and again. "What are you going to wear later then Chantelle?" Honey asked when she'd finished her toast.

"I'm not really sure, I have a dress upstairs but I'd like your valued opinion, if you please Honey!" she said getting up from the table and taking the dishes to the sink.

Gedd plodded on with the toast and he buttered some ready for Enid "I'll just go an' tak' these 'ere up to mi' little sister an' check on 'er. I might even see if the boy is awake, so you two stay down 'ere 'till I get back alright?"

"No argument off me love..." said Honey "Don't particularly want to see 'im anyway, I'm liable to want to smack 'im one!" Gedd's eyebrows rose. "Well... all the bloody trouble e's caused and upset an' that?" Honey said looking at Gedd. "I know e's yer nephew an' all but 'onestly Gedd 'e 'is a little sod an' no mistake. Wot are yer gonna tell Enid?"

"Dunno yet... I'll 'ave ter think on that a bit... I mean 'ow can yer tell 'er, 'er own flesh 'n' blood slipped 'er a Mickey Finn. Which I might add won't meant fer 'er any road."

Gedd left the kitchen and slowly walked up to his sister's room. He honestly didn't have a clue what to do tell her if she asked about her 'collapse'. He knocked on the door gently and could hear voices... what was Ben doing in his mum's room? Maybe he was trying to cover his own tracks Gedd forced a smile on his face and walked in.

"Ow's my girl this mornin' can't 'ave you bad on mi weddin' day. Enid... you alright love?" Gedd just looked at his sister, he wasn't feeling charitable this morning and if Ben kicked off he was liable to want to clout him one.

"Not too bad... I don't know what happened last night... I was just saying to Ben here... wasn't I Ben" Enid said as she looked at her boy. She had a pinched look about her and her face looked a little grey.

"I told Mum, it was probably a bug or something eh Gedd?" Ben said looking totally innocent.

Gedd could feel his blood boiling, little sod why he'd... "Er... yeah... probably" he managed to say gritting his teeth. "Ben, could I 'ave a word, outside like, while yer Mum eats 'er toast!" He said gesturing towards the door outside.

"Now you..." Gedd said as he stood nose to nose with Ben, his arms either side of Ben's shoulders. "I'm goin' ter asks yer just this once an' once it'll be... did you put owt in yer Mum's drink? Now think on lad, cos if yer lie t' me an' I find out I'll kill yer mi' self!" Gedd stared into Ben's eyes, and when Ben's face dropped, he knew that his own flesh and blood was about to lie to save his own skin. Gedd wasn't a small man and he looked quite wiry but he was incredibly strong.

Reviving a Rose

"Um... I didn't do anything to my mother or Mr. Rodgers..."

"I didn't ask owt about Mr. Rodgers lad, now did I..."

"No... but... I didn't do anything, maybe it's something they both ate?"

"Now don' yer go blamin' Honey's cooking BOY, there's nowt 'rong with it... I think you'd better go an' pack... I don' want you at mi wedding and I be thinking on again about the garage too!"

"You can't do that to ME, I'm family... my mother needs me!" Ben spluttered as Gedd words filtered into his warped mind. He stared Gedd in the face and said "You can't do that... I'll see you in court, it's mine... if I can't have what's mine no-one will." Ben pushed Gedd's arm away and stomped off to his room, muttering under his breath, his face flushed in temper. 'It's all her fault, if she wasn't here, none of this would have happened and the bloody garage would be in my hands by now!'

In Ben's 'own world' everybody owed him, and nothing was ever his fault. Chelly must have been telling porkies and everyone was against him, even his mother.

Actually Ben's poor Mum knew nothing at all. She was still totally oblivious, tucked up in bed finishing her tea and toast.

"Enid love?" said Gedd as he tapped on the bedroom door. "You finished pet?" He walked in and looked at his 'little sister'. Enid was sitting up in bed and had now got a little colour back in her cheeks.

"Ello Gedd love... yes I've managed t' get it down an' swallow a good draught of yer tea lad... 'Ere where's mi boy gone then? 'E's been good t' mi; comin' in t' check on mi an' that!"

Gedd mumbled something under his breath and went to open the curtains. "You feelin' up to dressin. an' then comin' down for a chat wi' Honey?"

"Sure darlin'... I'll go steady an' 'ave a bit of a wash... I'll meet yer in the kitchen in a mo' okay?" Gedd crossed the room and kissed Enid's forehead...

"See ya in a minute then love!" He said as he picked up the tray and left, closing the door softly.

22

Well, thought Enid, what was that all about. He'd never done that before, maybe he'd been scared last night and it fetched his soft side out. Or maybe Honey had brought his gentler side out. She was a lovely woman and Enid liked her. Now then, let's get dressed and find my boy.

With that she made her way slowly to the bathroom, and washed her face. As Enid looked at her reflection in the mirror, she noticed that her skin looked pinched, maybe she was 'coming down' with something. She'd see her doctor when she got home.

Enid washed and dressed at a leisurely pace and was ready after about 45 minutes. She left her room and made her way to Ben's, she knocked on the door twice "Ben... love it's me... you ready love?"

There was no reply, so she opened the door and walked in. The room was a 'tip'; all the drawers were open and the cupboards as well. Enid looked around her in astonishment 'Where was Ben?' She checked the bathroom, he wasn't in there, but then she didn't think he would be if all the drawers were empty. There were no cases either, this had her flummoxed and she lost no time in going to find her brother.

"Gedd... Gedd love... Ben's gone... I don't know where or when but all 'is stuff's gone as well?"

Gedd had been on his way upstairs to get changed for the wedding. "Now then... don't fret love... what's t'do Enid... what's wrong?"

"E's gone... my boys gone an' without a word an' all!" Enid clung to her brother and sobbed. She was feeling really rough and 'her' boy not being here was really starting to put the wind up her and she was frightened for him, she didn't know where he was or why he'd gone.

Gedd calmly led his sister back into her room. "Now love, you just sit down for a sec' an' I'll try an' tell yer what's been going' on okay!! I'll just get that nice young lady Chantelle t' sit in an all... female company an' that... won't be a tic!"

Gedd disappeared from Enid's room and asked Chantelle to come with him. He didn't think Ben had the guts to go, but then again if the Doc turned up with the results then Ben would have some serious explaining to do. He didn't think Ben had gone far though. Ben was the type to 'use' his mother; a lot, as a sort of personal bank amongst other things. No, that 'boy' wouldn't stray too far. Gedd hoped that Ben wouldn't muck-up the service, at the very least; he was hoping that Ben would have the decency to stay away.

Meanwhile back in Enid's room, she was sitting quietly, almost childlike, rocking gently. Waiting for her big brother to come back and explain everything.

Chantelle and Gedd came into the room to find Enid sitting on the bed, rocking back and for in an almost trance-like state. "You alright love?" asked Gedd as he shook Enid's shoulder gently.

Reviving a Rose

"Wha... Oh it's you... and Chantelle hello... wha... what's going on Gedd?" replied Enid.

"Well, it seems as if; you're Ben, for a joke I 's'pose, put something in a couple of the drinks..." Gedd explained.

"Why would 'e do that?" asked Enid.

"Well, we're all hopin' 'e did it for a laugh love... but it went a bit wrong." Gedd explained.

"What would 'e want t' give me 'stuff' that would make me bad for?" asked Enid.

"Well" Chantelle said softly, before Gedd started to speak "I think it was meant for me... and the other one, which made Mr. Rodgers ill, was supposed to be for Glyn."

"Why? Enid said, looking like a lost little girl.

"Because he is jealous of Glyn and I being together. Your son considers me 'his' and I told him NO! He didn't like it very much and there is past history between us which I would rather forget." Chantelle continued.

"He did somethin' didn't 'e... way back when... did you know 'im in college love?" Enid said worryingly.

"Yes Enid, I'm sorry he did. He treated me very badly and without going into detail, your son hurt me and I have been trying for a long time to get over it... I thought I was until Ben showed up here... I am so sorry Enid, really I am." Chantelle sat down next to her and held both of Enid's hands, they were very cold. Enid patted hers in return.

"'E 'urt you... didn't 'e... I knew somethin' woz up... but I didn't know what... Aw love... I am sorry... I'll leave now..." said Enid in tears.

"No... it's not yer fault an' we all want yer to stay..." Gedd said cutting into the conversation. "Ben left because he knew that the Doc had taken blood samples. Ben knows that we'll all find out what he put in the drinks and 'I' think he's a coward and too yellow to face the music... I'm sorry Enid love, but yer spoiled the boy 'cos his dad left and he's a bad 'un... Look... come on it's s'pose to be Honey and mi's wedding so can yer smile a bit love, for me?"

"Sure Gedd... I'll do mi best; you know I love you and Honey. I'll sort that boy out after... come on then... lets get dressed... you too." With that Enid shooed Chantelle and Gedd out, they had to get dressed and she had some serious thinking to do.

What had she done wrong? She'd always idealised her boy, maybe too much. Maybe she thought, she'd given into Ben too much and not reined him in enough. It was bad when his dad, Frank left, but Enid had been so proud when Ben went to college. He had been so popular too, so where had it all gone wrong? Was it in his genes, was it he really so much like his dad?

The person in question was at that moment stalking around the outside of Gedd's garage, Ben was absolutely furious. In his mind it was Glyn's and Chantelle's fault. If they had drunk; the right bloody drinks in the first place. Well he'd have been able to sort them both out, in different ways.

Ben was also mad at his uncle. Fancy telling 'him' that he couldn't have the garage; it was 'his'! Now, if something were to happen to Gedd, it would be his sooner rather that later. The cogs in Bens head were working overtime, and he was well on the way to planning revenge on all the people that, in his head, had stuffed up his plans. Ben scouted his way around all of the building and he grinned to himself. Perfect, someone, he hoped it was Glyn 'someone to blame' had left a window open.

Ben stuffed all his gear in his car, it wasn't as posh as he had wanted, but there was enough room. He had only managed to 'score' £2000 off his mother. She'd told him she didn't have anymore. Ben didn't believe it but would still have pinched her last £1 if he needed it.

After he had moved his car around the back, out of sight, Ben went back to the open window. He squeezed

Reviving a Rose

through and crept around, checking the flat out. He found some money in a locked tin in Gedd's bedroom. It didn't stay locked for long, he smirked to himself £500 for his troubles, not bad. Ben went down into the main garage and here he found what he was looking for.

There were two huge bottles of acetylene used for welding metal. Ben undid both valves and let them 'hiss' away. He returned to the flat and went to the little cooker. He then turned on both the rings and grinned to himself again.

Being the 'creep' he was, Ben flicked the catch on the window, so that it would shut. He stood back and admired his handy work. If someone opened the door with a key, maybe a spark 'metal on metal', it would definitely 'go off' with a bang and he hoped either Gedd or Glyn or both were around it did. The garage and male problem would both be rubbed out together, in more ways than one.

Ben really was one warped nasty piece of work, but he just couldn't see it at all. All Ben saw were two people in his way and that wouldn't do at all. Plus 'they' had put the wind up his mother, that wouldn't do at all either. She was supposed to think he was perfect. No-one was allowed to mucky the water.

Ben thought of nobody's feelings but his own and if someone mucked him about then he could get extremely angry and very dangerous.

23

Back at the Inn, the preparations for the wedding were well underway. The 'Regulars' had come back and were putting the seats out for the guests. Malcolm and Tim were arranging the rows in very precise lines. The ladies, Maud and Renee, were putting all the mountains of food out on the tables lining the whole length of one of the walls in the big hall.

"Don't the flowers smell lovely Renee?" said Maud.

"Ohh... yes they do and don't the colours look stunning too Maud?"

The ladies murmured to each other in a companionable way as they fussed and primped the room to perfection.

Mr. Rodgers came into the room and complimented the ladies on their 'sterling' work. "I say... Absolutely splendid, most becoming;" He said as he checked his tie for the 5th time.

"Mr. Rodgers" said Maud "You do look very smart... doesn't he Renee?"

Reviving a Rose

"Ohh yes... Just right for Honey I say.".

Mr. Rodgers had blushed a little and escaped on the pretext of checking on the very lady in question.

Honey was in fact upstairs, standing before her full length mirror. "You look beautiful Honey" said Chantelle "just lovely and Gedd is a very lucky man."

"Thanks love" said Honey, blushing. She turned slightly to check her suit. It was soft gold embroidered cloth which had been made into a two-piece suit. Honey had topped it off with a small pill-box hat. It was perched on her head at a slight tilt, with a little veil coming down over her face. She did look very 'chic' indeed.

There was a soft tap at the door and Chantelle opened it to see Mr. Rodgers standing there. "Come in Mr... Geoffrey... do come and see what 'our' lovely bride looks like." Chantelle said grinning broadly.

"My word... Honey you look stunning... an absolute vision, Gedd certainly won't know what's hit him." Geoffrey Rodgers walked proudly across the room and offered his arm. "Come on my dear, let's go and get you married off to your fiancé downstairs."

With that, Chantelle, Geoffrey and Honey made their way down to the large dining room where the service would take place.

Gedd and Glyn were both standing up by the large table that would serve as a sort of alter. The celebrant was there making sure everything was ready. She checked all the paperwork again and smiled reassuringly at Gedd, who was starting to look a little 'pasty'. Tiny beads of sweat were forming on his top lip and he swallowed.

Glyn turned to him and nudged his arm and said "Well they're here mate; you ready?"

"Well if I ain't ready now after all this time I need a good shakin' an' no mistake. I'm that nervous tho' d'yer thinks I look alright Glyn?"

"Sure Gedd" Glyn said patting his arm "Honey will be so happy and impressed that you scrubbed up clean!"

Gedd 'humphed' but he grinned too. He was so lucky to be marrying 'his girl' after the scare she'd had and he was going to make sure he looked after his 'best girl', so that they could share many more happy years together.

The doors opened and Chantelle walked down the aisle as the little organ was played. Glyn's eyes were like saucers and he thought he'd never seen her look more beautiful. She had a very delicate looking dress that looked like liquid on her.

It must be silk, it was a soft green which complimented the gold in Honey's suit. He wished it was Chantelle coming down the aisle to marry him instead of just escorting Honey.

Gedd caught sight of Honey as she walked slowly up the aisle, behind Chantelle, on Mr. Rodgers' arm. She looked stunning, absolutely beautiful and he was so proud that she was walking up to be his wife. The suit she had on looked spectacular and it suited her, she looked so refined and Gedd decided that Honey should have more occasions to wear nice clothes.

Honey made her way towards 'her Gedd' and she thought her heart was going to explode. He looked so handsome, and she felt a million dollars.

Chantelle made her way to the opposite side of the aisle but looked over at Gedd and Glyn. She had only seen Gedd in grimy overalls and the occasional apron! He definitely scrubbed-up well indeed. Glyn was in a well cut suit, he looked amazing. She'd seen him in tidy clothes before but never this hot. Chantelle was stunned, her heart was beating so fast and she was sure her skin was on fire. Surely everyone could see her face was scarlet.

"Ladies and Gentlemen..." the celebrant began... "We are gathered here today to join together this man and this woman..."

Reviving a Rose

Honey felt as if the service had lasted no more than 5 minutes. In actual fact it had been more like 20. She was glad it was being videoed because she couldn't remember any of it. Apart, that was, the feelings she'd felt, when she had seen the look on Gedd's face.

"I now declare before you all, that Gedd and Honey are now man and wife." The celebrant said with a huge grin on her face and well matched they were too, in her opinion.

Honey held onto Gedd's arm and walked proudly into the main function room where all their hard work had made the place look magical. The regulars' must have added a few more bits and bobs after she had finished.

All the other people watching thought the same thing too! Dr. 'Scotty' McArdle and Staff Nurse Susan Walker stood side by side and turned to each other at the same time. They both smiled and Susan felt her heart flip over, he really was a lovely fella she thought and what was more, he cared for his patients. The special care and attention that Honey had been given was above and beyond his 'work boundaries'. But where 'Scotty' was concerned his values were always the patient 1st and hospital and surgery management 2nd. Susan Walker had always known she liked the pleasant voiced medic, but having watched his care of Honey and Chantelle, whom she valued as friends now, her opinion has changed from respect to love.

The Doc was thinking similar thoughts to Susan's, but he didn't know how she felt. Still the smile had been warm and not the professional type, the ones that didn't quite reach the eyes. No this smile had lit up her face and she had flushed ever-so slightly. He needed to find out more. "What a' wonderful service, don't you agree nurse?"

"Please call me Susan doctor when we are out of work."

"... And you must call me Scotty then!" He said with a twinkle in his eye. Susan liked that, and also the fact that she could call him Scotty.

Susan would have to find out what his first name was, she was curious now, as she had never heard it spoken. The two of them followed on behind Honey's regulars as everyone made their way to the main function room.

"Wow... doesn't it look super" Scotty said as he guided Susan by the arm, towards the complimentary drinks and the well stocked buffet tables. They seemed to be creaking under the weight of all the food. There were at least 6 extremely long tables, decorated and draped. Mind you, you could hardly see it for the food. In the centre was a splendid wedding cake, which Mrs. Martha Crabbe from the gift shop in the village, had made. It was only two tiers but Mrs. Crabbe had been told that two would be plenty by Honey and Gedd, although they hadn't actually seen it until today.

"My gawd... it's wonderful" Honey said, giving Mrs. Crabbe a huge hug and kiss, Gedd kissed her on the cheek and agreed with his wife. "You've outdone yerself Martha its that bloody lovely... hey Honey it is an all love, 'int it?"

Glyn had also guided his partner into the function room. Chantelle could feel her arm tingle where Glyn's arm was, it felt very good. Her whole body was warming up.

"I think we've earned a drink... don't you Glyn?" She said moving over towards the table with the assorted drinks on.

"D'you know I absolutely agree, I'm parched" Glyn picked up two glasses of what he assumed was champagne. He drank a little "this is good stuff... I wonder who paid for it."

"I think I can answer that!" A voice said behind them. They turned round to find themselves looking at Geoffrey Rodgers. "Well I mean..." he continued. "I am

Reviving a Rose

the proud man who gave Honey away and normally the Father of the Bride buys the drink. So I decided to fill the position wholly. You know not just giving away the Bride but actually going the whole nine yards as they say."

He had puffed up with un-diluted pride, and Chantelle thought he looked every bit as proud as any father would have been in his place. "I must say too Chantelle, that you look absolutely stunning... doesn't she Glyn?"

"Yes I definitely agree with you there Geoff"

"I say... Geoff... I like that. I'm so used to Mr. Rodgers or Geoffrey, yes I like Geoff a lot. I think I'll have all my friends call me Geoff." Only Honey had called him that before and now he really liked it, so informal. "Now... where did the lovely Enid go?" He said to himself as he wandered off.

Glyn and Chantelle grinned and shrugged shoulders "You know what?"

"No... What?"

"I think Geoff is a little sweet on Enid. It's a shame that her son is such a bad penny"

Chantelle wished that Glyn hadn't mentioned Ben, but just his name had again made her feel sick to her stomach. Glyn noticed her slight pallor and could have kicked himself for being so stupid "Sorry"

"No... don't, just leave the creep out of it... he shouldn't be allowed to ruin this day" Chantelle said and took a deep breath "Come on... some escort you are, I need feeding." She grabbed his hand and dragged him off towards the mountain of food.

The whole village seemed to be in the Inn somewhere. They had spilled out of the function room and were sitting down in the lounge and dining room eating and drinking merrily.

"Good do 'init?" said one young lad who worked in the butchers.

"Aye... good grub an' all" replied his young skInny friend.

"Aye... they make a fine couple eh?"

"Yep Gedd sure scrubbed up well... never thought he'd marry though."

"Yeah... he was always in oily overalls at 'e's garage... weren't 'e?"

"Yep... wonder if he'll move in 'ere? Or mebbie even sell up the garage?"

They carried on at length discussing the newlyweds who were on their own little planet.

"Mam" said Honey's daughter Sonia "D'yer want to come an' get changed?"

"Inna minute pet... I'm just goin' to see a few more guests." Honey squeezed Gedd's hand and smiled, her face was glowing with pride and happiness.

"Not many left ter see, just Scotty and Susan over there and to thank Glyn and Chantelle for doin' such a grand job." Gedd had said as he followed his wife (he liked that) across the room.

Both of Honey's children were over the moon. They had met up on the way down to the wedding. They all got on well and were very happy with their parents. Both siblings were equally impressed with their mother's partner. They had told them both too, with much laughter, back slapping and more than a few drinks. Unfortunately there had been traffic problems and they had arrived late.

Honey's daughter had wanted to personally thank Chantelle for all the help she had given her mother over the last few months. She was also impressed at how Chantelle had done today, in supporting her mother with all that a wedding day entailed. Mind you, Chantelle was very happy to hand over the reins to Honey's daughter, once she had arrived 'en-mass' with all the others.

Reviving a Rose

Gedd and Honey walked over to Scotty and Susan Walker. Honey had taken a real shine to Susan and she hugged her warmly.

"Thanks fer comin' it's been an overwhelmin' day an' yer two bein' 'ere 'ave been all the more special." She turned to Scotty and as her eyes filled a little she said "if you 'adn't sorted me out. I won't be 'ere… I'm that grateful Scotty I can't tell yer!"

"No need woman" he said giving her a bear-hug and then kissing her on the cheek. "You're a special lady, Mrs Honeysuckle… Oops! Sorry Mrs. Williams, it's been my pleasure, I am glad t' have been asked to the wedding." He turned to Gedd and shook his hand firmly. "Look man you are very lucky t' have yon fine woman… I am so very pleased for yer both."

Gedd smiled and shook Scotty's hand again as he clasped his arm. "I know an' you'd better look after yer lady there… she's not so bad either."

"Give over" said Honey as she noticed Susan blush. Scotty looked at Susan as well and he thought she looked very fine indeed. Susan was floating on air, her Scotty; she hoped was looking at her as if he was going to dive right into her eyes.

"You do look smashing Nurse… sorry Susan and I'm that glad yer decided to come with me… May I ask yer tay dance?" They both swirled away totally oblivious to Gedd and Honey, and they didn't mind a bit. In fact Honey was hoping that the romance blossoming between her Doctor and his pretty nurse would grow and grow.

Susan was wrapped in Scotty's arms and she didn't want the music to ever stop. Unknown to her Scotty was feeling the same. Funny that, he'd never in a million years thought he would fall for a nurse, but Susan Walker was definitely special. He wasn't going to let her get away.

Meanwhile Gedd and Honey were looking for Glyn and Chantelle. They found them sitting near the buffet table. "You're feedin' Chantelle up there Glyn?" Gedd said as he pulled up two chairs.

"Yes" Glyn replied "she needs a little more flesh on her bones... more for me to hug!" He grinned like a naughty schoolboy, and Chantelle didn't have the heart to tell him off, she did however nudge his elbow.

"Chantelle love... I just wanted to say thank you... for lookin' after me when I was bad an' for all yer 'elp today!" Honey said as clasped Chantelle's hand in her.

"You are so very welcome Honey..." Chantelle said as her eyes misted over "You have done so much for me, you believed in me Honey and that means so much to me... you to Gedd... I would have felt so bad if you..." she couldn't continue as she was choking up.

"Not a problem" Gedd cut in "you are a very special lady. Anyone can see that... Glyn can and so can we... chin up love." Gedd gave Chantelle a hug and so did Honey. As they stood up Glyn squeezed her hand and nodded.

"You are special and don't you forget it."

Chantelle watched Gedd and Honey walk out of the room and then everyone decided, almost at the same time, to gather in the reception area. She listened to all the idle chatter and moved over towards Honey's daughter.

"There you are..." said Sonia, who was dragging a tired looking man with her. "This is my husband Stephen, and I know you two are Glyn and Chantelle. My Mam has said so much about you both; you know all the help and that!"

"Give them a chance love... you don't half talk fast... slow down and do it properly... Oh Son' where are the kids?"

Chantelle smiled and shook both their hands and she liked the look of Honey's daughter very much indeed. Glyn shook the man's hand and said

Reviving a Rose

"Hi I'm Glyn and you are Stephen... well... I caught that bit anyway" Glyn said has he shook Stephen's hand. The two men laughed and turned to the ladies. "We're going to do a bit of male bonding, over a pint"

Sonia raised her eyebrows and Chantelle nodded in silent agreement. "MEN!" they both said at the same time and then laughed.

"Sorry about that" Sonia said looking apologetic "I always ramble when I'm nervous... I am really pleased to meet you... Mam told me over the phone about the heart trouble, blood pressure thing. I was so worried, but she said look after the little ones 'cos she had a lovely lass taking care of her, oh and Dr. Scotty too!"

"Well actually, we all kind of pitched in, Gedd, Glyn an me. We looked after the regulars and Honey. Honestly I'm sure she'd do the same for anyone, in fact Honey has been a bit of an emotional support for me lately. So you really don't need to thank me. I'd do it again if she needed me." Chantelle said

"Well I'm glad you were all here. My Mam is a very special lady." Sonia said

"Yes I agree, even Dr. Scotty has a soft spot for her." Chantelle said

"Is that him over there, who's that with him?" asked Sonia.

"Oh that's Nurse Walker, she came with Scotty. To do all the checks on Honey, and she stayed with Honey and I when all the tests were being done. I think maybe 'Scotty' might be a bit smitten." Chantelle replied.

"Really, ooh we'll have to go and say hello... Oh I'd better go and check on my kids. Mind you, knowing my lot, they're probably under a table with their cousins stuffing their chops with goodies." With that Sonia went back into the function room on the hunt for children.

Chantelle looked around and decided to go and talk to Scotty and Nurse Walker. "Hello you two, what did you think of the service then?"

"Well! Not havin' gon' too many weddings, this one was very special. Mind you lassie, they are very a special couple. They've been thro' a lot both o' them and feel a lot for each other, then it's all for the better aye."

"It was lovely, wasn't it... the celebrant seemed to know them both didn't she? It made it seem so personal, I was very much moved." Susan finished speaking, and then realised that 'Her Scotty' was staring at her intently. It made her skin feel alive. If this is love, 'I love it' she thought.

Chantelle sensed the chemistry flowing between them. She wondered if they both had realised how much they actually felt for one and other. She wasn't sure but if Susan was looking for a female ally then she would gladly be there for her.

"Do you know that you're looking lovely Nur...? Susan.

I would be honoured if you'd have a wee dance with me, after the Bride and Groom have left." Scotty had forgotten that Chantelle was there, he only had eyes for Susan. How had he missed her at work, she was stunning as she was at work but now she was all his, and he felt very happy indeed. But the dress she had on looked as if it had been made especially for her and he was proud when she held onto his arm, he was going to lead her in for a very special dance, he was sure of that.

"I'd be glad to" Susan said shyly.

As they seemed to be away on a different planet, Chantelle began to move slowly backwards. She felt an arm go around her waist, for a split second she thought it was Glyn. But something didn't feel right. Infact it felt all wrong and alarm bells were going off inside her head.

24

"Having a nice time Chelly?"

Chantelle tensed up and all colour left her face.

"Come back slowly and don't try anything, I've got something to show you." Ben was feeling exhilarated, he had 'his Chelly' in his arms. That she was totally rigid with fear meant nothing to him. They made their way towards the main door and no-one seemed to notice. Chantelle was screaming inside and no-one was looking.

"Come on..." Ben said as he roughly dragged her outside and spun her round to his car... "You look lovely and just for me too!" He leaned closer to her, puckering up as he did and Chantelle felt absolutely sick.

Ben did try to kiss 'his Chelly'. Unknown to him though, they had been spotted. Enid and Geoff had walked out to the stairs, ready to watch Honey and Gedd, when Enid spotted her son.

"Geoffrey... Look its Ben... and he's dragging Chantelle outside... ooh quick do something!"

"I certainly will my dear" Geoffrey Rodgers had said 'my dear' automatically and later that evening he would be very glad he had, when he remembered it.

"Excuse me" he said as he touched Scotty's arm "Um... Ben... Yes I believe that's his name, Ben has just taken that lovely young lady outside, against her will I believe."

"Where to..." said Scotty letting Susan's arm drop. He almost ran out and most of the men seemed to be following him.

"What's t' do?" Said a voice from the stairs; It was Gedd and instead of looking full of happiness he looked annoyed.

"Your nephew has taken Chantelle outside and I don't think she wanted to go with him" Said Susan.

"Right!" said Honey "You lot in 'ere and we'll wait for the men to fill us in. No sense in all goin' out in the cold and you all got silk and next t' nothing on." So although the women wanted to see what was up, they followed Honey back into the main room.

Just as Ben leaned in to claim his kiss, he was pulled round so fast he nearly fell over.

"What the...?"

"No kissing the lassie, if yer ken my drift." Doc McArdle had spun Ben round and very efficiently got him in an arm lock.

"Gerroff... you're hurting my arm... I'll have you for assault."

"Don't think so laddie... its restraining yer, not breaking owt, so I'd just stop yer struggling or it might hurt a wee bit!" As he said this; 'Scotty' adjusted his grip and Ben 'Yelped'.

"Would some nice man kindly phone the police and we'll go and wait in the warm if you don't mind." With that Scotty almost frog-marched Ben back inside and all the male guests followed behind, blocking off any escape route. Well, nearly all. Geoffrey and Honey's

Reviving a Rose

Son and Son-in-law had stayed back. They had taken charge of the very shocked young lady. Who was still standing exactly where Ben had left her.

"Chantelle... come on my dear... it's me; Mr. Rodgers... Geoffrey... you're cold and we need to get you inside." Geoffrey Rodgers words seemed to seep slowly into Chantelle's frozen brain. She looked around as if her eyes had just opened.

"Come on pet" said Stephen, and he and Darren took her under the arms. Geoffrey Rodgers had taken off his jacket and draped it gently round her shoulders..

"Wha...? Where are we going?" Chantelle was slowly coming out of her shock.

"It's alright Chantelle... these young men are Honey's boys and we are escorting you back into the warmth of the Inn." Mr. Rodgers said He was really shocked at her pallor and that she was so affected by just one person. He had never seen anything like it.

"Why you little waster... why if I 'ad you in a room on m' own I leather yer 'ide." Gedd was fuming. He was ashamed to acknowledge that 'Ben' was related to him. "What on earth wer' you gonna do to our Chantelle... you sick in t' 'ead or what?" He was so wound up; he could cheerfully have given him a hiding. But that wouldn't do Enid any good at all.

The lady herself had walked into the lounge where Scotty had taken Ben. He was sitting in one of the large armchairs, with most of the village on guard it seemed.

"Oh Ben! What 'ave yer done boy? ... What 'ave yer done?" Enid stopped in front of her son and she didn't recognise him. He looked like 'Frank'. What a waste, she thought that after he'd left Ben would grow up to be a lovely boy. It seems that he had a lot more of his father in him and that was BAD!

Ben sat there saying nothing. His plan to take Chelly for a 'special' drive had been stopped. He just didn't get it. What were all the bloody village doing guarding him.

Chantelle's Journey

He'd done nothing wrong. They must all be in-bred, he thought and there was nothing wrong with him, surely they could see that.

Mr. Rodgers and Honey's boys had by now brought Chantelle back into the reception area, just as Glyn came out of the toilet. "What the bloody hell is going on?" He virtually ran across the hall and enveloped Chantelle. She sank into his arms, sensing safety but still not entirely with it.

"Seems Enid's boy was going to take her for a drive or something, but Dr. McArdle stopped him." Mr Rodgers said "He's in the lounge but I wouldn't go in if I were you. He's not going anywhere until the police arrive and most of the village seem to be on guard as it were. You had best look after your young lady Glyn... much safer I feel... Yes that seems the best idea I'm sure." Mr. Rodgers patted Glyn's arm and guided him and Chantelle towards the stairs.

Honey looked on as Glyn led a shell-shocked Chantelle up the stairs. She waited until they had reached the top before going into the lounge to find her 'new husband'. She found him alright, standing in front of his nephew.

"What the bloody 'ell d'yer think yer doin' boy, you damn well scared that young lass t' death... Well what yer got t' say fer y'self then?" Gedd was fuming, he really wanted to give Ben a hiding, and mind you it probably wouldn't do any good. He was from bad stock; it wasn't Enid's fault she fell for Frank Locke's charms.

Oh he'd been a smooth one and all the smarmy ways too! Frank had swept Gedd's little sister off her feet. But after a few years and Bens arrival, Frank's true colours emerged. Enid had stuck by him though, through many beatings and verbal abuse, she had still loved him.

Frank had finally left one night, after men he'd borrowed money off came after him. Enid had, never seen him again, she didn't even know if he was still alive

Reviving a Rose

or not. Gedd was still staring at Ben waiting for and answer, as Honey came up next to him.

"Gedd love... 'E's not worth it... come away an' let the police handle it!"

As soon as Ben heard that word he flinched, 'Police'. "You haven't got anything on me... I haven't done anything... I was just talking to Chelly..."

"Well why was she looking so bloody scared then... she didn't want to talk to you... did she?"

"I'm not saying anything else without a lawyer, so back off... Uncle Gedd" he sneered, and then with a defiant stare he looked away and would not make eye contact with anyone.

"Well man..." Scotty started saying "... it seems as there's enough people in here ter watch yon man, so I'll go and check on the lassie. Susan can yer fetch ma' bag from the car and come up to Chantelle's room with it... Gedd what's the room number again?"

"It's number 7 Scotty" Honey said instead of Gedd "An' I'll bring up a strong cup of tea."

"No Mum..." Sonia said gently "it's your wedding day and you're going on your honeymoon. Don't worry Mum we'll look after everything." She said as she gently guided Honey towards Gedd's side.

"Gedd... look it's time you two were on your way... I've told Mum we'll look after everything and that includes Chantelle and your guests."

Gedd was very moved, he liked Honey's kids but the way they had stepped in, made him feel very proud to be married to their Mum.

"Come on love..." He said, nudging Honey's arm. "It's time we left, your kids will do us proud I'm sure and the police are coming now. So we'd best get our goodbyes said and be on our way!"

Honey reluctantly nodded and began to thank everyone for coming. It certainly wasn't the departure she had imagined. Still, best make most of it. In the end Gedd and Honey had even shook the hands of the officers who had arrived to speak to Ben.

"Well thanks again everyone" Gedd said to all the people in the hall. "It's not the send off we'd thought but we're both glad you all came." And with that Honey and Gedd Williams left the Briory Bush Inn on their week long honeymoon. They were off to Scotland, Honey had wanted to see the countryside that Scotty had grown up in, and so off they went.

Back in the lounge Ben had now got a police officer either side of him and he was definitely 'not a happy bunny'. He was still defiant, as he remembered 'the garage'. "Now then Mr. Locke, would you mind telling us why you were trying to force Miss Adams outside against her wishes?"

"I wasn't... its lies... Chelly's been after me... it's all a load of rubbish... Just ask my Mum?" He whined on, and the little spoilt petulant boy, who always got his way, began to show through.

"That's not what a room full of witnesses say though is it?" The officer continued, his partner studied the young man sat between them and he didn't much like what he saw. "I think this conversation would be better conducted down at the station."

At the mention of the police station Ben's stomach flipped, and he did something stupid, he lost his temper. "I'm not going anywhere... Get your hands off me..." He snarled. "I want a lawyer... you can't do this" he tried to punch one of them, but as his hand went upwards a cuff came down and clicked shut. Before he could react again the other arm was firmly forced behind his back and also clicked into the handcuffs. "You haven't got anything on me!" Ben began to whine again and struggle.

"Excuse me officers" a voice said from behind them. It was Scotty and he was looking very serious. "I had a few blood tests done, a couple of the guests were taken

Reviving a Rose

unwell these last few days. It seems they had something put in their drinks. I believe that young man there put it in and if you ring me at the hospital on Monday, I will be able tey tell you exactly what it was. I believe at least two different substances were used."

"That's a lie" squeaked Ben.

"Thank you…"

"Dr. McArdle."

"Thank you Dr. McArdle, we will contact you accordingly."

"Mum… do something can't you!" Ben said as he was going out the door.

Enid Locke was staring in disbelief at her only boy. What on earth had she done wrong? Why had the sunshine of her life turned into such a nasty dangerous little creep? "Ben" she said "I'm sorry son, but I gave you so many chances and you've always let me down. I'm afraid you'll 'ave to face the music on yer own for this… How could you have made yer own Mum sick and Mr. Rodgers too? 'E's never done anything to yer; yer adn't even met 'im before this wedding?"

"It wasn't meant for you it was for…" Ben realised what he really said and shut up.

"Come on then, we can do this easily or the hard way, you decide?" The police officer said as he escorted Ben outside and into the waiting police van.

"Well what a to-do" Geoffrey Rodgers said as he guided Enid back into the function room. "Do you mean your son had put some substance or other in our drinks the other evening?"

"I'm so sorry" Enid said as she stared brokenly at the floor. "It wasn't meant for us yer know, it was supposed to 'ave been drunk by Chantelle and Glyn. Ooh it fair makes me shudder, t' think mi' own flesh an' blood could do that t' another person. It gives the chills I can tell yer."

Mr. Rodgers put an arm around Enid's shaking shoulders. "There, there Enid, it's not your fault! Ben is an adult and you cannot be held responsible for his behaviour."

Enid was grateful for the support shown to her; all the guests had voiced the same opinion as Mr. Rodgers. Why on earth her son had turned out like that, she wondered. Maybe he did take after Frank too much, the thought made her shudder.

"Enid... Perhaps! A Medicinal Brandy" Mr. Rodgers said as he led her to a seat.

Enid was glad of that, as her legs felt like jelly. Mr. Rodgers scooted off to get Enid a large tot of Brandy. He found that he rather liked her company even if she was a little bit of a rough diamond. Geoffrey Rodgers found her intriguing; she had a delicate quality around her and a calm nature. He hadn't had much female company, because all of his time spent at the school. Maybe in his twilight years he just might find someone to enjoy 'Rose Cottage' with him.

Meanwhile Dr. McArdle had made his way up the stairs to check on Chantelle. He turned at the top just in time to see Susan following him with his bag. He could also see Ben being escorted out of the front door, 'Good Riddance' to bad rubbish' he thought and waited for Susan to catch him up.

"Right Susan, into nurse mode for a wee while, but I must check on something first." And so saying Scotty McArdle kissed Susan Walker smack on the lips. Then he walked off towards room 7 leaving a shell shocked nurse standing at the top of the stairs. Susan quickly got herself together and followed Scotty to Chantelle's room.

Glyn had been sitting on Chantelle's bed, cradling her and gently rocking back and forth. It seemed like ages had passed since he'd almost carried her up the stairs. But in fact it had been less than ten minutes.

Reviving a Rose

"Shh... it's alright "Boss-Lady", I've got you... he's gone love." Glyn said it over and over like a mantra; eventually it seemed to be getting through to Chantelle's shocked mind and she slowly started to relax.

Scotty and Susan found Glyn still rocking Chantelle as they entered the room. "How's ma patient Glyn?" Scotty asked as he put the medical bag on the dresser.

"I think she's still in shock, but she seems to be relaxing a bit now. I've been rocking her for ages!"

"Right nurse if you could just find a nice wee vein for me." Scotty said as he filled a syringe. Susan pushed up the sleeve of the cardigan that Glyn somehow managed to get onto Chantelle.

"Right sweetheart, I'm just getting your arm ready for a small injection, the doctors just going to give you something to help you relax and hopefully sleep, alright?"

Scotty came over to the bed and listened to Chantelle's heart, it was racing and she looked very pasty indeed.

"Now lassie, just you try and calm down a wee bit for me, I'm just going tey give a wee injection in yer arm. It'll calm ye doon and let yer sleep okay!" He wasn't really asking her, it was just medical speak. How could such a miserable rat of a boy turn this dependable young lady into such a mess? Scotty just didn't get it at all. With the injection given he wiped the arm and helped Susan and Glyn to get Chantelle into bed.

"Now Glyn..." he said standing up and rubbing his lower back slowly. "If you want t' stay with yon lassie, just try and keep the room quiet... I'll come back and check on her in the morning."

"Don't worry..." said Susan automatically putting everything back into the doctors' bag. "She's made of strong stuff. If you want any advice just give me a ring, I'll leave my mobile number on the side for you okay?"

"Thanks guys... I really mean it... she means the world to me... if that creep had..."

"Well he didn't man, so don't ye fret now... anyway! yon laddo is in the back of a Police van now. He's got a lot of explaining t' do" Scotty cut in sharply.

Glyn stood up and shook Scotty's hand and gave Susan a quick hug. They both left quietly and Glyn settled down in a chair by the bed. He wasn't going anywhere, his 'girl' needed him and he intended to be there when Chantelle woke up.

The party downstairs seemed to draw to an early close. The departure of Gedd and Honey had taken a little of the spirit away. But when all the commotion happened concerning Ben, it sort of went abit flat. The villagers and Regulars started to clear and pack up and Sonia, Victor and their families helped out too.

Sonia made it her business to thank everyone for coming and making her Mum's and Gedd's day special. She really felt sorry for Enid though. It wasn't her fault her son was such a scum-bag.

"Enid... there you are... I just wanted to thank you for coming, Gedd was really glad you came and so was my Mum."

"I'm ... sorry... so sorry Ben..."

"Shh... it's not your fault you know, you can't live his life. We are all glad 'you' came anyway."

"Hear, hear... I've been trying to buck her up a bit... hence the medicinal brandy." Mr. Rodgers said a she patted Enid's shoulders.

"Is it alright if I stay... only there's bin' such an upset I don't want t' overstay me welcome!"

"Of course you're staying, and don't worry about the bill either."

Sonia said, she really did wish for Enid's sake, that Ben hadn't been her son, still 'there's nowt as weird as folk', at least that's what her Mum said anyway. So the wedding party ended more or less, there and then.

Mr. Rodgers escorted Enid up to her room and bid her goodnight at the door. He wasn't a man of impulse but

Reviving a Rose

he was quite smitten with Enid. Having never actually dated before he was unsure how to proceed. Maybe he would seek some advice in the morning from either Honey's son or Glyn; they both seemed like sensible fellows. With that thought in his head he toddled off to bed to sleep extremely well, considering the days events.

Enid was curled up in her bed, but she was wide awake, there were so many things going on in her head, she didn't know what to do. She hopped out of bed and nipped into the bathroom. As she did, she heard a soft tap on the door.

"Who is it?" Enid wasn't the bravest of women and she wasn't even sure if she'd open the door or not!

"It's Sonia... Enid I've brought you up a cup of tea and a little something to help you sleep. I hope you don't mind?"

"No... No of course not" she replied opening the solid oak door to let Sonia in. Sonia in fact had 2 cups of tea on a little tray.

"I thought you might want some company... what a day it's been." Sonia bustled over to the dresser and gave Enid her cup. She sat down beside the dresser on a chair and had a good sip.

"Thank you very much... it's so good of you after..."

"Look Enid, I've said before love, it's not your fault okay and no-one here blames you at all. Maybe the trip in the police car will do your boy some good!"

"I hope so" Enid said as she sat shaking slightly "E' used to be such a good boy, what happened?"

"Who's to know love?"

They both sat there in a companionable silence. When they both had finished Sonia gave Enid a small bottle, which she'd had in her pocket.

"Take one of these, with a sip of water, when you get into bed Enid. I checked with the 'Doc' and he said it shouldn't do any harm. If anything, it'll help you relax.

If you need anything else, just give me a shout, I'm in the 'Big room' Number 12 okay, night love." Sonia put both tea cups on the tray and smiled at Enid as she left. "Don't forget... if you need me at all, for anything, honestly, I really mean it... call me okay."

"Thanks again dear... so much... I think I'll 'ave a bath and pop into bed, if it's alright... I really appreciate it... night."

The door closed and Enid turned the key in the lock. 'Now then, let's fill mi bath' she said to herself.

25

The following morning was like the calm after a heavy storm. Most of the guests who had stayed at the Inn slept late. They all gradually stated to appear downstairs after 10 o'clock. Sonia had been up for awhile, she had her Mum's and Gedd's interests to look after. Her husband Stephen had taken the children to the near-by park to burn off some energy.

Glyn woke up to the smell of bacon wafting up the stairs. For a brief second he thought maybe Honey or Gedd was cooking. Then he remembered why and where he was and realised it couldn't be either of them. He was feeling really hungry; he hadn't had much the day before. Events had seen to that, so his stomach growled angrily.

As it rumbled again Chantelle was beginning to stir in the bed.

"Hiya 'Boss-Lady', you okay?" he said kneeling down by the bed. He picked up one of her cold hands and rubbed it gently.

Chantelle's Journey

"I feel a bit muggy... what did Scotty give me last night?"

"Just a mild sedative... you scared a few people you know... me especially, I could have wrung that little wasters neck... but I wanted to stay with you!"

"Well I'm glad you did, can I have a cuddle please?"

Glyn didn't need asking twice, his tummy forgotten for now, he cuddled up beside Chantelle. He stayed on top of the covers though.

"You smell lovely..." Chantelle said as she snuggled into his strong arms.

"Don't think so... I've been sat in that chair all night, in the same stuff I had on yesterday..."

"Why didn't you join me?" Chantelle said looking slightly lost.

"Couldn't sweetheart... just in case you had a bad dream and thought I was 'him'."

"I would never think that... even filled with drugs... Your body tells mine every time we're together, that I can feel safe... and if my body's happy then so am I..." She finished with a wobbly smile. "Glyn, surely you can feel that, can't you?"

"Yep... but I need food... So I'm reluctantly going to leave you for a mo' to get some bacon sarnies. Do you want some?"

"Yes please... but only if you bring them, with some coffee and you stay to help eat them!"

"Not a problem "Boss-Lady" be back in a tic." Glyn was going to be the fastest waiter ever; he didn't want to leave Chantelle alone... not for a minute.

He pushed the kitchen door open and Sonia looked up. "Hiya Glyn, smelt the bacon then?"

"Yep... sure did. Chantelle has woken up and we both need feeding please."

Sonia laughed; he looked like a naughty schoolboy. But she was glad Chantelle had an appetite though.

Reviving a Rose

"Sure Glyn... Pull up a chair and I'll whiz up a couple of sarnies okay. Tell you what, you get the coffees instead and put 'em on the large tray over there!"

Glyn did as he was told, Sonia had her mothers' ways and she definitely knew her way around the kitchen. It was no more than 20 minutes before Glyn was back in Chantelle's room. They both sat in comfort on the bed and munched away. After demolishing all that Sonia had cooked they finished their coffee, with much finger licking and wiping of chins, they both laid back and grinned.

"Oh... I'm stuffed... I feel enormous"

"Get over... you look good enough to eat... but I'm full of bacon." Glyn said as he kissed Chantelle gently and she snuggled in close for the second time that morning.

"I'm so glad you ran me off the road."

"I'm glad I got you plastered at the cottage."

They just laid there gently caressing each other between light and soft kisses and smiling.

"Glyn get in under the covers, you look cold... you're shivering."

"I'm not cold sweetheart... it's you making me shiver... you send my body wild... don't you know that yet?" He said slightly accusingly, but flicked his eyebrows up and down so that Chantelle giggled and kissed him again.

"You do the same to me... I have never felt so safe and sexy at the same time... its mind blowing."

"Glad to be of service m'lady" Glyn said doing a mock bow, as he stood up from the bed. "Much as I would love to continue, I think the 'Doc' is coming back to check on you. So I think it best he doesn't find me in your bed ravishing you!"

"I would mind a little ravishing!" She said rather coyly. But she understood why he wouldn't. That was the difference between Ben and Glyn. Ben just took what he wanted when ever he wanted. But Glyn always

Chantelle's Journey

put her wishes first. Chantelle realised then, just how much she loved him. Did he really feel the same about her though?

Before she had a chance to ask the bedroom door was knocked quite forcefully.

"Hello in there... Sonia tells me the patient has devoured some rather tasty Bacon sandwiches. I guess that means she's feeling a wee bit better then." Scotty had come in and Chantelle was glad now that Glyn hadn't got into her bed. It would have been a bit embarrassing to say the least. Glyn was in fact perched on the edge of the bed. He'd moved away as soon as he had heard the knock.

"How's yer feeling then lassie?" Scotty said as he entered the room and started to check her eyes, chest and blood pressure.

"Fine... honestly... I just feel so relieved he's gone. My nerves were getting a little frayed to be honest... Anyway I've got Glyn with me, so how can I not feel safe?!"

"I agree lassie... I wouldn't tangle with him! Well, you seem alright all things considered... I'll leave you in his capable hands."

Glyn stood up and thanked Scotty again and firmly shook his hand.

"Not a problem Glyn... I'm here to help. I'm just away tay check on Enid Locke... D'yer ken what room she's in by the way?"

"I think its 9... and thanks again Doc;" Glyn said as he opened the door.

'You're welcome' floated down the hall as the doctor went to find the other lady who'd been upset by a certain young man.

Glyn gently closed the door and returned to the bed. "Come on... time you were up and about... doctors orders." He tugged the covers off her body and dumped them at the end of the bed. She squeaked and sat up. Glyn feasted his eyes on her firm body. She had the longest old fashioned nightie on that he'd ever seen, but somehow it made her look even lovelier as it clung to her body.

"Come on... into the bathroom with you!" He reached a hand out to her; she clasped it and hauled herself up.

"Only if you share a shower with me?" she said cheekily as she nipped into the bathroom. Glyn didn't need asking twice and as his belly was nicely full, he could think of nothing nicer than sharing a shower with his 'Spitfire'.

"Move over darling, make room for one more" Glyn said as he kicked her still warm nightie which had fallen to the floor. He only just remembered, before shedding his own clothes, to lock the door. He then followed Chantelle into the now steaming bathroom.

"Move over you!" he said stepping into the bath "give us a little room eh!" Glyn said as he lightly smacked her pert bottom.

"Ouch... that wasn't very nice... carry on like that and you'll have no kisses at all..." she said swatting Glyn with the 'scrunchie'.

They stood body to body as Chantelle slowly soaped Glyn's chest. Moving slowly lower and lower, she washed, touched, and caressed his throbbing manhood. Her eyes widened as it grew between her hands.

Glyn felt on fire, his knees were in danger of giving in and he wasn't sure if he could hang on. "Oh God... that is so good..." he said gasping as Chantelle soaped all around his groin. "... Have you any idea what that is doing to me?"

"I think your body is showing me just how much you're enjoying it..." Chantelle said breathlessly "... I've never done this to any man before, but you bring out the devil in me... I just want to please you."

"You're doing fine... honestly sweetheart I don't think I can hang on for much longer... so I think it's my turn."

Glyn took the 'scrunchie' off Chantelle and began to soap her. He liked to be in charge, but having her take that the lead just then had been mind blowing, she was definitely 'all woman'.

Chantelle's body was tingling from the top of her head to her toe-nails and everywhere in between. Especially her most secret place, her very insides were convulsing and tensing, but with exquisite pleasure. Her wet and now wanton feminine place was aching to be filled.

"Glyn! Please...," she gasped as his hand rubbed where the 'scrunchie' had been "... I need you now... please... no more!"

Glyn snapped off the shower and carried her to the bed. He was going to show Chantelle just how good making love could be, when both people totally trusted their partners.

"I'm going to love you so totally, you won't know where you are "Boss-Lady"." Glyn said in a very gentle voice, almost a whisper. He lay down next to her still wet body and began to rub some baby oil all over her. In gentle circular movements, he moved from legs to stomach to breast. When he reached her neck Glyn stopped, and wiped his hands.

"Ready for your private lesson now?" He said as he nipped her lips and kissed her face.

Chantelle groaned, and pulled Glyn down onto her slick body. She could feel her whole body wake as soon as Glyn's solid erection touched her. They both began to explore each others bodies, hands seemed to be everywhere and they were clutching and pulling and teasing.

She thought the shower had been erotic, but now Glyn was moving south, Chantelle's brain felt like it was going to explode. His hands parted her still wet legs and slowly his fingers began to move up into her moist core!

Reviving a Rose

"Ooh... I feel... Ooh Glyn please don't stop; it's wonderful..."

"Here to please 'M'lady'." Glyn said as his fingers quickened their pace. Chantelle was writhing beneath his touch. She found herself out of control and totally primeval. She squirmed and bucked as her climax began to build. Faster and faster Glyn's fingers went and her body was gripping them desperately, trying to stop them leaving her. Glyn was so turned on he nearly 'came' all over her.

"Glyn... now... please I can't stand it!" A breathless Chantelle pleaded to be filled and released from the tense coiled spring she had become under Glyn's control.

He entered her firmly and pushed in right up to the hilt of his manhood. Chantelle gasped, wide eyed and shocked, but she had never felt so alive before in her life.

On and on Glyn pushed and retracted, faster and faster until they both exploded in myriad of emotions and the whole universe, it seemed to Chantelle, had gone with them.

It was a full 10 minutes before either had enough breathe to speak.

"Wow..." Glyn said "... your body seems to know what it likes!"

Chantelle lay on her back staring at the ceiling. Her whole body was still tingling and she felt absolutely fantastic. "It must be your expertise!" she said, as she groped for his hand. Glyn held it and gave it a quick squeeze.

They turned to each other, at the same time and shared a delicate soft kiss which seemed to seal their bond. "Glyn... you know I love you... don't you?"

"I wasn't sure... but I sure hoped so. I love you so much Chantelle, but I didn't want to scare you with too much emotion; I know how fragile you've been."

"Thank you Glyn... for believing in me and loving me... it's like your love is healing all the hurt... I feel so blessed that you love me... I just want it to last..."

"It will last" Glyn said strongly "... if we both nurture it and love each other the love will last, trust me!"

"You know I do."

They moved together and lay in each others arms, it felt beautiful. Glyn had never felt so content before in his life. And Chantelle was so amazed that this strong stunning man 'loved' her and would continue doing so, for a very long time.

They had no idea how long they had stayed there, after declaring their mutual love for each other. But eventually Glyn got up.

"Where are you going?" Chantelle said slightly sleepily. It amazed her how tired you got after making love.

"Got to go to the bathroom "Boss-Lady", nature you know" Glyn said over his shoulder as he went to empty his groaning bladder.

Chantelle got up too; she went over to the dresser to sort her hair out. 'God' it looked a mess! It was fuzzy and all over the place. She had a rosy tint to her cheeks, they looked flushed but not like a fever. Glyn came back in and stood behind her.

"Pass the brush!" she did so and with firm strokes he worked his way through the tangled 'post love making' mess. Chantelle found it very relaxing. She leaned back onto his chest and sighed; he held her close and kissed the top of her head.

It was much later after they had made love again, that Glyn and Chantelle got dressed and went downstairs in search for more food. She marvelled at how hungry you became after showing the man you loved, just how much you loved him.

Glyn was thinking along similar lines, and he felt on top of the world.

26

On entering the kitchen they both smiled and lips were licked in anticipation. Sonia was every bit as good in the kitchen as her Mum and the smells wafting through would make anybody salivate.

"Oh hiya both… just knocked up a hearty stew… I know it's the wrong food 'post wedding', but I thought we all needed comfort food… y'know… Dumplings and Crusty bread as well."

"Don't… you'll have me diving in the pot, if you're not careful." Glyn said sniffing appreciatively.

"Sit down both… I'm just taking some out to Mum's 'Regulars', I'll be back in a tic." So saying Sonia took a large tray through to the lounge and gave them their stew. Chantelle could hear the thank you's and compliments from the kitchen.

"Well… they seem to like it!" Sonia said as she came back. She dished up three hearty bowlfuls and sat down to eat in companionable silence. Between mouthfuls Chantelle asked where the children were.

"Stephen's taken them home. He's going to come and get me when Mum and Gedd come back. It was too much for them, and they were getting bored and restless."

"It's been a funny couple of days to say the least, hasn't it?" Glyn said between mouthfuls.

"Yeah it has that... I hope Mum and Gedd enjoy themselves, bit of a rough start to married life!" Sonia commented.

"They're made of strong stuff, both of them, they seem totally made for each other." Chantelle said as she dipped her bread in the juices left in her bowl. "Is Stephen going to look after your children?"

"God no... they'll drive him mad. No, 'his Mum', Lucy will have them no doubt, he'll go back to work for some peace. They're good kids mind, but oh they could drive a saint up the wall sometimes..."

They had all finished when a face appeared round the swing door. "'Scuse me." It was Maud Pennington, one of the 'Regulars' "Mr. Rodgers, sorry Geoffrey and Enid have come down. They said the aroma has managed to reach upstairs, and their stomachs need filling... Have you got any stew left?"

"Of course... Maud, could you take some cutlery out and I'll fetch two big bowlfuls through... Do you or your party want anymore, there's plenty left?"

"Goodness me no... we can't move. Why, Malcolm has said he can't possibly do any gardening for at least three hours." Maud chuckled as she went to let Enid and Geoffrey know they hadn't missed out on the fantastic meal.

"Thank you so much for asking on our behalf Mrs..."

"Maud love... just call me Maud."

"Yes well... Maud I must say Enid and I are most grateful for your kindness" said Geoffrey.

"Not a problem Geoffrey, not a problem at all. Now I must get back to Malcolm, he needs persuading that

Reviving a Rose

his garden is calling." She gave them, their cutlery and fetched over the basket with some crusty bread still in it. "See you both soon I hope... Bye."

Maud shook both their hands and went back to her husband. She thought that Mr. Rodgers would be a nice addition to the village, when he moved in. And Enid was a lovely but shy lady.

"My goodness Enid isn't this wonderful. I can feel it sticking to my ribs, isn't that what they say about wholesome cooking." Geoffrey said as he made short work of his stew.

"It's lovely; Honey's girl can sure make a good stew. She definitely takes after 'er Mum. What a lovely girl!"

"I agree... Enid would you like to walk off your food with a stroll around the village. I could show you the cottage that Chantelle and Glyn have worked on for me?"

"That would be smashing Geoffrey, I'd love to... I think those two make a nice couple don't you?"

"Well they certainly seem well matched. And from all the work done for me they work well together 'at work', if you see what I mean."

"'Corse I do, silly man. You don't 'alf talk daft sometimes. Mind you, you are the most 'Gentleman' I've ever met, if you don't mind me sayin'." Enid stood up, quite surprised by her defence of Geoffrey. But she did like him; even if he was 'posh', it wasn't his fault.

Geoffrey Rodgers was bowled over by the compliment and her defence of him. Well he had never had a woman stand up for him before in his adult life. The last lady who'd done that had been his mother, what a severe woman she had been. He was sure that was why he found it hard to talk to women. For some reason though, Enid was different. Maybe it was because she came from a different background.

They took their bowls through to the kitchen and said their thank you's.

"We're just off for a stroll, to work off the effects of your fine cooking Sonia. I have to say that your cuisine is of the highest order..."

"What 'e's trying t' say..." Dived in Enid... "Is that yer food was 'bloody fantastic', 'Cuse the language folks."

Sonia said she didn't mind at all, and she was well pleased with the compliments. It was a nice change to cook for others, instead of just her family.

Enid and Geoffrey went off to find their coats. It was a little on the 'raw' outside, so wrapping up was definitely the best plan.

Enid enjoyed the slow but steady journey to the 'cottage'. When they finally reached it she gasped in awe. "Aww... it's lovely... d'y'know it looks like it fell off a choclit' box don't it?"

"Yes... it's definitely picturesque, I agree." Geoffrey was pleased Enid liked the look of his new home. Somehow it felt important for her to like it. "Would you like a tour, my dear?"

"Wot... oh yes please... that would be smashin'."

As he opened the little front door he stepped aside for Enid to go in first.

She was dumb-struck... Enid had never seen such a pretty room. The soft colours and curtains made it feel snug and cosy. The little fireplace was gleaming. It had a few logs in the grate, ready to go. She could imagine the wonderfully intimate vision of a blazing fire, with the curtains nearly closed and snow slowly drifting on the tiny window ledges.

"It's stunnin' Geoffrey, they must 'ave done a lot of work. What was it like when you first saw it?"

"Certainly nothing like this, I can assure you. It was a little tired and the garden was so over-grown, I didn't even know how lovely that could have become. Glyn and Chantelle have put in so much work, it's much more than I ever had expected. Do you know what Enid? I can't wait to actually retire and potter around here and explore this wonderful countryside."

Enid was really envious; she would have enjoyed that too! "You must be so proud of your little 'ouse now Geoffrey, I know I would be. Can we see the garden now?"

"Certainly, come through this way. I do like the little windows; they give this place so much character don't they?"

"Oh yes... Ohh I say wot a fabulous garden and a little stream too!" Enid said as followed Geoffrey out into the beautiful garden.

The autumn colours were at their best. The Willows, which framed the stream like the sides of a picture, were wafting gently and their leaves were turning from green to a soft brown. The roses in the flower beds swayed slightly and showed off their beautiful array of colours.

"Aww... ain't they lovely..." Enid said as she moved over towards them and took a good sniff. "... They smell so beautiful too!"

"Yes... I must agree Enid, they are exceptional aren't they! And to think, they were all hidden away under lots of brambles. Chantelle did a sterling job tidying the place; I believe her flair for re-decoration extends to this splendid garden, as well as the cottage."

"I reckon you're right there Geoffrey! She's a lovely girl too, can't figure out 'ow my boy did so badly by 'er?"

"There, there, dear lady. Some things just can't be unravelled, no matter how much you dwell on it! I think a cup of tea is in order, what do you say?"

"Ooh... that sounds smashin', come on then!" Enid returned to the cottage, as she did so she brushed past the herbs, and they released their own distinctive aromas.

"Cor 'erbs as well, I wonder if Sonia would like some fresh ones for cooking." As she spoke, Enid realised that this was not her garden to pick and choose, she looked down-hearted.

"Now then..." Geoffrey said as he noticed her expression "I think that is an absolutely splendid idea. We shall pick some after our cuppa, shall we?"

"Can't fault yer there, can I? Come on; where's mi' tea?"

Enid was quite happy to carry the herbs. While Geoffrey locked-up and slid his hand under Enid's elbow. She looked round, and he sheepishly said "just to steady you, I'm sure you can't see over the top of that impressive bouquet."

She smiled shyly and Geoffrey blushed ever-so slightly. He was well on the way to being smitten. 'What would his colleagues and students think of 'Crusty Old Rodgers', with a delicate woman on the end of arm! He found he liked the idea a lot, and so they continued in a comfortable silence all the way back to the village.

27

Whilst Geoffrey and Enid were slowly exploring his 'new home', and getting to know each other, Chantelle and Glyn had long since helped Sonia to clear up dinner and wash the dishes.

In fact, they hadn't even missed the senior guests at all. They had been getting to know and like Sonia. She was very much in the same mould as her Mum and that was fine by them.

"Look you two 'ave done enough, why don't you go for a walk or something?" said Sonia.

Glyn looked at Chantelle and flicked his eyebrows up and down. She giggled and nodded her head. They were getting so attuned to each other that they just knew what the other one was thinking.

Coats were found; along with scarves and gloves, it was getting a little raw outside.

"See you later guys." Sonia said as they waved from the back door.

Chantelle's Journey

Glyn tucked Chantelle's arm through his and they strolled off down the lane, towards the garage then said "I don't think Gedd's been near the garage at all this week. D'you think we should check up on it and make sure it's secure. I'm sure it is, but better safe than sorry."

Glyn didn't know about the 'trap' that Ben had left. They walked together in a comfortable silence, no words were needed their bodies were as one. It didn't take long before they reached 'Gedd's' garage, they both went around to the back. Glyn fished around in his pocket for his key. He put it into the lock and turned it.

In a split second the 'kitchen' exploded, shortly followed by the main blast of the garage. As a fireball erupted from the doorway, Glyn and Chantelle were both blown across the tarmac. The 'Bang' had deafened both of them for a split second and there they sat on the ground with their ears ringing.

"Chantelle... you okay?" Glyn's only concern was for his 'Spitfire', he didn't care about himself.

"Yes"... she said shakily... "But Glyn your face... it's bleeding!!"

He put his hands up to his face, it felt wet. He rubbed it, to try and dry it.

"No don't"... Chantelle said as she rang 999 on her mobile. "There are lots of cuts Glyn you might have glass in there... leave it for the ambulance guys to sort... here put my scarf against it." Chantelle took her scarf off and placed it gently onto his face. She had never been so scared.

"What happened?"

"There must have been a leak or something!" Glyn's face took on a serious look. Maybe the 'something' was Ben! God, it didn't bear thinking about how sick that boy could be!!

They both tried to stand up, being very careful not to make Glyn's face bleed even more. The sirens of the

Reviving a Rose

ambulance came closer and closer and then came flying round the garage, closely followed by a fire-engine. The fire was quickly and professionally put out, and then followed the painstaking process of finding out 'WHY?' had it happened.

The ambulance crew treated Glyn, luckily they had said the cuts were superficial, they also told him he'd been very lucky. If Glyn had set off the spark inside, he would have been a fire-ball too!

Chantelle winced; she clung to Glyn's arm. Reality set in and she realised just how close she had been to losing Glyn forever. She began to weep silently and was shaking as well. The ambulance crew packed her into the ambulance along with Glyn. Just a check-up, they said, just to be on the safe side.

The whole village seemed to have descended on what was left of the garage. There were lots of mutterings between them as they tried to figure out why Gedd's garage had 'gone-up' in flames. It was a mess, that would take a while to clear up and that was for sure.

Glyn and Chantelle were sat next to each other in the Casualty Department. Glyn's face had been cleaned up and lots of little Steri-strip plasters were dotted about on it. Chantelle was feeling slightly better now, she clasped Glyn's hand tightly and he returned the pressure.

They both heard a familiar voice and sat up a little straighter... 'Scotty's Face' appeared as he pulled the 'Cubicle's' curtain back.

"Well what the blazes have you two been up tay?"

"The garage went up, just as I put the key in." Glyn said

"What! Exploded ya mean?" Scotty replied scanning the two charts on the clipboard.

"Yes, it would seem so. A huge fireball blew us both across the back yard."

"Wow... Have you got Guardian Angels or what?"

"I'm not sure Scotty, but I think we must have. I dread to think what could have happened if we had gone inside."

Chantelle hadn't said anything, so Scotty leaned closer to her and checked her eyes. He had seen her in shock twice before, and although she looked a little peeky he wasn't unduly worried.

"Looks like another sleeping draft for you hen! And mebbie one for Glyn as well… Hey man, where are you going ta' sleep, the accommodation went up too didn't it?" Scotty said

"I'm not sure… we left as the fire brigade were damping down. I guess I'll have to throw my plight at Sonia's disposal."

"No you won't…" Chantelle said, suddenly springing to life. "… You can bunk in with me. I'm not letting you out of my sight… I could have lost you Glyn and I couldn't cope with that." She clung to his arm and looked down at the floor. Glyn lifted her chin up, so she had to look straight at his face.

"I'm not going anywhere without you, and if you are offering to share your 'boudoir' then I'll certainly take up the offer!" He said; jiggling his eyebrows. It had the desired effect, Chantelle smiled, all be it a ropey one.

"Right you two… I'll away and get yer drafts and then see if I can arrange a lift back to the Inn." Scotty told them as he finished writing up their notes. He was very impressed with the attention Glyn paid to Chantelle; they certainly made a striking pair.

It was nearly 6 o'clock by the time they had got discharged and returned to the Inn. Both were cold and needed to clean up, so they headed up to Chantelle's room. Luckily for Glyn; Sonia had dug out some old clothes of Gedd's. They weren't Saville Row, but they would do for now.

Glyn was thankful that he and Chantelle were okay, so the thought of 'old clothes' didn't bother him. He had his wallet and he realised that he would have to come clean about his money situation. As most of the village it seemed had wrongly assumed; all of his worldly goods had been burned in the fire.

He followed Chantelle and stepped into No. 7, slowly but firmly closing the door behind him.

"God Glyn, I have never been so scared in all my life. I'm so glad you didn't go in; I couldn't have coped with that... You know how much I love you, don't you?"

"Yes" Glyn replied, as he enveloped her in his arms and buried his face in her hair. "You smell smoky do you know that?"

"So do you" the muffled response came.

"Chantelle I love you too, when you flew across the backyard, my heart nearly stopped. I couldn't bare it if you'd been very badly hurt, you are my life." Glyn was glad that his face was still in Chantelle's hair, because tears were coursing down his cheeks. He sniffled and straightened up, holding his 'love' at arms length he gathered himself ready to tell her all about his past, present an d future. "Chantelle, we'll have a scrub and then you and I need to talk."

She was wrapped up in her own Inner-glow and assumed he wanted to talk about the future. Well that was fine with her, any life with Glyn after today, had to be a bonus.

The shower wasn't really that big, but somehow they both managed to fit in again, without falling out the bath. Chantelle just stood there and let the water wash all of the day out of her hair. Glyn gently soaped her back and checked her for bruises. He also very gently washed her hair. It was very relaxing and Chantelle was almost sleeping.

It took her a few minutes to realise he had stopped. Glyn was just standing there, totally nude, looking at her face. He cupped her face with his hands and very gently brought his face to hers and kissed her.

Chantelle's toes curled and sweeping hot sensations flowed all around her body. She returned the kiss and it deepened. Glyn's arms moved to surround her and she felt completely safe. "You are so special..." she began.

"Shh... just be still and let me hold you." He said, and rocked her in his arms.

With the shower now turned off, they both rubbed each other dry with big fluffy towels, and Glyn led Chantelle back into the bedroom. He wrapped her up in the huge bedspread and sat her down on the bed. She noticed the seriousness about his manner and sat very still. Whatever he had to say, she wouldn't speak until he had finished.

"Now, where do I start?" Glyn said, more to himself than Chantelle. "I'm not as poor as you would believe. In fact, I am very solvent." He let this fact sink in and then continued. "I know you thought the Mercedes wasn't mine... well it is. I'm not just an ordinary 'brickie', I own my own company!"

Chantelle continued to sit quietly and when she said nothing Glyn continued.

"Have you ever heard of Matthews Construction Limited?"

She shook her head.

"It's mostly based in the Midlands. I started it when I was 26. My father encouraged me; he's been in the building trade for over 40 years... Anyway, I decided to get my hands dirty again, and get a feel for the amount of grafting I ask from my employees. I saw your ad on the net and as it was so far from my usual stomping ground I took it. I'm glad I did too, because I would never have met you otherwise."

Chantelle nodded, thinking she was glad he'd answered her job ad. Glyn never took his eyes off her face. What was she thinking, he had no idea, but he must be honest with her.

"I never intended to deceive you, but you didn't ask about my life. At first I thought it was because you were shy, but I'm not sure now. I have to tell you Chantelle I'm probably worth roughly £40 million. But it doesn't alter how I feel about you. In fact I'm scared it will push you away, am I wrong?"

His face said it all, love mingled with fear. Chantelle loved him totally and although the thought of all that money scared her, she had loved him when she thought he was 'skint', so surely she could get used to a little money couldn't she!

She leaned forward and wrapped the bedspread and her arms around him. "I love you Glyn, with or without money. In fact I thought you had nothing left after today. I was, am prepared to share everything I have with you. I was going to ask you if you wanted to become my partner, ready for the next job, whatever that turned out to be."

"Yes" Glyn cheered and hugged her back. "I knew you were special, the moment I first laid eyes on you. Will you marry me PLEASE, and make me the happiest and proudest man alive?"

"Of course I will, I love you with all my heart. I would be honoured to be your wife."

They both fell back on the bed enveloped in the bedspread and kissed each other in silent commitment. The day had finally caught up with them and they both fell asleep in each others arms. What a day that had been, from one extreme to another.

Glyn thought his heart would burst, he couldn't wait to tell his dad, Glyn was sure he would love Chantelle too!

Chantelle was ecstatic too; fancy her 'Glyn' a millionaire. That was going to take time to get used to, but with Glyn's love it would be an interesting journey.

28

The morning arrived fresh and cold and the 'newly engaged' couple were still asleep in each others arms. There was a soft tapping at the door; Chantelle struggled to dis-entangle herself from the bedspread. "Hang on a sec', just coming"

Sonia was standing by the door holding a large tray. It was groaning under the weight of toast, 'fry-up' and a huge pot of coffee. Enid was standing behind her, shyly holding the plates and cups.

Chantelle opened the door and gasped! "Wha... Thank you for this, but we would have come down..."

"No, you both needed 'mothering' so Enid and I decided that 'Breakfast in bed' was the order of the day, so here we are."

Glyn was slowly coming around, he could smell good food. His nose and stomach had never failed him. "What's this... ladies you are pure gold."

He was so grateful that he had put his boxers on before he left the bathroom last night. He studied Chantelle

Reviving a Rose

and she had a slight flush about her cheeks, Glyn liked what he saw.

"Wot a mess... we went round this mornin' and 'ad a look at the garage. Gedd's gonna be heart-broken when 'e gets back... d'yer know wot 'appened there Glyn?" Enid had been so shocked by the state of the garage she had been physically sick. Gedd had worked so hard to build it up too!

"I'm not sure... the fire brigade are investigating... but it definitely exploded, as we both can testify. It blew us across the backyard." Glyn told them as he deftly slid on the 'old gear' that Sonia had found him.

"Well I 'ope they find out soon. Gedd will be crushed t' see 'is garage lookin' so done in." When it came to family, Enid wasn't shy and she loved Gedd so much.

"Don't worry Enid," Sonia said placing a comforting hand on her arm. "I'm sure it's insured and I'm sure the entire village will pitch in to get it back to normal."

Enid nodded, not quite believing it, but she was impressed with the way the villagers had turned out yesterday.

"We'll leave you to it... enjoy your breakfast both... see you later, don't rush okay!" Sonia guided Enid out and left Chantelle and Glyn to enjoy their food.

It was then that Chantelle realised she hadn't mentioned 'the engagement'. Mind you, she wasn't sure if Glyn had wanted to say anything just yet. He seemed to have read her mind and said

"We didn't tell them, did we?" Glyn was grinning like a Cheshire cat, he was certain he would explode with happiness. "Come here you, my wonderful 'Bride-to be'. Have I told you today how much I love you?"

"No silly... we've only just got up... I love you too!!"

"We'll have to get a ring" Glyn said "I wasn't very well prepared last night. I'll have to do it again properly."

"You don't have to Glyn, with what happened yesterday I think you proposed beautifully and I don't need a second go. You're enough, without the ring!"

Glyn was warmed by that, 'His' girl wasn't materialistic she just loved him, and anyway Chantelle had said she loved him before she knew about his wealth. He was a very happy man!

It didn't take them both long to eat everything on the tray and as Glyn had thought and smelt, it was really good food.

When they both eventually came down with all the dishes, it was nearly afternoon. But Glyn felt really refreshed and 'alive'. He held the tray as Chantelle pushed open the swinging doors so they could get into the kitchen.

"Hi you two... it's nearly 'alf a day gone... how yer feeling?" Enid asked, as she stood by the sink, up to her elbows in bubbles. "I'm just 'elping Sonia out a bit. I must say it's nice t' be wanted."

Chantelle took the tray from Glyn and joined Enid by the sink. "Where's Sonia then?" She asked.

"Gone t' the cash 'n' carry for more food. Seems yesterday 'as made a lot of people 'ungry; Sonia's cooking loads!"

Glyn was just about to 'announce' the engagement, but Chantelle stopped him. She shook her head slightly, and he arched and eyebrow in reply.

After helping Enid, they both decided that a walk around the village would help the massive late breakfast go down. They passed 'Martha's Curios' and wandered on down the picturesque street. All the houses were well worthy to be on postcards, and most had thatched roofs too!

They stopped outside a very quaint; looking jewellers. It had small windows and there were small trays of beautiful rings on velvet trays.

Reviving a Rose

"Come on "Boss-Lady" we've got a ring to find." Glyn took Chantelle's hand and led her into the shop. It was beautifully decorated; the walls had soft gold lamps which directed the light up and although it seemed quite small. The addition of light rugs on the stone floor added depth and charm to the interior.

Glyn noticed a little gold bell on the table, he pressed it once. It 'pinged' and the clear note pierced the room like an arrow. Seconds later an old distinguished gentleman entered, from what they assumed was his sitting room.

"Good afternoon folks, how can I help you?" The shop owner said He was no more than 5ft tall, but was dressed in a well fitted 3 piece suit. In fact he looked immaculate, and his appearance certainly added to the shops 'aura'.

"Yes we hope so... I... we... have come to find an engagement ring." Glyn was normally straight forward and knew what he wanted, but today he felt like a nervous teenager.

"Certainly Sir... Madam, I'd be happy to oblige. My name is Mr. Thomas and it would be my pleasure to help you both find the perfect ring. Do come over here and take a seat!" Mr. Thomas showed them to a cosy little corner with three chairs and a small table. It had lighting above it and a small mirror. They both looked at it thoughtfully.

"Oh that" Mr. Thomas said as if reading their minds "that mirror is for the lady to see how the ring sits on her hand, from another one's perspective so to speak."

They both settled down and smiled secretly to each other. Chantelle had never been so happy; she honestly thought her heart was going to burst with excitement.

"Now then... what sort of ring were you looking for, anything in particular? A Solitaire or something else, and the stones are very important too! Would you like just Diamonds or Diamonds and others as well?"

Chantelle didn't know what to say, she was flummoxed. She just didn't know what she wanted. Glyn however had ideas of his own and he wanted her ring to be spectacular.

"Have you got Solitaires on Platinum bands, and also the ones with three stones? I think they're called 'Trilogy' rings or something like that."

"We do indeed..." Mr. Thomas said as he got up off his chair. "I'll just bring a selection over for you now. Would you both perhaps like a cup of tea or coffee whilst you are waiting?"

"Thank you that would be lovely..." Chantelle said "coffee would be fine, wouldn't it Glyn?" She looked deep into his eyes and the love that shone there almost over-whelmed her. He was positively glowing with pride and emotion. Glyn took her hand and kissed her ring finger.

"Coffee would be perfect, just like you." She blushed, captured his hand and returned the kiss. She whispered softly 'I love you so much'. He was her soul-mate and they both waited excitedly for the rings to appear.

"Mrs. Thomas, could you possibly make a nice pot of coffee for our customers out here, we're looking for a special ring!" Mr. Thomas called through the door at the back of the shop. A muffled reply came back and he seemed pleased with it, Mr. Thomas scurried off on his quest. They seemed to be a very nice couple and he always enjoyed finding the 'perfect' ring for his customers. In fact he had a very good eye and almost all the rings he found were what 'his' clients wanted.

It only took 10 minutes or so, but while he looked the coffee arrived and they both sat and drank, both completely at ease now. Mind you Chantelle's stomach was doing back-flips.

"Now then..." Mr. Thomas said as he re-joined the couple... What do you think?" He placed 3 trays on the table and moved the coffee tray. A green baize cloth

Reviving a Rose

was placed across the table and Mr. Thomas placed 3 different types of ring on the cloth in front of Glyn and Chantelle.

Chantelle was enchanted; they were beautiful, each in its own individual way. The 1st ring was a 'Solitaire' and the stone shone and twinkled as it caught the light.

"Now that one is what you would call your standard engagement ring. It is a whole carat, white diamond and it is a brilliant cut stone, which catches the light spectacularly." He passed it to Chantelle and she slid it onto her finger and studied it.

"What do you think Glyn?" She said as she turned her hand to catch the light.

"It's stunning; but you must have a look at the others too."

Chantelle took the ring off and placed it back on the cloth. The 2nd ring was a cluster of diamond and around the edge were five small rubies. It almost looked like a flower and it was such a pretty setting too!

Chantelle picked it up and held it to the light. The colours danced and sparkled and it was very beautiful. She didn't feel that it was the ring though, so she replaced it next to the first one. This ring picking business wasn't as easy as she thought.

The 3rd ring was the 'trilogy' ring and as soon as Chantelle had placed it on her finger she knew, this was 'the one'. It was simple but stunning and it seemed as if it belonged on her hand.

"Glyn?" she said and as she looked up from the shining facets, her eyes were shining "what do you think?"

"Well if your face is any judge I think you've found it. If you're happy then so am I."

Chantelle was literally grinning from ear to ear. This was the best day of her life, by far and she felt like she was floating. It all seemed a little surreal, she was euphoric and Mr. Thomas knew that the trilogy was the perfect ring for his customer. He would never say so, of course, it wasn't his way. Mr. Thomas took pride in himself and his ability to find 'the ring' and he had done it again.

"Mr. Thomas?" Said Glyn "Is there a similar ring for me, which would compliment that, for the wedding. I would like to reflect and enhance Chantelle's ring by wearing its partner, so to speak!"

"I'm sure I can find what you're after. Please excuse me." Mr. Thomas replied as he stood up and went on his personal search again.

Mr. Thomas was pleased with his assessment of the 'newly engaged' couple in his shop. Not many men would think of their own wedding ring. In fact! Most men just opted for a plain band almost as an after thought. The young gentleman obviously adored his lady and was proud enough to show it by wearing a similar ring to hers. He smiled to himself and picked out a large ring with 3 diamonds set into it. They weren't as large as the trilogy, but when placed next to it on the green cloth, they looked as if they had been made to be together.

Chantelle clapped her hands together in delight "Ooh... they're perfect, they look made for each other, like partners!"

"I agree... they look super Mr. Thomas. While we're here could you also find a wedding band for Chantelle?"

"Please..." Chantelle said... "Just a plain band for me I don't want to detract from the beautiful engagement ring. It would be criminal, besides I have my mirror image in Glyn wearing his."

"I think that is a very good idea." Mr. Thomas said scurrying off again. He returned in seconds with a tray of simple but lovely wedding rings. "Chantelle, could you put your ring on for a second, so we can find a matching band the same width."

Glyn said... "I'll put it on properly later, on one knee the whole 9 yards!!"

Reviving a Rose

"You don't have to Glyn, you've already asked me!"

"I know but I didn't have a chance to show you off. You actually glowed when I asked you before, so I want our friends to share it too!!"

Chantelle felt so loved and she was so proud of Glyn, because he wanted to share their special moment with the people who had become their friends.

"Mr. Thomas" Glyn continued… "I think this one is perfect, could you please put them in some boxes and I'll dig out my card."

"Certainly sir… No rush… Take your time, these things should never be rushed you know." Mr. Thomas replied.

He picked up the rings that weren't wanted and left the 'chosen 3' on the baize cloth. He was a happy man today. Not only had he sold 3 very expensive rings but the couple concerned looked radiant and that Mr. Thomas felt was the best part of his job. It was at that point that Mr. Thomas' wife re-appeared.

"Ooh… what a lovely choice you've made… absolutely stunning!" She then started to clear away the coffee tray promptly and efficiently and then returned to find the boxes for the rings.

She was proud of her husband today, 'Oh yes' he had found some beautiful rings which matched the couple so well. Mrs. Thomas was a very happy lady. "Have you both come far?" She asked.

No! The Briory Bush Inn, we were at Gedd and Honey's wedding…" Chantelle began.

"Ooh yes wasn't it lovely, didn't Honey look a treat. Gedd's a lucky man alright." Mrs. Thomas said as she brought 3 boxes over and gave the rings a quick polish, before putting each one into the blue velvet cushion and closing the lid gently. Mr. Thomas re-joined them and gave Glyn a folded piece of paper.

Glyn read it and one of his eyebrows went up but he said nothing. Chantelle was worth the price and so much more. What was more important to Glyn was that she hadn't looked for a really expensive ring that was over the top. Yes Glyn didn't mind a bit. He pulled out his wallet and handed his platinum visa card to Mr. Thomas. He in turn nodded and went off to finish the transaction.

When Glyn had his card back he stood up and shook Mr. Thomas' hand firmly.

"Thank you so much for your advice and guidance, the rings are just perfect."

Mr. Thomas beamed, not only had he guessed correctly but he had also sold some stunning and expensive rings today. Yes, he too was a very happy man.

Chantelle stood up and because she was so happy she kissed not only Mrs. Thomas but also Mr. Thomas. Who was slightly surprised but not upset? It wasn't often that a pretty lady kissed his cheek, and Chantelle was definitely pretty.

"Thank you both so much... this has been an unforgettable experience and your kindness has made this so special."

"You are entirely welcome." Mrs. Thomas said as she gave her a hug and then moved onto Glyn as well. 'What a lovely couple.'

"Well... thanks again!" Glyn said as they put their coats on to leave.

"It was our pleasure!" The Thomas's said as they showed Glyn and Chantelle to the door.

"Cup of tea my dear?" Mrs. Thomas said after they had left.

"Lovely..." he replied... "What a splendid idea... the perfect end to a profitable day." And patting his waistcoat Mr. Thomas put the 'snip' down on the shop door and turned the sign to 'Closed'. A cup of tea would hit the spot alright and they would enjoy it together.

Reviving a Rose

Yes Mr. Thomas was glad he was a jeweller today, very glad indeed.

With that he followed his good lady into the back of the shop to have his well earned tea.

29

Chantelle tucked her arm through Glyn's and he smiled. He leaned over and kissed the top of her head. She squeezes his arm in return, as they both walked 'as if on air', slowly back to the Inn.

They decided to go straight up stairs to get changed. Glyn wanted his proposal 'just right', so he ordered some clothes on his phone, they would be delivered shortly by courier. He didn't mind paying a little more for them as he had no clothes left from the garage. Being rich certainly had its advantages sometimes, and this was one of them.

He pulled on a pair of cords that Sonia had found for him and a large T-shirt. Chantelle giggled when she saw it, because it had a motif on it, which read 'love me' with a very cute looking rabbit sitting in a basket.

"Oh Glyn..." she said with tears in her eyes "... you look so cute!"

"Come here and say that" he replied.

Reviving a Rose

So she did. Chantelle stood on tip-toes and punctuated her speech with kisses. "You... Look... So... Cute"

Glyn kissed her back "So do you "Boss-Lady" and you don't even need a bunny rabbit to do it either."

They wrapped their arms around each other and both sighed, totally content in each others arms. Glyn would have stayed like it too but Chantelle said her tummy needed filling, so reluctantly he released her and they went in search of food.

Both had a surprise when they nearly reached bottom of the stairs. "Honey... Gedd... what on earth are you two doing here?" They said almost together.

"We 'eard 'bout the garage an' you two, so we came 'ome" Gedd said with his arm around his wife's shoulder.

"Yeah" Honey chipped in "we couldn't stick sittin' about not doin' anythin' so we both said 'let's go 'ome' an' we did."

Chantelle flew down the remaining stairs and enveloped Honey in a bear-hug. With tears in her eyes and her heart full of love for this lovely lady who had taken her under her wing. Then she hugged Gedd as well. Glyn shook Gedd's hand so hard nearly fell off.

"'Ere you'll pull it off not so 'ard man."

"Sorry Gedd, I don't know my own strength sometimes."

They all made their way towards the kitchen. Sonia flew into her mothers arm and squeezed her fondly.

"'Ello mum, back so soon!" she said tongue in cheek.

"Cheeky devil, you know I can't stay away from my kitchen fer long. Whatcha bin' up to in there mi' girl? Come on show me and we'll all 'ave a brew eh!"

So while Sonia filled in her mum with the goings on in the Inn, Glyn and Chantelle told Gedd all they knew about the garage. He looked gutted and said it didn't matter as long as they were okay.

They both said apart from a few cuts and bruises they were fine. Chantelle made Gedd smile by saying

"I didn't know you let people have flying lessons at the garage!"

"Yes" continued Glyn "they were stunning too, we both flew full across the back lot."

"Oh don't..." Honey said "it doesn't bear thinkin' on what 'appened, did anyone tell yer after?"

"The police are investigating, but it wasn't an accident. The Fire Investigation Team said that Gedd's two cylinders in the workshop were both fully open, and so was the cooker too!"

Gedd was shocked, who would want to do such a thing. Then a thought struck him. No... it couldn't be his waster of a nephew Ben! He wouldn't be that vindictive would he?

The police said they would be in touch Gedd, but they didn't know how long you'd be away on honeymoon. I'd give them a ring tomorrow if I was you." Glyn said

"Good idea that" Gedd replied "I'll sort it out in the mornin'. Well come on Honey lets get brewin'."

So they all sat in the kitchen and quizzed Gedd and Honey about their very short honeymoon.

Sonia stood up and as she hugged her mother again she said

"Well now you're back to take the reins again mum, I'll be off in the morning. I think the kids will be pleased to have their 'mummy' back. Stephen has a heart of gold but only so much patience. I think I'll let him off the lead early." She chuckled and they all laughed with her. Honey was proud of her girl, and the way she had stepped in.

Sonia was quick to point out that Enid had been a 'god-send' and that she deserved equal praise. Honey and Gedd were pleased with that and Gedd went off in search of his sister. Sonia said that she that she had gone up to her room for a nap and with that Sonia excused herself and went upstairs to pack her case ready to leave in the morning.

Reviving a Rose

Glyn and Chantelle felt now wasn't the time to mention the ring, but they decided that when evening meal was finished, Glyn would propose again in front of the regulars and everyone else.

"Enid!" Gedd said tapping her door "You awake love?"

"Umm… ooh is it?" a muffled voice said

"It's me love yer big brother!"

The door flew open and Enid sailed into Gedd's arms. "Ooh I'm that pleased yer 'ere. All sorts 'as been goin' on an' yer poor garage an' all!"

"I'm not worried one bit 'bout mi' garage, I'm just glad Glyn and Chantelle weren't killed… Enid I'm sorry to say this but I think Ben might have had something to do with it."

"I'm not sorry Gedd, 'e's a bad 'un an' I reckon if the guests 'adn't grabbed 'im, 'e'd 'ave taken Chantelle off."

"What?"

"Yeah 'e tried t' tek 'er from the reception just after you two left. The police came an' arrested 'm"

"What d' 'e want wi' Chantelle?"

"Seems he wen' out wi' 'er a few years ago an' he thought she should be 'is, so 'e tried t' tek 'er wi' 'im. Sonia's husband an' someone else stopped 'im, an' then the police carted 'im off. I'm not upset, I'm angry, 'e's ruined 'is life and mine…"

"No 'e 'asn't, your life is fine 'ere. You can stop as long as you like. In fact you can stop 'ere an' 'ave a job wi' Honey if yer like! I said she needed a 'and an' it seems you've just solved t' problem, that's if yer wan' it?"

"Corse I do, I'd love to stop. I really like it 'ere. It's quiet and peaceful and best of all I like Honey a lot, she's like the sister I never 'ad." Enid hugged Gedd fiercely and it was decided then and there. She would stay and help run the Inn with Honey and her brother, for as long as she wanted. Another thought popped into her head as well. If she stayed in the village she would

Chantelle's Journey

see more of Geoffrey Rodgers. Yes, Enid was more than happy to live here in Chettle, for as long as she was wanted.

Gedd went back downstairs, a very happy man. Not only had he got a beautiful wife in Honey, but now his little sister was going to stay. He was so glad she was out of Ben's clutches; Gedd would never let that boy hurt his mother again.

Honey was busy doing what she liked best, and that was 'rooting around' in her freezer, looking for something to cook for dinner.

"'Ow would you like an extra pair of 'ands?"

"Wot, you offrin'?"

"No... I mean a permanent pair on the end of someone you like!"

"Stop bein' so cryptic, just tell me Gedd, I'm tryin' t' get somethin' fer dinner 'ere!"

"'Ow d'yer fancy Enid comin' t' live 'ere in the Inn an' 'elpin' yer?"

"Ooh, that'll be smashin' Gedd, she's a diamond that one. It'll be great 'avin' a 'and. I'm sure we'll rub along t'gether just fine."

Gedd snuck up behind Honey and as she stood up he cuddled her from behind.

"Know wot Mrs. Graham? You are smashing, and I love you lots and lots." He spun her around and planted a kiss on her surprised face.

"Yer not so bad yer'self Gedd." She said kissing him back.

Meanwhile Chantelle and Glyn went back upstairs and sat on 'their' bed looking at the ring.

"It's beautiful Glyn. I can't wait to have you put it on my hand."

"I know, it's making me a bit nervous but you're worth it."

They both grinned like naughty children and then there was a knock at the door.

Reviving a Rose

"Who is it?" Glyn said.

"It's me lad..." Gedd replied "there's a fella 'ere says 'e's got some stuff for yer, it don't 'alf look posh!"

Glyn opened the door as Chantelle hid the ring box under the pillow. "Yes... it's mine, I ordered it on line. All my clothes went up along with your garage mate."

"Corse they did, sorry Glyn if I can give yer..."

"No, there's no need Gedd" Glyn interrupted quickly... "I'm quite solvent you know. In fact I'm a lot more solvent than you or Honey know. I'm not quite as poor as you thought..."

Gedd looked puzzled so Glyn continued "... remember the BMW, well it was a gift from my 'boss'. But he also happens to be my father. He owns Matthews Construction Limited."

Gedd was still looking puzzled; he just stood there scratching his head.

"Look Gedd, I wanted to spread my wings a bit and get back down to manual grafting, so my workforce could see that I knew what I was talking about. If I'd done a certain job then they would see I had their perspective in mind... get it? You know like getting my hands dirty and earning respect."

"Well you certainly did that lad!" Gedd said finally find his voice. "But if yer not skint, wot were it 'solvent' yer said, wot's that in money terms then?"

"Well without bragging, I could rebuild your garage for you by next week. That's the workforce available to me, and you can pick the colour!"

Gedd looked stunned; he thought he'd be rattling around with Honey in the Inn for months. "Ow the bleedin' 'eck can yer do that then?"

"Well, I phoned my father last night and asked if he had any crew available if I needed them. But I wanted to check with you first 'Partner'?"

"Wha...!" Gedd's mouth dropped open.

"I know you want to slow down a bit and enjoy married life. Well I'm giving you the chance to relax and work when you want. Oh, by the way, the plans include a small cottage, on the site, in keeping with the rest of the village."

"Yer mean... you'd build a bleedin' cottage for me 'n' Honey next ter mi new garage and I could work when I want t'?"

"Yes... if that's what you both want?"

Chantelle's head was whipping between the two men like she was watching a tennis match on TV.

"If we want... just wait till I tell Honey, she'll be gob-smacked." Gedd left the delivery man standing in the open door way with a huge grin on his face.

"You don't need anymore employees do you?"

"Sorry, but I'll let you know if I do, okay." Glyn said as he signed for his clothes. They were as smart as he had thought and he was sure some eyes would be wide open when he escorted Chantelle down to dinner.

"Glyn, what shall I wear?" Chantelle said as she looked at his fine new wardrobe. She didn't think any of her clothes came up to Glyn's standard.

"What had you got in mind love?" Glyn said "You would look fantastic in a potato sack!"

"Thank you... I think, but I don't own one and I would like to look good for you when you get down on one knee!"

"Oh yes... I forgotten..." he ducked as a pillow sailed past his head. "Only kidding "Boss-Lady". I took the liberty of asking Sonia's advice and we thought this..." He said as he revealed a stunning dress from beneath the other clothes, "... would suit you M'lady." Glyn bowed and placed the garment into Chantelle's open arms. She gasped; it was stunningly beautiful and simply cut. It was emerald green with tiny straps and a matching light knitted scarf.

Reviving a Rose

Chantelle was just about to ask about shoes when Glyn produced them from behind his back, just like a magician.

"Ta Da... Do they meet with your approval madam?"

Chantelle just looked on in an awed silence. She was stunned, not only had Glyn got the dress right, but the shoes matched perfectly. She would feel like a princess when they went down to dinner.

"They're wonderful and so are you!" She flew into his open arms and held him tightly. Glyn didn't mind a bit, he would have been quite happy to stay there all night.

"Come on, let's go and see if Honey's in shock, Gedd must have told her by now." He said as he breathed in Chantelle's scent. Kissing the top of her head he released Chantelle and they made their way downstairs.

30

Chantelle led the way into the kitchen, she found Honey sitting at the table with a large mug of tea in front of her. Gedd was sat down too, but instead of the shock on Honey's face he had a grin of pure joy. It seemed to be trying to split his face in half.

"Well…" he prompted "watcha think then mi girl, it's a heck of an offer eh?"

"Yes…" Glyn cut in "what do you think Mrs. Graham, oops sorry Mrs Williams, can we tempt you?"

"Oh gawd… yer scared the life out of mi then lad, don't go creepin' in and doin' that. I have t' be takin' the wife's tablets at that rate." Gedd caught his breath and stood up. He shook Glyn's hand, pumping it up and down and he was still grinning too! Honey just sat there looking at the pair of them. Well what a turn up for the books this was.

"I don't know wot t'say! I mean I know wot I want t'say but it's not comin' out." She knew she was babbling, but there were so many emotions flying around in her

Reviving a Rose

head that her tongue which normally had no trouble moving about, had just gone on strike.

Chantelle sat down beside her and put her arm around Honey's shoulder. She squeeze it re-assuring Honey and said softly "Glyn's not kidding you know, he'd never do that to you two. It's a proper offer, what do you want to do Honey?"

The three in the kitchen all stared at Honey and she cleared her throat. "Well for a start I need a new brew! Mi tongues stuck fast and I'm that stunned 'onest!"

"Tek yer time love, its fer both of us t' agree or nowt 'appens." Gedd said gently as he rejoined his wife at the table.

Glyn rubbed his wrist; Gedd was still a strong man, even at his age, and the shaking he'd given it had rattled his bones. It was fully 10 minutes and two more mugs of tea before Honey finally gave her opinion.

"I think we'd both be soft in t' 'ead if we let this opportunity slip by. An' Enid could live 'ere without us trippin' over each other."

"Is that a YES then?" Glyn said.

"Corse it is silly" Honey replied and they all hugged and jumped up and down as though they'd won the lottery.

That was how Enid found them all when she came down from her room.

"Wha's goin' on 'ere then?" she said looking at the four extremely happy people bouncing round the kitchen like a whole gang of 'tiggers', all that was missing was stripes and tails. Gedd spun round and whirled his sister into the group.

"He's only gonna rebuild the garage an' make a new 'ome for Honey an' me as well."

"Wot?"

"Glyn's loaded... sorry Glyn it came out wrong... look Enid love, d'yer still want t' live 'ere?"

"Yes... But..."

Chantelle's Journey

"No buts love... you'll be livin' in and not trippin' over us two. The Inn will be your baby too! Honey's still the boss like you'll be like a live-in manager... 'ow d'yer fancy that eh?"

Enid was overwhelmed and shocked at the same time. She thought she would burst with happiness. She not only had a new life here with family, but a proper job and 'her own place', she felt as if the whole world had just opened up for her like a flower.

"I think its bloody fab, I do that! Congratulations all. I think I'm gonna cry I'm that 'appy for us all."

"Well pet..." said Honey "Make yer first decision as manager-to-be, an' go an' crack open a bottle of bubbly."

They all shook hands and hugged. Then Honey took charge and reminded them that dinner was soon to be served.

"Honey" Glyn said "do you mind if Gedd and I announce all the new developments to the 'regulars' tonight. Then I can explain it more?" He didn't add that he would also be proposing as well, Glyn thought that would be the icing on the cake, so he left well alone.

"Well, I think I'd better get changed if I'm going to be introducing my new partner tonight don't you Chantelle?"

She thought he'd meant her for a second but she saw a wink and smiled at him as she winked back.

It was much later, after Honey and Enid had served a lovely dinner that Gedd stood up and got everyone's attention.

"Scuse us folks but Glyn and I 'ave summit t' say and we 'ope yer gonna like it?" It did the trick, the whole room went silent and all the faces looked up at Gedd. Glyn stood up next to him and gave an encouraging nod.

"Well, yer all know 'bout mi garage goin' up an' all that, but wot yer don't know is that Glyn 'ere has been a bit of a dark 'orse. He's not as poor as we all may 'ave thought. In fact e's stinkin' rich... sorry lad... but 'e 'is, an' 'e wants t' re-build mi garage wi' us as partners. Well wot d'yer think 'bout that then?"

The place erupted with cheers and clapping. The regulars were all beaming and they all shouted congratulations at the same time. It took a little while to calm down but gradually the noise dipped and Glyn looked at Gedd nodded and then began to speak.

"I asked..." Chantelle held her breathe "Gedd and Honey," she swallowed "if they would also like a new home. Don't worry..." he said quickly "I don't mean away from here. If the plans are approved, the garage will have an addition. We plan to build a cottage on the plot as well, so that Gedd is close to his work if he wants to work, and Honey isn't too far away from here..."

"What about the Inn?" Maud Pennington said interrupting Glyn.

"It's alright love..." Honey called back "Gedd's sister... Enid 'ere will be livin' in and we're gonna run the place between us."

"Oh!" Maud and the rest of the regulars seemed shocked but really pleased. They had all thought Honey was working too hard trying to look after them; especially after her fainting spell before the wedding. Glyn rubbed his palms down his trouser leg, now to the 'other' announcement. He cleared his throat and addressed the room again.

"I do have one other thing I need to say, if you could all just give me your attention for a minute..."

Chantelle could feel her stomach knotting up, but she was tingling with excitement. Gedd and Honey looked at each other and shrugged. Whatever it was they hadn't been told, so they both sat down and looked at Glyn.

"I think after the last few days, you all know how I feel about a certain "Boss-Lady" I worked for, on Mr. Rodgers' cottage. Well today..." he took Chantelle's hand and got her to stand up next to him. "We both went to buy a very special thing..."

Honey grabbed hold of Gedd's arm and Enid grabbed the other one. Geoffrey Rodgers sat upright in his chair and all the regulars were agog!

"I bought a very special ring today. And I would now like to ask Chantelle in front of all my friends, if she would do me the honour of becoming my wife?"

Everyone was cheering and clapping and shouting out, it took a full 5 minutes to settle down. Glyn got down on one knee and took Chantelle's left hand in his.

"Chantelle, you know how much I love you, and now I would like to let everyone else see it too! I would move heaven and earth to keep you by my side and I would be honoured and so unbelievably proud to have you marry me... So... Chantelle will you make me the proudest of men and marry me?"

He took the ring out of his pocket and slid it onto her wedding finger. Glyn then took her hand to his mouth and kissed it gently. He then stood up.

Chantelle had tears streaming down her face but she was glowing with happiness. "Yes... yes please Glyn, you know too, just how much I love you and I would be just proud to be your wife. I will go anywhere you go and do what ever it takes to make you happy."

"You've already done that" Glyn said as he stood up. The room went mad, they rushed up to congratulate the happy couple, and then a 'pop' sounded. Enid had brought some champagne in and some glasses.

"Well" she said "this is definitely time for a posh drink eh!"

Geoffrey Rodgers and the regulars all toasted the newly engaged couple and Glyn wrapped his arm round Chantelle's tiny waist, to pull her closer, if it was at all possible.

Reviving a Rose

Honey and Gedd were very pleased indeed. They looked upon Glyn and Chantelle as family and they were well matched.

The door into the restaurant opened and Scotty walked in.

"What's t' do then… free drink… I'm off duty I have one wi' yer!"

"Oh Scotty"… Honey said". .. Glyn an' Chantelle; 'ave just got engaged 'int it smashin'?"

"Aye it is that, I'll add my congratulations among the rest too!" Dr McArdle walked over to the happy couple and hugged Chantelle as he said 'well done'. He then clasped Glyn's hand and told him that he was a lucky man and to look after his woman."

Glyn said he had every intention of doing so, as he shook Scotty's hand. "Why are you here anyway Scotty? Not that you're not welcome?"

"Well! The truth be told; I just wanted t' check on Honey, after all the excitement and upsets."

"No need man…" said Gedd. She's t' get 'elp, mi sister Enid is comin' t' live 'ere and 'elp run the Inn."

"Well I'm pleased on that score" said the Doctor truthfully. "I don't fancy seeing ma friend back on ma patch, at the hospital."

Everybody was floating on good news and bubbly. Chantelle had never in her life been so happy. Her new ring felt heavy but it sparkled brilliantly on her hand. Glyn looked at her and nodded his head sideways. Nobody noticed them slip off to room 7. Glyn closed the door softly and pulled his lovely fiancée into his arms.

"I love you 'Boss-Lady'; you have filled my heart so much, it could burst, thank you for loving me."

Chantelle looked up into his beautiful face and smiled "You're entirely welcome my love and ditto to the loving me bit!"

They kissed and rocked gently in each others arms. Healing and filling each others hearts. Today was the start of a new life and for Glyn and Chantelle the journey couldn't start soon enough. Glyn had 'Revived His Rose' and he was a very happy man indeed.

THE END

Or is it?

About the Author

Sally Loveday has been a very keen writer of poetry, this has always been her first love, especially where children are involved. She has had her poems published on the web, with some commissioned works going as far as Canada, Pakistan and Germany.

She also has written lyrics for her own CD 'Matilda Mine'. Showing how diverse Sally has become to achieve her goals. At present is working on songs for a stage show, based on the Welsh involvement in the Spanish Civil War.

Writing this book has given her a new purpose and feeling of achievement. In other ways, it was a way of proving to herself, friends and family she can write a book, that is enjoyable to read. Sally hopes to show the reader that she has an understanding of the complexities of romance.

Printed in the United Kingdom by
Lightning Source UK Ltd., Milton Keynes
139634UK00001B/38/A